Praise for *Private Heat*

It "deserves praise for sheer action and suspense . . . Bailey has a good, sassy sense of humor." In this "hard-boiled homage . . . there's no denying his narrative drive, which keeps the reader moving right along until the last page."

—*Publishers Weekly*

"First-novelist Bailey delivers a well-constructed, action-packed thriller. . . . A series to watch."

—*Booklist*

"No doubt, Bailey will quickly gather many devoted fans (including myself) with this action-packed, well-crafted thriller. His vivid characters and brilliant sense of humor won me over."

—*The Mystery Review*

A "knockout debut private eye novel . . . Full of high speed, adrenaline-charged action and vividly drawn characters, Bailey's classic hard-boiled effort is a real gem, easily a candidate for best first private eye novel of the year honors."

—*Lansing State Journal*

Praise for *Dying Embers*

"Buckle up and enjoy a wild ride through the mean streets of Grand Rapids."

—*Publishers Weekly*

"The second Hardin thriller is packed with sharp dialogue, stark violence, and details of real-world investigatory work. An intriguing new voice for mystery fans."

—*Booklist*

"Bailey, himself a retired P.I., imbues his second [novel] with that reassuring been-there-done-that confidence, plus considerable style and brio."

—*Kirkus Reviews*

"Bailey's at his creative best in the book's last half, as violent confrontations and frenzied, frantic action on the gritty streets of Grand Rapids lead to stunning revelations and an explosive conclusion."

—*Lansing State Journal*

Praise for *Dead Bang*

"A hard-hitting novel . . . [It] goes far beyond the usual mystery, combining espionage, intrigue, and thriller elements into the detective formula. Perfect . . ."

—*Midwest Book Review*

"This is gritty, smart storytelling that forces the reader to participate in the story rather than simply observe it. Fans of hardcore detective novels will enjoy this latest installment in the Art Hardin Mystery series."

—*The New Mystery Reader*

"All the time *Dead Bang* is fast, lively and surprisingly informative and ingenious. . . . If you like your mysteries peppered with the bizarre and hilarious, with side dishes of history, then *Dead Bang* is a dead-on read for you!"

—*Rebecca's Reads*

"In the third book in his Art Hardin series, Robert Bailey does not disappoint. This tale keeps the reader racing along with howls of laughter and seat of your pants excitement."

—*Reader Views*

DÉJÀ NOIR

Also by Robert E. Bailey

Private Heat
Dying Embers
Dead Bang

DÉJÀ NOIR

A Detroit Mystery

Robert E. Bailey

ignition
books
San Diego

Publisher's Note

I had the pleasure of working with Bob Bailey as his literary agent and then publisher. Few authors could match his wit or determination. This book was written by Bob, but the version you have in your hands also contains editorial contributions from his wife, Linda Lyons-Bailey, and his friend Joseph M. Erhardt. Throughout the editorial process, with Bob no longer here to do battle over word choice, plot points, and style, Linda and Joe fought to ensure that Bob's voice and words remained true to what he would have wanted. Their contributions are greatly appreciated.

—Andrew Zack, Publisher
Endpapers Press

DÉJÀ NOIR: A Detroit Mystery
Ignition Books®

LCCN: 2018968269
ISBN-13: 978-1-937868-76-5 (trade paperback)
ISBN-13: 978-1-937868-77-2 (epub)
ISBN-13: 978-1-937868-78-9 (Kindle)

Cover design by Labelschmiede (via 99Designs.com)
Cover Image: Ambassador Bridge Lights © Jill E. Kulchinsky (Dreamstime); Man © Alexey Makhinko (Pexels); Woman © Mircea_dfa (Dreamstime)

Ignition Books are published by Endpapers Press, a division of Author Coach, LLC.

Ignition Books is a registered trademark of Author Coach, LLC.

The First of
Many Stories

Last Call

I KNEW IT WAS MORNING because my office was dark. The three-story blue neon cross on the skid row mission across the street turned off at five. I was trying to remember if I'd saved a "wake-up call" in the file drawer's pint when my office door started to rattle.

I opened my eyes to listen harder—definitely the door rattling. Sometimes the vagrants from across the street came scrounging for copper, aluminum, or whatever.

The first floor had been a drugstore-cum-karate studio. Both of them closed up in the eighties—thirty years ago. My insurance and travel neighbors had long since gone, and plans to turn the third floor into apartments had never been finished. The city owned the property for taxes, and nobody came looking for rent. The electricity was on—maybe to service the fire alarms. I hadn't called to ask, and I didn't have the inclination. So, all in all, the price obliged. Except now some meathead was screwing with my door.

And knocking! *Frog!*

I sat up and mauled my face with my hands. Tan morning light drilled dusty rays through holes in the shade.

"Yeah, yeah," I said. I pulled the pillow off the desk blotter and stuffed it into the bottom drawer of the file cabinet. I'd sold my sofa about six bottles ago, and now I sleep with my head on the desk—the chair rocks forward a little so my legs don't get numb.

I stood, tucked in my shirt, and wedged the revolver from the top of the desk into my belt at the small of my back. Now they were twisting the doorknob and shaking the door. "Frog's sake, tie a knot in it, will ya?"

I padded out of my office and through the waiting room in stocking feet. I snapped the lock and eased the door open a crack, blocking it with my foot.

The gray shadow on the other side of the frosted glass morphed into a woman—maybe twenty-two, and thin as a stick. She had a black pageboy hairdo and looked freshly dressed for an evening out in a little black dress, heels, and a boa wrap.

Her eyebrows arched into question marks. She asked, "You Raymond Kerze?"

"Why?"

"On the door." She pointed a finger with a bright red nail that had been nibbled to the quick. "Raymond Kerze, Private Investigator." Her hopeful face dropped into panic and her eyes darted up and down the hall.

"Yeah," I said—not what I was thinking—and looked at my wristwatch just in time to remember that it was only right twice a day. I took my right hand off the revolver and swung the door open. "It's a little early. Maybe you could come back later."

She brushed by me. "Okay if I wait?"

"The chairs are dusty."

She beamed me a bright smile and pushed the door shut.

"Yeah," I said. "Sure." *Frog!*

She sat, folded her arms, and put on a customer-service face that hid her feelings from view.

It seemed like a mile back to my desk. I dug the pint out of the file drawer and headed back through the waiting room to the crapper.

I flushed the toilet to be discreet while last night's liquid dinner posted bail and then stepped over to the sink. The pint held a precious quarter inch of bottom-shelf bourbon. I added water, took a slug, and swished it around my mouth—just enough to get the taste, but not enough to get well. I swallowed and scrubbed my teeth with my finger.

I had to squat down to get my full face in the mirror. Lately, it hasn't been worth the trouble. Crappy booze and crappy sleep had added an artificial decade to my two-score-and-six, and the battered leathery face in the mirror wasn't the one I remembered as my own. Still, I could stand straight and see enough of my jaw to shave. I used the dregs of my jug to splash on the divots left by my aged disposable razor. Grizzled, wiry hair stood out from my head like I'd stuck a finger in an outlet. I pushed it back from my face with some limited success. Parallel hair is overrated anyway.

All right! Back at my desk, tie on, coat buttoned to hide the stain on my tie, and she's planted across from me. "So how can I help you, Miss . . . ?"

"It's Misty," she said, still smiling. Then, like a cold slap, "I want you to kill me."

I let my chin fall into my hand and closed my eyes. After a moment of mentally playing back what I'd heard, I said, "You realize I could still be sleeping?"

"I can pay."

I opened one eye. "Really?"

Her forehead wrinkled and her eyes squinted while she shook the contents of a small black clutch out onto the desk.

"Why come to me?" I asked.

She straightened singles as she took them from the desktop and pushed some coins around with her finger. When she looked up, high tide rose in her brown eyes, a single line of mascara plowing down her cheek. "It's eleven dollars and sixty cents. It's all I have. I came to you because in the neighborhood, they say you help people."

I hate it when they cry. This probably wasn't a prank, because you usually don't get juice with jokes, so throwing her out by the scruff of her neck didn't seem right. I kept a stack of fast-food napkins in my top drawer. I gave her a couple and said, "Sure."

She gasped, "Oh God, thank you," into the napkins.

I stood, walked over to the window, and snapped up the battered shade—nothing moving on the street but wind-blown trash. I said, "You don't mind dying on a full stomach, do you?"

She held a compact mirror in her hand and wet the napkin with her tongue to scrub her cheek.

"Personal thing with me," I said, "I never kill anyone before breakfast."

"I can wait here until you get back," she said.

"Better if you come with me."

"I know you got your methods," she said, and bobbed her head for emphasis. "And I respect that. But maybe, just this once, you could do it now and then go get breakfast. You could throw me out the window and tell the cops I ran in here screaming. And jumped."

I looked down at the street. "Nah," I said, "only one story—might not do the job. A swan dive off the roof would get it done, but leave the money."

"You have to come with me," said Misty, her eyes very large. "You have to throw me off." She karate-chopped the air with both hands. "I'm Catholic! I can't kill myself."

"And what about me?" I said. "What do *I* tell them at the Pearly Gates?"

She wagged her head in the negative. "You're not really doing what you're doing." She placed her palm flat on her chest. "Because I'm doing what I'm doing."

"But not really." I stared at her until she looked away.

"Sort of," she said.

I said nothing.

She snapped open the mouth of her rat-sized purse and began feeding it the bills and change. "I'm sorry," she said, her voice very small. "I have to do this." She stood and turned toward the door. "You don't have to help me."

I coulda kept my mouth shut. I shoulda let her walk out. It woulda been smart, but Coulda Shoulda Woulda left for San Jose the second her first tear dropped. I said, "Eleven bucks may not be much to you, lady, but it's more than I got, and I need the work."

She sniffed, smiled, and flung the boa over her shoulder. "You're not what I expected."

"You're kind of a surprise too, Misty," I said. "I don't know if I can help you. But if you leave, I know I can't. And if I throw you out this window here, the cops are going to screw around until after lunch."

"Stairs go all to way to the roof?" she said.

"Roof door's locked and connected to the fire alarm."

Misty turned and waved a backhand at me. "I can't go out on the street. Not alive. That's why I came so early."

I sat at my desk, stretched out my palm to offer the other chair, and said, "Maybe if you'd explain a little."

Misty marched back to the desk and, fists on her hips, announced, "I'm not in the mood for a lecture!"

"This is the economy job," I said. "Eleven bucks, you just get whacked, no lecture."

Her eyes went narrow and her lips taut. She snapped open her purse, grabbed the money, and threw it at me. The bills scattered on the desk like cheap confetti; the coins caught me square between the eyes.

"I expect my! Money's! Worth!" She spun about, giving me the dramatic I've-Turned-My-Back-On-You spiel.

I rubbed the place where a quarter had pecked my forehead, surprised not to find it embedded and sticking out like a hood ornament. "Yeah," I said. "I'm starting to get a feel for the work already."

She turned back in a couple of jerks, eased the chair away from the desk, and sat tentatively—her butt on the front of the chair and her weight on her feet. "I owe money to a Mob guy," she said. "I'm late. He's got this big mean bastard that comes around when you don't pay."

"Benny Slick?" I said.

Misty shrugged.

"Old guy, liver spots for hair and hooked up to an air bottle? Sits in the corner booth with his back to the wall down at Genie's Wienies on Conant Street?"

Misty nodded.

"Big mean bastard is Meat Hook Marty."

She let her head tilt to one side.

I shook my head. "You don't want to know how he got that name."

"Well, do you see now?"

"Good news is, we got time for breakfast." I bent over and went to work picking up the cash. "Marty works late, so he don't start lumbering around until noon." I rubbed my forehead with my finger. "And the Slickmeister doesn't claim his booth until after the lunch rush is bussed off the tables."

Misty closed her eyes and gave her head a couple of silent wags. "Oh, all right," she said. "What is it with men and their fascination with food?"

"A good meal lasts longer than sex," I said, although I couldn't remember having had either one recently.

She rolled her eyes. "Oh, let's go," she said. "And if we run into that meat-hook monster, I want my money back."

THE LIQUOR STORE ON THE corner opened at seven and a line of the usual suspects had already formed. I looked at my watch—same time as the last time. I said, "We gotta stop up here at the corner."

"That's breakfast?" said Misty.

"That's pretty snippy for someone up to her"—I waggled my fingers—"frilly little neck to a shylock. So were the ponies running a little slow?"

She barked something at me through a rabid Doberman face, which I didn't get, because a dump truck had come roaring up behind us. The next thing I knew, she bolted past me for the street. I got an arm around her just before she ate a chrome bulldog and swung her up on the curb. Someone in the liquor-store line yelled, "Olé!"

As soon as I put her back on her feet, Misty laid a roundhouse smack on the side of my mug and said, "Push, don't pull. My God you're thick, *Raymond*."

My bell still ringing, I said, "If Meat Hook Marty bothers you, I think you can take him. So what's this about?"

"Not horses," said Misty, straightening her dress. "Just one horse's ass, my ex, and he's still running. I borrowed five hundred to post his bail."

"This is about five hundred dollars?"

"Five hundred, five million." She shrugged. "Same amount if you don't have it."

"But you get the bail back," I said.

"The judge called it 'absconding.' Weasel waited until a week before the trial, emptied the checking account and sold my jewelry. The judge kept the bail money."

"Let's get in line," I said.

She wrapped the boa around her neck twice. "I'm freezing."

"How much you behind on the vig?"

"The what?"

"Vigorish," I waved and shrugged. "The interest."

"Three weeks," she said with a sigh, "a hundred and fifty a week."

"Nine-fifty, that's still not an impossible sum."

"I paid the vig for eight months. I got laid off at my waitressing job. You got my last eleven bucks, and I wouldn't be standing here in this stupid line if you had just done your job."

"Well, ah, I—"

"Nothing!" Misty slashed a backhand past me. "All you had to do was *nothing*."

Jimmy Crates—Crates because he pieced together abandoned shipping pallets and dragged them down to the truck terminal for sale—piped up from the front of the line, "If you guys are gonna stand there and argue, come take my place in line." The roofing hammer clipped to his tool belt and his ham-sized biceps made him a neighborhood peacekeeper. Gray-blue eyes peeked out from under the vee-tent folded brim of a battered ball cap; the rest of his face disappeared in a woolly union of curly red hair and gray-streaked beard. "You're disturbin' the neighborhood here."

I looked around. The neighborhood consisted of a liquor store, a boarded-up Monkey Wards store, and wind-blown trash. Another dried-out scab on the face of a battered Detroit.

Misty started talking. "Who the—"

"The man is Jimmy Crates," I said. "And he's absolutely right!" I shepherded Misty to the front of the line to an approving murmur from the crowd, though someone did mumble, "Nice tits, honey."

Anyway, I knew most of them. Jesus, Cheaters, Gimp, and Eddie, who was waving around his pre-paid cellphone, trying to sell individual minutes for profit and booze. At seven on a Sunday morning. "Sorry, Jimmy," I said. "We didn't mean to be upsetting you."

"Right," said Jimmy. "We always work good together. But, ya know, hangin' around here with this little bird—no offense to you, ma'am—I don't know, Ray."

"We're gonna get our business done and move along," I said.

Jimmy took a triumphant stroll to the back of the queue and caught a couple of high-fives along the way. "You got that straightened out," someone told him. Others just nodded or settled for, "Yeah."

"'Little bird?'" Misty asked.

I tapped my index finger against my lips. "We're next," I said. I looked up into the camera, the door buzzed, and we stepped into a shower-stall-sized bulletproof plastic booth that served as the customer-service area. Grumpy Al sat in his wheelchair with the dregs of a fat cigar screwed into the corner of his mouth.

"One at a time," said Al, his voice all gravel and sludge.

"It's just me, Al," I said. "I don't want to leave my sister outside. She's kinda chilly."

"Ba, ah, hah." A wisp of smile blew across Al's prune face. "Sister? Like you had a mother, Ray."

"We had different mothers," said Misty.

"I'm only waitin' on one a ya," said Al. "Then you both leave. Nobody else gets in until you're both gone."

"A pint of Kessler's," I said. He rolled out to a stack of cartons and turned back with the pint in his lap. I asked Misty what her birthday was.

"July sixteenth," she said. "I don't think he's going to card you, so you don't need me to buy your booze for you. Except, I guess I already have."

"See, there you go soundin' mean again." I looked at Al and told him that I wanted two bucks straight on seven-sixteen.

"You're supposed to fill out a bet slip," said Al as he pecked the number into the state lottery machine. He rolled the cigar stub around his mouth once and announced, "That's nine dollars and eighty-six cents."

Misty said, "You have *got* to be kidding."

The metal transaction drawer rolled out, I dropped in ten of Misty's singles, and it snapped back into the wall like a frog reeling in a fly.

"That's your plan?" Misty asked. "I should have set my money on fire."

The drawer spit out my pint, two lottery tickets, and fourteen cents. I handed the tickets to Misty. She crumpled them up and dropped them on the floor. I cracked the lid on the pint, chugged in a slug, and chewed it. Al said that I couldn't do that in here. I swallowed and the warmth spread downward. The sand came off my eyeballs. I offered Grumpy Al a toast, "Pluck your magic twanger, Froggygremlin," and took another slug. Al started pounding on the window and yelling that he could lose his license.

I had half a jug left. I screwed on the cap, stashed it in my pocket, and nearly lost some fingers reaching for the change. I pounded on the closed drawer.

Al said, "Fuck you, now I gotta rewind the security camera."

I said, "Al, I know where you live."

The drawer eased back out with my change in it. "I thought you was leaving it," said Al, his face sullen.

"Keep it," I said. "Buy yourself a couple of them nickel cigars." I snatched the lottery tickets off the floor and stuffed them into my shirt pocket. Al buzzed the door and let us out. We stepped around the corner and I said, "Eight blocks."

Misty looked up Grand Boulevard toward the expressway. This early, you could hear the traffic. She gave me an astonished face and said, "I'm in heels."

"You're the one that dressed to the nines so you could French kiss a Mack truck."

A breeze disturbed her hair and she patted it back in place. "A girl wants to look nice," she said.

I got an ugly flash of what she would have looked like after a three story half-gainer into a sea of cement. I kept it to myself. Instead I said, "You do look nice. We can walk slow and you can show off your outfit."

She smiled.

"But we need to get started because sometimes they run out of those little pinwheel cinnamon rolls."

"If you hadn't wasted my money on those lottery tickets, we could've taken the bus," said Misty.

"Two bucks straight," I said. "A thousand dollars if you hit. You pay off Benny and his gargoyle, and you have a whole new ball game."

"That's ridiculous," she said. "It can't happen."

"But it can happen."

"In the movies."

"It can happen," I said. "Right here. Today."

"Well, yeah," she said. "I suppose."

"So," I said. "The drawing is like twelve, one o'clock. Something like that. So, until then we show off your outfit and you don't play in traffic."

"After that?" she asked.

"I kack you like a stray cat."

HALF A BLOCK PAST THE first bus stop, a City Transit bus shooshed to a halt beside us and the door swept open. The driver, Henry Lee Stevens—his Michelin Man body topped with a chunky black face sporting gold teeth and silver hair—gave me a frown and made one nod toward the back of the bus.

Misty said, "But we don't—"

"All aboard," I said. "We've got a friend in need."

On the seat directly behind Henry Lee we found two men in their late teens or early twenties. One had a swastika tattooed ear-to-ear on his shaved head. The other sported flaming Waffen SS lightning bolts inked to the side of his neck. Both were decked out in white T-shirts, jeans with suspenders, and finished their uniforms with heavy work boots with the prized red laces—a self-testimony to a history of mindless violence. Lightning Bolts sat next to the window. Swastika sat on the aisle.

A moat of empty seats insulated them from the rest of the passengers.

We took the seat directly behind them. I ushered Misty in first so I could sit on the aisle. The swastikaed genius who sat before me told Henry Lee that he should be driving the bus from a seat in the back row. The fellow beside him turned in his seat to face Misty, but dog-eyed me as he made a slow lick in the air with a fat, wide tongue.

Misty leaned forward and folded her arms so that her elbows rested on the seat in front of her. In a sultry voice she said, "Hi ya, big boy. I bet you got a great . . . big . . . knife." The smug sneer on Lightning Bolts's face drooped into wide eyes and an open mouth. He bared a large switchblade knife from his hip pocket.

The Mensa candidate wearing the swastika also turned to Misty and said, "I got something big for you too, honey."

Misty slowly ran her finger down the ridge of Swastika's nose while she said, "Sweetie, I just wonder if you've ever had sex with anyone but your mother."

Lightning Bolts looked me square in the face and snapped his knife open. He turned his head to Henry Lee and said, "*Knee-grow*, you gonna drive this here bus or step out for a bucket of chitlins?"

I banged their heads together as I stood. The tick of their skulls sounded like the crack of a police baton on the sidewalk. The knife hit the floor and the vacancy light flashed in their eyes.

I grabbed the one on the aisle by the arm and the back of the neck, turned my back to the windshield and swung him past me. He tumbled down the stairs, through the open bus door and out onto the street. I started back for the second man, but Misty had moved up and was sitting beside him. She pressed the handle of the knife into his palm and tried to get him to take a grip. She said, "Show me some guts, tough guy. Show me *my* guts."

I got a forearm around Misty's waist, pulled her out of the seat, and stood her in the aisle. Before I could turn back, Lightning Bolts jumped from his seat and crashed out of the bus. He was holding his head and screaming, "Fucking crazy people!"

Henry Lee closed the door, pulled away from the curb, and spoke into the PA system. "Raymond Kerze, ladies and gentlemen, late of our city's finest and now working as a private detective. If your spouse is a lout, give Ray a shout."

Henry Lee reached out a hand and I shook it. We got a round of applause and a smattering of whistles. Misty and I sat. In a falsetto voice, I squeaked, "Hi ya, big boy. I bet you got a great . . . big . . . knife!"

"Quit complaining," Misty said. "If he'd killed me, it would've saved you the trouble. You could tell Saint Peter whatever you liked. You could knock back a couple shots with him."

"You promised to leave Saint Peter in peace until after the morning lottery drawing."

Misty flashed a feline smile. "I only promised not to play in the street."

"You knew what I meant."

"I know what you're trying to do," said Misty. "I suppose it's really very sweet. But I had all night to think this through."

"This money you owe," I said. "You want these people out of your life? Pay them and never darken their door again."

"I paid them nearly five thousand dollars," said Misty. "I don't have any more."

"Benny Slick isn't looking to hurt you. He sure wouldn't decorate a bus aisle with your intestines over five hundred dollars."

"Nine hundred and fifty."

"Talk to him," I said. "Even he'd tell you, 'dead customers don't pay.'"

"I talked to him," said Misty. "And that's exactly what he said." She nodded and flashed me more arched eyebrows. "He put a little more emphasis on the 'dead' part."

I chuckled and waved a hand. "C'mon, he has to maintain a certain—well, ya know—reputation. But he offered you an out, didn't he?"

"Oh, yeah," said Misty. She tilted her head and scrunched up her nose. "All I had to do was spread my legs."

I shrugged and looked at her sideways.

She straight-armed my shoulder. "Not him, you goof!"

"Well," I said, "It wouldn't have lasted as long as a dirt nap. And I don't think that old geezer . . . I mean, he drags around that oxygen bottle." I squeezed shut my eyes to press the idea into my skull and decided, "Hell, it would probably kill him. That'd be some 'dead' for ya."

"Professionally!" said Misty, adding an elbow for punctuation. "He said that he'd roll it all into a new loan, which would make the interest three hundred a week, and that I could work it off as an 'escort.' Something about—I don't know—Top Lights or something."

"Top Hat Night Lighters?"

"Yeah."

"Wow!"

She backhanded my shoulder.

"Just a minute," I said. "To Benny, that's a legit offer. And the Lighters are a very high-end outfit. Lots of gals—"

"Prostitutes!"

"Yes. There *is* that," I said. "This is our stop."

Misty pulled the cord. Henry Lee dropped us at the curb in front of the City Suites hotel.

"So you used to be a cop?" she asked, as she stopped to adjust the strap on the heel of her shoe.

"Used to be."

"What happened?"

"Had a disagreement," I said. "This is it. We get our continental breakfast."

"We're going to get in trouble," said Misty, smoothing her dress. "We didn't stay there. They're going to throw us out or call the cops."

"I'm sort of the part-time house dick here," I said. "I'm the one that throws the bums out. So far, I haven't had to call the cops."

I held the door.

"So, what was the disagreement?" she asked.

"They said I drank too much. I said I couldn't get enough."

"You got fired?"

"Twenty years," I said. "I got retired."

The manager stood behind the reception desk, sorting receipts. I waved. "Little Joe! The haps, dude?"

"Usual stuff, different day," he said. He sported a rug on his head and a rail-thin body which, to the casual eye, made him look a decade younger than his two score and ten. "I need to talk to you before you go."

The breakfast "continent" was a small, airy alcove off the main lobby that in less politically correct days had been a cigar stand. Misty went for the French toast and orange juice. I like the frosted cornflakes and scored the last three of the cinnamon rolls. We claimed one of the half-dozen tiny pink and white striped tables. I went back for a cup of coffee. The table rocked a little so I shimmed up one of the legs with a folded-over menu.

"So," I said, "where is this missing boyfriend now?"

Misty shook her head and shrugged.

"Maybe we could find him. I could explain how much he needs to pay this money."

"He wouldn't pay," said Misty.

"I'm real good at explaining," I said. "It's sort of a specialty."

"I don't know where he's at." Misty shoveled in a bite of French toast and seemed to be chewing her thoughts as well as her food. She swallowed and said, "I got a card from Vancouver. You know, in Canada."

"That *is* a long way."

One tear stumbled slowly down the edge of her nose. "Wasn't from him," she said. "Board of Health—said he tested positive for HIV."

I put my hand on top of hers. "Sorry."

A storm gathered on Misty's face. "I know he's alone and afraid," she said, and lurched to her feet. "I still love him," she gushed and retreated to the ladies' room, her high heels clattering on the tile floor.

I snuck the pint out of my coat pocket and poured a couple of glugs into my coffee. Stirring it in, I started to have some real strong feelings for her ex myself. I took a drink—relished the mellow sweetness—and closed my eyes to savor the peaceful warmth as it spread through my chest.

Little Joe stalked over on his pipe-stem legs looking like a heron wading in the shallows. "Ray," he said, his voice blithe, "who's the twist?" He nested his narrow keister in a chair. "I think I'm falling in lust."

"The 'twist' is my sister," I said.

"No offense," he said, showing me his palms. "You really don't resemble, ya know."

"Yeah, she got the good looks," I said. "I got the ugly temper."

"Speaking of which," he said and fished a business card out of his pocket, "this guy has turned into a problem." He passed me the card.

"Bella Photography," I read. "Vincent Bell?"

"Yeah," said Little Joe. "Guy ran an ad in the paper for gals interested in a modeling career. He rented one of the conference rooms over the weekend to take the pictures."

"Legit?"

Joe shrugged. "I know he charged them for the pictures. Had little cuties lined up in the hall for two days."

"And?"

"He skated the bill," said Joe. "I've been calling the number, but it's a service and he ain't calling me back."

"How much?"

"Three hundred."

"Take him to small claims court." I bit off a chunk of a cinnamon roll and washed it down with a slug of coffee. "File a complaint with the Better Business Bureau. He'll pay."

"I can't really do that." Joe closed his eyes and whined, "It was sort of off the books."

"Ah," I said. "You need me to explain it to him."

"I'll take half, if I can get it now," said Little Joe. "What you get is up to you. On the books, the room would have been five yards, plus tax."

Misty strolled up wearing a fake smile and red eyes. Little Joe jumped to his feet.

"Misty," I said, "this is Chuck DeSimone. Chuck, this is my sister, Misty."

Little Joe reached and took Misty's hand with his right and patted it with his left. "I am so pleased to meet you," he said. "Around here, Ray's family is our family."

"Ya know," I said, "Misty's looking for a job right now."

"Gee," said Little Joe with a shrug, "all I got is housekeeping right now."

Misty said, "Well—"

"But, in a few weeks," he said, chopping the air with his finger, "my hostess, in the restaurant, is going on maternity leave. Might just be a couple of months for you, but you'd have some breathing room to find something else."

"Who knows?" said Misty. She turned her head to scorch me with a laser stare. "I could be run over by a bus by then and not have a problem in the world."

I put on my how-could-I-be-so-stupid face. "I know," I said, and threw out an open palm. "That pal of ours that takes pictures for modeling?" I shook my head. "Bella something?"

"Oh, Vincent!" said Little Joe. "Yeah."

"Maybe Misty could use your phone to set up a photo shoot. We don't have anything planned until after noon, and Misty's all decked out."

Misty leaned back in her chair, gave me one raised eyebrow and said "Sure" like the hiss of a cobra. Little Joe showed the way with a sweep of his arm and they tottered off to the desk. A vision of a stork leading Alice to the Mad Hatter's tea party came to mind. I called after them that Misty should say she saw his name in the paper and went to work on my already-soggy cornflakes.

On my last cinnamon roll, Misty returned to the table wearing the first hopeful smile I'd seen on her. She said, "He can see me right away." She showed me a scrap of paper with a scribbled address.

"Yeah," I said. "Great!" Guess my feigned enthusiasm didn't quite sell it. When I reached for the paper, her smile hardened into an accusation.

She pulled the paper away and said, "What's going on?"

"He's ducking Little Joe because he skated out on a room rental."

"So, you used me?"

"No," I said. "He really does take pictures for modeling agencies."

"You bastard!" She picked up her plate of French toast.

I held up both hands in surrender. "Okay, I didn't want you to know. I needed you to be sincere so he would give you the address."

"You wanted me to lie for you?" Misty's lips took on a curl and the arm with the sticky breakfast coiled.

"I wanted you to be truthful. We're going to get your picture taken." I waved my hands. "For God's sake, you're a knockout, Misty. Gimme a break."

She eased off on the plateful, but didn't set it back on the table. "I want the truth, and you can start from the top. You call him Little Joe and introduce him to me as Chuck?"

"His name is Charles, most people call him Chuck." I shrugged.

"What's Little Joe?"

"Eight the hard way," I said, chuckled, and nearly strangled myself on a sip of coffee.

"Who—what?" she said, leaning toward me.

I dabbed my mouth with a napkin. "He's got eight kids. Four boys. Four girls."

Misty shook her head, her eyes vacant.

"Dice," I said. "What's two ones?"

"Snake eyes?"

"Right. A pair of sixes is boxcars, and two fours are . . . ?" I pointed a finger.

"Little Joe!"

"Bingo," I said. "His youngest daughter was born with a club foot and a cleft palate. He needs his money."

Misty holstered her plate on the table.

LITTLE JOE HAD LENT US his car, a rolling testament to duct tape and coat hangers with a bungee cord holding up the rear bumper. Lucky for us, Misty could drive a stick. I haven't had a driver's license in years. She'd tossed her high heels on the back seat, and off we went.

We had to park so far out in the lot at the Grandview Mall, I wondered why we had bothered to drive in the first place. Our photographer had staged the shoot in front of the whale fountain, sort of a convex chrome suggestion of Moby Dick with water spouting from the blow hole.

Vincent Bell turned out to be Vinney LaRoaka, a small potatoes bunco artist who lacked the gift for grift to be a real con man. In his late thirties, he had a lot of nose, no chin, and a ponytail gathered off a wreath of black hair that ringed his head at ear level. The top of his head, bare and sweaty, gleamed as shiny as the fountain. With his excursion into photography, I guessed Vinney had given up trying to perfect the Pigeon Drop.

Half a dozen perky young ladies stood in a queue, each clutching a sheet of paper like it was a lifeline to golden tomorrows. Vinney had set a camera on a tripod next to a couple of those light-inside-silver-umbrella things. Looked pretty convincing, but two mall security guards in state police uniforms with private security patches had Vinney off to the side and were chewing on him like dogs with a bone.

"The mall is private property, Mac. You gotta pay to do business here. You need a permit."

"I got one of those," said Vinney. "Crossed in the mail. Honest to God!"

"Pack up and get out!"

"I can't go to the mall office," said Vinney, shrugging while he spread his arms. "The ladies are here. I can't leave the equipment."

One of the guards spoke into the hand-mic clipped to the epaulet of his shirt. "Eight-one to base, I need you to call the city police."

"Wait, wait," said Vinney. "If you can get the form, I'll fill it out and pay." Vinney offered his open palms. "Again, I mean. I trust you. We can straighten this out."

"Stand by," the guard said into the radio. Then, to Vinney, "I get back here, you got sixteen hundred dollars or you're gone. If not,"—he made a single nod of his head—"you get busted for trespassing and they impound your gear as evidence."

"I'll be here," said Vinney. "But I have to write you a check."

"Then you better be gone," said the guard, "because you don't take pictures until the check clears."

"Okay," said Vinney. "Cash."

"Don't take any pictures until we get back." They left.

Vinney watched the guards until they rounded a corner and then smacked his hands together. "Okay, ladies, this is going to be fast. Gimme the release forms and sixty dollars. You'll get the proofs in a week."

Misty rushed up and asked if he could squeeze her in before those "big bullies" came back.

"You bet, baby," said Vinney. "I'm going to make you a star."

My plan to impersonate Misty's agent lasted until Vinney laid eyes on me. Stepping backwards in haste, he threw up his hands and implored the heavens, "Mamma mia, Sweet Jesus, tell me what I did."

"You're a waste of skin," I said.

"Kerze, I'm legit," said Vinney, "and besides, you ain't a cop no more, so this ain't your business."

"My business is the three-hundred-dollar room tab you left at the City Suites."

"Tell the manager to call me in a couple days."

"He's been calling," I said. "But you don't call back."

A smug smile set sail on Vinney's face. "Tell him to sue me," he said.

"Can't," I said. "Was off the books. You got a conference room at half price."

"Well, that's just too bad then, ain't it?"

"For you," I said. "I bought the debt. Now you owe me."

"I don't owe you jack shit."

"You owe me three hundred, today." I picked up his camera and folded the tripod legs. "How much is this worth?"

"All right, all right," he said. "C'mon. No camera, no money."

I let him take the camera back.

"Call me. A couple days, we'll work it out."

"Let's work it out right now," I said. "How about an installment plan?"

"Yeah," said Vinney. "That's the foundation of America. But it's gotta be small payments that go for a long time."

"How much?"

Vinney dug into his pants pocket and then looked at his palm. "I got fifty cents."

"How about a quarter?" I said.

Vinney leaned toward me, made his face insolent, and said, "How about a nickel?"

I forced a smile. "Perfect." I cracked the knuckles on my right fist. "I'll beat the three hundred dollars out of your narrow, froggy ass at a nickel a pound. I get the first installment today."

Vinney turned to run, but my right hand clamped onto his ponytail and lifted until he danced on his toes.

"Kerze," he begged. "For God's sake!"

I took the camera and tripod out of his hands and handed it to Misty. "We don't want to break that."

"Ray?" he said. "It's three hundred doll-laars."

"The smaller the amount," I said, "the bigger the insult."

He produced a rubber band-wrapped roll of bills from his hip pocket and peeled me off three hundred, mostly twenties. I let him get his heels on the ground and let go of his hair. He took the camera from Misty, adjusted the tripod legs, and sighted through the eyepiece. I dealt three twenties off the stack, tucked them into his shirt pocket, and said, "Make her a star."

Vinney motioned me to the side, turned his head away from the ladies, and fished the money out of his shirt pocket between his index and middle finger.

"Ray," he whispered, handing me back the money. "There's no chip in the camera . . ."

MISTY GROUND HER WAY INTO third gear and said, "You're no different from that Meat Hook guy!"

"I think there's a big difference," I said.

"How?" she said, waving her hand like she was shooing a fly off the windshield. "You threatened to beat him, so he paid."

"I would have appealed to his higher virtues, but the man is a maggot sandwich. And, had I been Meat Hook Marty, I would have given Vinney a gratuitous beating after he paid and then stolen the rest of his money."

"You let him get away with the lie that the camera 'suddenly' broke and couldn't save images."

"The ladies had a dream. They got their money back and they got to keep their dream."

"I had that dream too," said Misty.

"And you can still have it. Just pick a photographer whose best work isn't his own mug shot."

"I don't need a dream," Misty said. "I don't have a future."

I looked at my watch—same time as before. "Ain't noon yet, so you don't know," I said. Misty turned right onto Grand Boulevard. "Hotel's the other way."

"I just want to pick some stuff up down here," she said. "I couldn't pay the rent, so the landlord locked me out of my room. I've been sleeping in the laundry room and I left a couple bags of clothes."

"Don't need your jammies for a dirt nap," I said.

"Salvation Army," she said, "if you don't mind taking care of that for me."

"For eleven bucks I'll put them in a mail box if I can't find a trash can."

Misty laughed. I laughed. But when we arrived at her building, we walked straight into Meat Hook Marty. He wasn't laughing.

Marty's head looked like an inverted bucket parked atop a granite boulder. He wore an impeccably cut, double-breasted black wool pin-stripe suit, a black cashmere turtleneck—sort of his way of saying "I do *too* have a neck"—and a fifty-dollar gold piece suspended on a fat gold chain.

He reached for Misty. I intercepted his hand, giving it a good shake with both of mine. Misty disappeared into the building, leaving Marty and me on the street. I said, "Marty! How the hell are you? How long has it been?"

Marty watched Misty disappear, gave me a sad sigh, and cranked his vice-like grip onto my hand.

"Gee, Kerze," he said, "let me see." He gave my hands a pat that would have splattered a turtle. Numbness spread to my elbows. "Last I saw you, you busted me for boosting car radios and sent me to reform school."

"Great to see you," I said. "What are you doing now?"

"Business, Kerze. And you are no longer a policeman. So it isn't your business."

He released my hands, and I looked at them to take inventory because I couldn't feel the digits.

"Business good?" I asked.

"Yes, it is," said Marty. "And I'm going to business school three nights a week to finish my MBA."

"Career taking a new direction?"

"Hardly," he said. "I'm thinking payday loans, car title loans, and check cashing."

"Benny has become a forward thinker."

"Benny is a very charming antique," said Marty. "I may have him freeze-dried and displayed in his booth as a curio."

"Nice to catch up with you," I said, "but I gotta go."

Marty closed his eyes and shook his head. "No, Ray," he said. "You know we're not done. You've stuck your nose in this."

"She's a client," I said, "and she left. I think she was on her way to pay Benny."

"She doesn't have any money," Marty said. "I know because I bought her that dress and gave her cab fare, but not so she could go see you."

"She came to my office this morning. I took a small retainer."

Marty took a firm grip on my shoulder. "Ray, I know how you collect strays. I saw you talking to the guards when I was in juvy. It made things better for me." He gave me a gentle pat on the cheek. "Kerze, you old bastard. You have a good heart, but this is business. She had a date last night. She didn't show up. The Night Lighters aren't happy, and Benny is furious. What can I do?"

"Let her go," I said. "You bought a lady a nice gift. I won't tell your wife."

"It's a matter of respect, Ray," he said. "When respect fails, all I have left to work with is fear."

"I can't let it happen."

"This isn't about you. And by the way," Marty said, squinting and scrunching up his nose, "do you have any idea what you smell like?"

"Booze?"

Marty reached into his pocket and produced a wad of money that would choke Babe the Blue Ox. "You should be so lucky." He peeled off two Benjamins, folded them, and stuffed them in the hanky pocket of my jacket. "Look, Ray, forget about this. Be a friend. Go get some steam. And, for God's sake, burn that suit."

"You gotta listen carefully, Marty," I said, measuring my words. "I. Can't. Let. You. Do. This."

Marty put away the money and whispered, "Okay, Ray."

He produced a set of brass knuckles, his face long and sad as he slid them onto his fingers. "I'll give you a beat down. Everybody will know that you're still a stand-up guy."

I LOOKED AT MY WATCH—time for a drink. As I tipped up my pint I saw Misty perched on the edge of her roof like a gargoyle. I thought better of waving her down.

Five flights of stairs later, it felt like I was breathing razor blades. I stepped out onto the roof and said, "Who are we trying to kill, you or me?"

Misty had set her shoes and purse on the ledge and dangled her bare feet into the five-story void. "Just a little shove."

I parked Marty's shoes next to hers and took a seat on the ledge. The cement felt warm on my backside. Pigeons swooped below us, dropping whitewash on passing yellow taxicabs.

"Shoes?" she asked.

"And a watch."

"Whose?"

"Marty's," I said.

A police car and an ambulance rounded the corner with their lights and sirens on full whoopee. They screeched to a halt right below us.

I pointed down at the spectacle. "Marty," I said, and took a beat to think about it. "Marty had an accident."

"Really?" she said, knitting up doubt with her eyebrows.

"It's like he got mugged," I said. "A couple of big guys with pipes or bats or something."

"You were there?"

"Yeah, but what could I do?" I shrugged. "A couple of guys. With clubs!"

A smoke smile drifted across her face. "You beat the shit out of him."

"Nah," I said. "Marty and I go back a long way. He just wanted me to take care of his shoes and watch. Stuff like this gets lost in emergency rooms."

Misty slowly shook her head, keeping her eyes riveted on mine.

"Sometimes," I said. "Anyway. Marty said to give you this. Two hundred bucks." I gave her the money Marty had stuffed in my pocket. "Said he understands that you can't do the escort thing, but you need to talk to Benny again."

"I don't believe you."

"No?" I said. "That really is two hundred bucks. But, okay," I shrugged. "Marty's jaw may be dislocated, so what he's really sayin' is kinda up for grabs."

"You're not telling me everything."

"There's a lot of that going round, Miss They-bought-me-this-dress-and-I-had-a-date-and-didn't-show-up-and-I-spent-my-cab-fare-on-a-detective. Did I leave anything out?"

"Whatever." Misty swung her legs back to the roof side and stepped into her shoes. "Maybe I'll win the lottery, too." She stowed the money in her purse.

"I'll drink to that."

"*You* don't drink to celebrate," said Misty. She headed for the roof door.

I picked up a paper bag from the trash shifting around on the roof and plopped in Marty's shoes and watch.

The roof door swept open and out stepped Donnie McQuinn, my old patrol partner—a six-foot blue muffin with sergeant's stripes. He said, "Jesus! Kerze, the man of the hour. There's still time. Jump and do everybody a favor."

"Donnie!" I said. "You're a good man. I don't care what your wife says."

"Which one?" he said. "They're all ex-wives now, anyway."

"Donnie, Misty. Misty, Donnie," I said.

"That's *Sergeant McQuinn*, thank you." He pecked his trigger finger at me. "I've been looking for you for two hours."

"I thought you quit drinkin'."

"And the ambulance crew thought you two were jumpers. What are you doing up here?"

"Misty lives here," I said. "She wanted to show me the view from the roof."

"Maybe you were hiding out," said McQuinn, deadpan.

"Wouldn't have been sitting on the ledge," I said, and offered McQuinn a pull on my pint. "It's all right, alcohol kills the germs."

McQuinn massaged his face with his hand.

I took that as a "no" and put the pint in the bag with Marty's stuff, handed the bag to Misty, and turned my head so I could give her a wink.

"Why is it," said McQuinn, "I'm following a trail of shit all day, and when I get to the end of it, there you are?"

"Gee, Donnie." I shrugged.

"It's because it's *your* shit trail," said McQuinn. He took a notepad out of his pocket and thumbed it open. "Take a little bus ride this morning, did you?"

"I don't drive anymore," I said.

"And?"

"I took the bus," I said. "I have a part-time gig as the house dick down at the City Suites."

"And?"

"We had breakfast."

"Nothing remarkable?"

"My cornflakes got soggy."

"On the bus!"

"I didn't get the cornflakes on the bus."

McQuinn gave me a grimace and a groan that sounded like a growl. "We'll get back to that." He licked his thumb and flipped up a page. "You were at the mall today?"

"Yeah," I said. "Misty wanted her picture taken. She got all dolled up. A guy scouting for fashion models."

"How'd that go?" said McQuinn. Butter wouldn't have melted in his mouth.

"Didn't work out," I said. "The guy had problems with the camera—something like that."

"You think he was telling the truth?"

"How would I know?"

"So you were holding him off the ground by his ponytail to test the wind speed?"

"Who told you that?" I tried for incredulity.

"Mall security," said McQuinn. "They called and said the photographer was trespassing. They said there'd been an altercation."

"They file a complaint?"

"They took it as a favor."

"I guess that leaves the photographer," I said.

"Vinney LaRoaka," said McQuinn. "If he said water was wet, I'd check. Right now, he says he wasn't at the mall."

"So, there you have it," I said and took Misty by the hand. "We want to go check the lotto numbers. Misty just told me she thinks she's going to win."

McQuinn shook a finger. "Not so fast. Downstairs, I got one Martin Milazzo, AKA Meat Hook Marty. The best I can make out—he's not speaking very clearly just now—is two hard cases took the wood to him."

"So, he's mobbed up," I said. "Could be an internal Partnership matter."

"Also downstairs, I got a couple of hard cases who could have mistaken him for you," said McQuinn. He unfurled a plastic evidence bag with a switchblade knife in it and asked, "This look familiar?"

Marty and I stood about the same height and carried the same bulk, but that's where the resemblance ended. It was more like McQuinn wanted me to incriminate myself.

I made a circle with my index finger and he spun the bag so I could see the other side. I squinted and bent at the waist to get my head close to the bag. When I straightened up, I announced, like an epiphany, "Switchblade knife!"

"That's it, Kerze," said McQuinn, his face red hot against his sandy hair. He stuffed the evidence bag with the knife into his pocket. "I had your back, but now it's all on you. Maybe a cruise on the SS *County Jail* will dry you out."

"Well, it ain't mine!" I said. "I just shoot 'em. The coroner cleans 'em."

"Hilarious," said McQuinn. "Let's see how funny this is: I got two guys in the back of the squad car. I just picked them up around the corner. Same guys filed a complaint this morning. Said they got roughed up on a bus. The bus driver gave me the knife, which a passenger found on the floor. And I got to say the description could have been you or Marty, but I don't think Marty rides the bus."

"I saw the knife," said Misty.

"All them knives look alike," I said. "How do you know it was *that* knife?"

"Shut up, Ray," said McQuinn. "We're going downstairs. If you say one word on the way, I'm going to hook you up."

I said nothing. Didn't help—they put the cuffs on me anyway when I got downstairs. McQuinn could hold me for seventy-two hours. By then, Misty would need a drink. And that's only if I could find the cheap bordello where Benny would have her tied to a bed.

YOU NEVER KNOW WHAT TIME it is; they don't want you to know. They had my watch, my belt, and my gun. My universe had been reduced to a metal table and two wooden chairs in a room with a mirror that was a window on the other side, but no clock.

McQuinn would talk to Misty—trip her up and get her to say something stupid—then hit the coffee pot. He'd round up the lieutenant and shoot the shit about ball scores and then head for the restroom with the sports section. By and by, he'd get a fresh cup of coffee and a stale donut and head for the room on the other side of the mirror so that he could watch me.

Guys who go to sleep are usually guilty—finish the donut and close the case. Guys who pace around the room and move the furniture are hiding something—finish the donut and have a second cup of coffee while they badger themselves into a real dither. Guys who sit at the table with their hands folded and stare at the window like they know you're watching have won the game—pitch the donut, go straight in, and take your best shot.

McQuinn marched in and set Marty's shoes on the table in front of me.

He took the chair across the table and stared a hole in me for what seemed like a long time. Finally, he said, "Nobody 'has it coming.' That's the difference between us and them."

I said nothing.

He said, "Maybe not for you, so much. Anymore."

I still said nothing.

His beaming Irish face clouded into a sneer. In twenty-some years, he had never shown me that face. "Maybe you need a drink?"

"I don't want a drink."

McQuinn fell back into his chair with his mouth open. I felt stunned, not that I had said it, but that I meant it. For the first time since Sheila, my wife, had passed, I didn't want a drink—that frozen hollow brick, buried in my chest, wasn't begging for a splash of warmth.

After a sullen calm, McQuinn confessed, "I know you did it."

I didn't answer. I couldn't guess which "it" he meant. He hadn't mentioned the skinheads from the bus, so I thought it best not to open the subject for discussion.

"Broken nose, broken jaw, broken right knee," said McQuinn. "You should just sign your work. How long did it take, three seconds? He had to be on the bricks before he got a good grip on his brass knuckles."

I did my best check-the-pot-while-holding-four-aces face.

"I'm not thinking robbery. Marty still had eleven grand and change in his pocket, and a pound of gold bling around his neck. He says a couple of guys with bats attacked him, but his descriptions are a little thin. If it ever got around that one old drunk took him out like a vandal stepping on a Halloween pumpkin, his street moniker wouldn't be 'Meat Hook' anymore."

I cleared my throat.

"So," said McQuinn, "get the fuck out of here and take the shoes with you. Marty said he asked you to look after them. The watch is in property and they'll give it to you with your stuff. Your gun is in ballistics. If it comes up clean, you can pick it up in a week."

McQuinn remained in his chair, and I walked around him. When I got to the door, he said, without looking around, "Ray, I don't get you two—I mean you and Misty. Maybe you should think about it."

I opened the door and told the empty hallway, "It ain't like that, Donnie." I let the door fall shut on its own weight.

I DIDN'T WANT TO LEAVE through the squad room. It's hard to watch old friends muddle through pretending they don't know you. I took the narrow outside stairwell from the basement property room to the street.

Lightning Bolts and Swastika waited for me at the top of the stairs.

They had bookend bruises on their heads that, at first glance, my brain tried to make into tattoos. Swastika had some scabbed-over scuffs on his arms amid a general motif of skulls and daggers. They stood at the ready, hands balled into fists, with sinister sneers on their faces which they, no doubt, practiced in the mirror when not being obnoxious in public.

I stopped about three steps from the top and set the bag with Marty's shoes and watch on the ledge under the black steel pipe hand rail. I said, "You two froggin' idiots have *got* to be kidding."

"Yeah?" said Swastika. "What are you going to do, bang our heads again? This time I'm watching."

"This time the cops are watching," I said, pointing out the video box mounted on the corner of the precinct building. "At least we won't have to sit around in interview or wait for a lineup." I loosened my tie and started up the remaining steps. "Take your best shot. If we hurry, we can get lunch at the county courthouse. At the jail, all you get is chicken salad and Kool Aid."

"Whoa," said Swastika. He shot a glance at the camera box, then stepped back and threw up his open palms. "Peace and chicken grease, dude. We were getting along fine until numb nuts here snapped out his knife."

"She said she wanted to see it," said Lightning Bolts. "Misty even said so."

"Misty?" I said.

"Yeah, she told that big Irish cop that she asked to see it, said it was a joke, but it all turned into a big mistake."

"Misty?"

"Yeah, the cop said that was like fifty-fifty. If he charged you with assault, he'd have to charge me with CCW. Jeez, I mean, it's not even a gun."

"Where's Misty?" I said.

"She said she wanted to see the river from the bridge," said Swastika. "The cops took her back to her car."

I looked at my watch. "What time is it?"

"You ain't getting out of this by acting crazy," said Swastika.

I shook Marty's watch out of the toe of his right shoe. It had a black face with no numbers, one gold hand, and a diamond at twelve o'clock—an idiot watch that probably cost a fortune. Close as I could figure, it was either five minutes after noon or nearly one o'clock. "You guys got a car?" I said.

"Love to take you for a ride," said Swastika, his teeth showing, "but didn't we meet on a bus?"

"What time is the lottery drawing?"

"Don't know," said Lightning Bolts. "We just got in town." He beamed a bright smile. "We're starting a new chapter."

"There's a million froggin' idiots in this town," I said. "You'll do just fine."

Swastika clinched his eyes and held his hands out, emphasizing each word with a downward chop. "What's—With—the frogs!?"

"Right you are," I said. "My apologies to froggies everywhere." I wrung my hands together and cracked the knuckles on my left hand, then the right. "Also, I meant no insult to the rest of this city's idiots."

"See ya around," Swastika said, with a wink and a nod. "Real soon!"

They started down the street. I picked up Marty's shoes. Lightning Bolts turned around and said, walking backwards, "Misty said you know the Mob guys."

I shrugged. "A million idiots."

"Could you tell 'em we didn't tune up that Mob dude?"

I waved a hand. "All they care about is who gets Marty's action."

I HAD TO HOOF IT all the way to the cab stand at the Continental and it still cost twenty-two of Vinney LaRoaka's three hundred bucks to get to Genie's Wienies. Twenty-two dollars is the price of three pints of vodka and reason enough to strangle Benny, but today I didn't care. Time was up for Misty, and probably Benny as well. I felt a rush of relief when I saw him enthroned in his booth and holding court as usual. From behind the hot dog counter, Big George gave me the evil eye as I advanced on the old reprobate.

Benny Slick—Benjamin Schlezik—looked like a dry twig wearing a Sears permanent wrinkle suit. He suffered from an enlarged heart and had to drag around an air tank on a trolley. As he slowly evaporated, the air tank got ever larger. His skin looked like a sheet of crumpled parchment and his neck rattled around his shirt collar like a soda straw in a bucket.

I looked again at George—shaved head, biceps sculpted on the iron pile at Jackson Prison, and wearing a white T-shirt and bib apron to complete his image of a counterman instead of a shylock's doorman. He nodded, and I slid into Benny's booth and said, "Hey Benny, been a long time."

"Fuck you, Raymond," Benny said. "Eat shit and die."

"You ain't still mad about that usury bust," I said.

"Why would I be mad?" said Benny. "That happened ten, fifteen years ago. Besides, I'm still a shy—" He smiled and had to adjust his cannula. "But you ain't a cop."

"Life moves on," I said.

"Yeah, now you're a drunk. Why are you wasting my time?"

"Misty."

"Short hair, big eyes, and a daisy tattooed on her neck?" asked Benny.

"Yeah."

"Never heard of her," said Benny. "And if I had, it wouldn't be your business. Get the fuck outta here."

"She's a client," I said. "I'm trying to help her."

"You want to help her?" Benny laughed, but it turned into a coughing fit that left him gasping. George hustled over to the table and glowered at me while he pulled Benny straight and turned up his air flow.

Benny composed himself and patted the hand George still had on his shoulder.

"It's okay, George," said Benny. "I'm fine." George stalked back to his lair behind the counter and Benny drilled me with his now bloodshot eyes. "Here's the advice of an old man: Run away from that crazy broad as fast as you can. I tried to help her and I got nothing but trouble."

"Five thousand dollars for a five hundred dollar loan?" I said.

Benny shrugged. "She knew the deal. Who else was going to lend her the money? I kept telling her to get her shit together and pay it off. She didn't do it. She just kept paying the vig. Then she lost her job and couldn't pay nothin'."

"Five grand?"

"Listen," said Benny. He spread his palms. "I told her to leave the bum in jail."

"But you lent her the money?"

Benny's face fell blank and he leaned back in his seat. "That's what I do. And I'm done talking to you." He leaned forward again, his head and neck weaving like a cobra in a basket. "You want to talk, talk to Marty."

I took Marty's shoes out of the bag, shook his watch out and laid it on the table next to the shoes. "Marty's going to be on the bench for a while," I said. "He had an accident."

Benny's eyes latched onto the shoes. For a long moment, he said nothing. Heat gathered in his face and his upper lip curled.

"You think—" Benny sputtered. "You can—" His whole body began to quake. "Just walk in here and threaten me?"

"It's not a threat," I said. "It's a favor. Marty didn't want to lose his shoes and watch in the emergency room. Maybe you can have George put 'em under the counter."

"Get out!"

"We need to talk about Misty."

Though clenched teeth, Benny said, "You need to make your peace with God. You don't have much time."

"We're all pressed for time. That's why I took a cab instead of waiting for the bus."

"I'm connected, you dumb bastard," Benny said. "If Marty's out, there's no shortage of muscle."

"And word gets around," I said. "They're probably on their way here right now."

Benny allowed himself a smile. "When they get here, you're going for a ride."

"Somebody's going for a ride," I said, "but I think it's you. Because without Marty to run interference, there's half a dozen made guys who want your book."

"I was here when this was a pool hall." Benny hammered the table with his index finger. "I was here when this was a launderette, and I'll still be here when you're fish food."

"Then we got time to talk about Misty."

"What *is* it with you?" Benny exclaimed. "This broad, she is nothing but trouble. I had to call in favors to get her into the Night Lighters. They had her fixed up with a diplomat. But she was a no-show and now everybody's pissed. She woulda met somebody to take care of her, instead of that tattoo artist bum that left her holding the bag."

"And you supplied the bag," I said. "And now, we have so little time."

Benny reached into his inside coat pocket and produced a battered leather notebook and a pair of dime-store reading glasses. With the cheaters perched on the tip of his nose, he thumbed a few pages. "Nine-fifty, today," he said. "You buy the paper. You can do whatever. Or Friday, she gets the sawbuck blowjob concession behind the bus station."

Five hundred pounds of Mafia—in the form of two button men wearing silk suits and pompadour haircuts—ducked through the front door. They had purpose in their step and when they got to Benny's table they looked at me and said in unison, "Get lost."

"Fuck you, Jerry," said Benny. "I'm doin' business here. Who's this mug you're with anyway?"

"This is Ricky. He's Ruffalo's nephew."

"He's a friend of yours or a friend of ours?"

"Benny, you ain't got no friends. Bill Junior's calling you in."

"So what?" said Benny. "I was on Black Bill's crew before you were the bastard son of a wanna-be goomba and a taxi dancer."

"Thanks, Benny," Jerry said. "I was feelin' bad about this for a minute."

"Go sit down and feel bad quiet-like," said Benny. "George will get you some lunch. I don't want you drivin' out here for nuthin'."

"I'm sent for you," said Jerry.

"Unless Black Bill sent you, you're sent for lunch," said Benny.

"Black Bill is away for a while, and he's as old as you, so he ain't likely comin' back. In the meantime, Bill Junior is here and Black Bill says he's in charge. So you can leave here through the door or through the front window. I don't care which. You're goin'.""

"This is what I get?" said Benny. "This is respect? This is honor?"

"This is it," said Jerry. "You get what you get."

Benny ripped a page out of his book, folded it, and pushed it across the table to me.

"So, you're paid," he said. "Go and sin no more, or at least leave the ponies to pull the ice wagon."

"Thanks, Benny," I said. I left, even though I wanted to hang around and see how many steps Benny had to take before his suit started moving.

DANNY'S BAR AND GRILL HAD old dark paneling that sucked up the light and fixtures that dated back to the Vietnam War. The only deference to modern times was a flat-screen TV mounted next to a row of bottles covered with dust, their labels turning brown at the edges. Local news was covering a local crisis, and that crisis was Misty.

Misty had the bridge to Canada lit up like the Las Vegas strip. Traffic in both directions was blocked by police cars and fire trucks with their lights rolling and flashing like a pinball machine ready to give up a free game. Misty had parked her backside on the rail right where she had one cheek in Canada and one cheek in the US of A. Only the prevailing winds would decide who got to clean up the mess.

"The TV is for the customers," said the bartender, a rangy fifty-year-old with tinted hair combed back in a greasy wave. The name on his shirt said "Kelsey."

"I just ducked in to use the restroom," I said.

"That's for the customers too."

Twist my arm, then. "Whiskey, twice," I said. "Whatever's on the bar."

The news station had a boat on the river and was channeling live pictures of Misty perched on the rail, zooming in and out so that you got a sense of the several hundred feet to the water. Her hair and dress fluttered in a strong breeze. Her face washed vacant, like her brain had taken her mind somewhere else.

I went to the head, returned, and knocked back a shot, but it felt like slugging a sock full of burs down my throat—no warmth, no sense of peace.

"What is this?" I said.

"Canadian Mist," said Kelsey.

"More like German *Mist*," I said, wondering if Kelsey knew the German word for *crap*.

"You making some accusation about the bar stock?" said Kelsey.

I ignored him and pointed to the TV. "The girl with half her ass in Canada's named Misty."

"No shit," said Kelsey. "You know her?"

"Yeah." I fingered the second shot but pushed it away.

"They said on TV she wanted to talk to some guy," said Kelsey. "The cops were looking for him."

My stomach grumbled. "Can I use your phone?"

McQuinn MET ME AT THE curb and we roared off with lights and sirens. He said, "I thought you two were on the roof looking at the view?"

"I guess I get to see the view from the bridge now."

When we got to the Ambassador Bridge, they asked for my passport. I laughed. McQuinn told them we'd stay on the American side and we took an electric maintenance cart—the only thing we could weasel through the stopped vehicles—out to the middle of the bridge.

At the international border, McQuinn handed me a bullhorn. "Has a crappy battery," he said. "Just keep pushing up on the battery cover with your thumb and click the trigger until you hear it squeak, then you can talk—but you gotta hold it like when you got the squeak."

"Maybe you got one that works?" I asked.

"Chief has it over there by the news crew," said McQuinn.

The rescue and police had formed a half-moon line about fifty feet from Misty. She said she'd jump if they came any closer. The wind ripped right along up there, and you could see through the metal mesh decking to the water below.

I took a step past the line and got the bullhorn to squeak once. Misty turned her head and smiled. I set the horn on the deck and walked out to Misty. I heard a commotion from behind—McQuinn grappling with a couple of rescue types that wanted to haul me back to the line.

I climbed up on the rail and sat on the American side of Misty. Lucky for us, the wind pushed in our face. The boats below us looked like bobbers on a fishing line.

"Life sucks," I said. "I'm gonna jump with ya."

"You wouldn't tease a girl, would you?" Misty asked.

"On three?"

Misty took a deep breath and squared her shoulders.

"You know they got a boat down there with a TV camera and they're takin' pictures up your dress."

Misty laughed. "Bullshit."

"No," I said, "I saw it on the news channel. You're wearing black underpants."

Misty let go of the rail long enough to backhand my shoulder and tuck her dress between her thighs.

"See," she said, "now I know you're lying." Her face colored red. "The dress cost eight hundred bucks and the cheap bastard wouldn't spring for underwear."

"Oh, my," I said. "That *is* breezy."

"Count!" said Misty.

"All right," I said. "Ready? One!"

Misty closed her eyes and wriggled her backside on the rail.

"Oh, yeah," I said. "I talked to Benny. He gave me this." I dug Benny's page out of my inside coat pocket and handed it to Misty. "He said, 'Go and sin no more'—and something about ponies and ice wagons. I think he's gettin' senile."

Misty held it in one hand and squinted while the wind flapped the note. "I can't read this," she said. "Some of the letters look backwards."

"It's in Ukrainian," I said. "Russian alphabet. The numbers are Yiddish letters. Benny and his family were driven out of their home by a pogrom in the thirties. Having that sheet means you're paid."

"Did I really win the lottery?" Misty asked.

"I haven't had a chance to check the tickets."

"Then, why would he do that?"

"Long story," I said. "But, basically, he liked you and he hated your boyfriend."

Misty handed the note back. "I don't have any pockets. I left my purse on the bridge and they took it with this little robot thing that looked like a tiny tank with a grabber arm."

"What difference will it make if we both go in the drink?"

"Count!" she said.

"Two."

"Wait," she said, "just one thing."

"Sure." I liked the "wait" thing. I hoped it would be a long thing.

"You introduced me to people as your sister?"

"A little fib," I said. "I'm a detective, a trained fibber. I tell fibs to get to information that people would conceal. It's called permissible decept—"

"No, no," said Misty. "Most old guys with a much younger lady tell people that she's his niece. You know—wink, wink—a niece."

"What do you mean, *old*?" I said.

Misty rolled her eyes and made one wag of her head.

"Yes, I'm old," I said. "Older than you, anyway. Saying that you were my sister was sort of shorthand for, 'This is Misty and she's important to me.' I never thought of you as 'wink, wink.'"

Misty sidled over to me, hooked her arm though mine, and hugged her head to my shoulder. "You are a sweet man," she said. Then she squared her shoulders, arched her back, and closed her eyes.

"Okay," I said. At this point, she could drag me over. If I held on myself, I wasn't so sure I could hold on to Misty. "I get a question."

Misty sighed and looked at me sideways. "Now what?"

"The whole Meat Hook Marty and Benny thing is taken care of. So why are we still sitting on this rail?"

"You wouldn't understand."

"Try me. It's a long way down, and I think the water's cold."

Misty tightened her hold on my arm. "I'm worse than a leper. I can't have a man. I'm stupid. If I had children, they'd die before they had a life."

"The postcard you got in the mail?"

"Yes," said Misty, her body convulsing.

I held on with both hands and hooked an ankle around the rail support.

"I thought about that," I said. "You had a blood test and—let me guess—it came back negative."

"They said I had to go back for another test in three months." Misty wiped her flooding eyes on my sleeve.

"Did they send you the results on a post card?"

"No," said Misty. "It came in a plain envelope."

"Postcard with bad news, envelope with good news." I paused for dramatic effect. "Makes you wonder, doesn't it?"

Misty scrunched up her face until her eyes made slits. She slowly turned her face to me. "You don't think my ex—"

"I'm just sayin'," I said.

Misty looked away and let her mouth fall open.

"You know your ex. Would he do something like this?"

She looked down at the boats. "He had a mean streak. That's how he got in trouble. The linen supplier stopped service to his tattoo studio for non-payment. When they sued him, he put sugar in the gas tanks of four of their delivery trucks. He didn't know they had video cameras."

"Okay, he was pissed at them. And it's good he got out of town, because all the laundry outfits belong to the Mob. But was he pissed at you?"

"We were arguing. He wanted me to leave with him. I wouldn't. I said I had my job and friends. He said"—she teetered her head from side to side and made her voice gruff—"'Oh yeah, the men you flirt with at the restaurant.'"

"So, a jealous type?"

Misty shrugged.

"Maybe he thought he could keep you from moving on," I said.

"That weasel," said Misty. She shook her head. "I'll kill him!"

"Maybe you should call the Vancouver Health Department first?"

"Let's have the cops call 'em."

"They'd lie," I said. "Permissible deception, remember? Basically, they'd tell you anything to get you off this rail. You'll have to call them yourself."

"Do you think Little Joe will let us use his phone?"

"I think we'd have to get off this rail."

"Now I'm afraid to move."

I turned my head, slow and careful. When I caught McQuinn's eye, I gave him the nod. Before they grappled us off the rail, I asked Misty, "What's with the tattoo on the back of your neck?"

She rubbed her head on my sleeve, like a cat, and purred, "Well, detective, there's a mystery for you."

The Second of Many Stories

The Boxer

SHOULDA CREPT UP AND gotten the claim ticket off Teddy right away. But I seen 'em—three of 'em—with bats. And they beat Teddy for a long time. And I just—couldn't move. He was screaming. And he begged them to stop. And they let him lay there and scream, and when he passed out, they pounded his brains into the pavement.

I shouldn't still be alive. I should be dead like Teddy, but I'm afraid of that, too.

And I knew he was dead and that creeped me out, and what if the guys we were supposed to give the hard drive to hadn't left? What if they were still around? If they were gonna beat Teddy to death, I knew they were gonna beat me.

So I sat up against the wall outside the parking garage where we were s'posed to meet them. Couldn't go back in. Couldn't leave. I didn't know what to do. I felt sick, like I was gonna puke.

I saw the first cop car pull in, then the second one, and then a tan car with blue flashing lights and two guys in suits, one black and one white. And that's when I really shoulda left, because this big Irish cop that almost busted Teddy and me over that business on the bus, he snuck up behind me and grabbed me by my T-shirt.

I scrabbled around with my feet to keep from getting drug to my knees. The big sergeant had hold of my shirt, and he wasn't letting go.

He pulled me down the block and back up into the parking garage, up to where Teddy was laying in a pool of blood, and then my head started hurting, too.

"Detective Jackson!" yelled my cop.

The black cop from the tan sedan turned around. He saw the tattoo on my neck and his eyes went all narrow and ugly and his nostrils flared. Other guys in the Struggle have been nearly beat to death by black cops in police stations. I wasn't about to say nothin' that might land me in there.

"Yo, McQuinn," said the black cop. "What's this?"

"Found this guy just standing around down the block." McQuinn let go of my shirt.

The white guy from the tan sedan stepped forward. He wore a suit so wrinkled it looked like he'd popped a brown paper bag and put it on. He flashed a badge in front of my face.

"Detective Paul Finney." He jerked a thumb at the black cop. "This is Detective Tony Jackson."

Detective Jackson balled his fists in the pockets of one snazzy suit. "So, what do you know about this, *boy?*"

I'd seen kinder eyes on a pit bull. My throat got so dry that, like, nothing came out. I swallowed hard. "Who says I know anything about this?"

Detective Jackson drilled me with his eyes. "Not *who*," he said, staring a hole in my neck. *"What."*

Detective Finney stepped in front of him. "What's your name, young man?" he said.

"John," I said.

"Last name?"

I looked at the concrete. I always hated this part. "Doe."

Detective Jackson rolled his eyes and McQuinn snorted.

"Your *real* last name," said Jackson.

"I don't know my real last name," I said. "They found me in a trash can at a gas station when I was a baby. John Doe is what's on the court papers. Most people just call me John or JD."

"Well, we already know *his* name," Detective Jackson jerked his head at Teddy laying crumpled and bloody on the concrete. He held up a plastic bag with fresh blood smears on the inside of it. It had Teddy's wallet in it. I could see our last thirty bucks sticking out of the top of the wallet.

I stared at it. Talking to them might be my only shot at getting the hardware Teddy didn't bring to the meet.

"If anybody saw anything," I said, "they're gonna have to, like, tell about it in court, right? And it will be in the paper, right?"

"This is a murder," snapped Jackson. "What do you think?"

Finney said, "Yeah, sometimes these things end up in the papers. In the small print. On the police blotter. And that's months away, when you testify."

Jackson showed me a face that promised a beat-down. Finney looked and sounded like he was half-asleep.

"What do you do with his stuff?" I said.

"We keep it for evidence until the murder trial," Finney said, "assuming you help us catch these guys. After that, it gets released to the victim's family."

"Only to family?" I asked. *Fuck*, I was gonna be stuck up here forever.

Detective Jackson's eyes narrowed. "Are you family?"

"No!" I said. "I don't know this guy. I never seen this guy at all. I was over there waiting for a bus." I pointed outside and down the block.

Off to my left, McQuinn shook his head *no*. Was there even a bus stop over there?

"Right," said Jackson, stepping way too close. "Here's Theodore Sorenson with a swastika tattooed on his head, and you've got fucking lightning bolts on your neck and you two don't know each other. What happened, some homeboys not like your tattoos? Some yo's? Some *Negroes*?"

I backed off, feeling all flush with heat. I tried not to yell, but it came out yelling anyway. "I wasn't! Here! I wasn't here, and you can't make me say I was! I didn't see nobody!" My eyes started watering and my nose started running.

The detectives looked at each other and Finney shrugged. "He's got a bruise on his head but no blood on him."

Sergeant McQuinn said, "That bruise is from this morning. Not relevant to what's going on here. Also, he was hanging around and not running off."

"McQuinn," said Jackson. "Give this *boy* a ride. Take him wherever he wants to go."

Sergeant McQuinn stepped up to them and they had their heads in a huddle for a few minutes. Then McQuinn grabbed my arm. "Come on, son," he said.

My head felt dizzy and my feet felt like blocks of wood, like they weren't my feet. He pulled me along by the elbow. I don't even remember getting stuffed into the squad car.

"They just only see that tattoo, and they hate me," I told him. But he acted like he didn't understand my words. "Teddy's already dead. They beat his head into hamburger! And they're going to do me next."

"Who's they?" Sergeant McQuinn asked. He pulled the patrol car over to the curb and dug a spiral notepad out of his shirt pocket.

"Everybody," I said. "Even you. You look at me like you want to puke when you look at me." My head throbbed really bad and I heard a whooshing sound. I touched the bruise on the side of my head. It hurt and the skin felt hot.

McQuinn adjusted his rearview mirror so he could see my face through the screen that divided the front seat from the back. But I could see him too—his mirrored sunglasses, his gray mustache, and the lines that punctuated his leathery, I-own-your-ass cop face. "You have Nazi lightning bolts tattooed on your neck," he said. "How'd you think people would take it?"

"They're called sig-runes. They're like two esses—stands for *Schutzstaffel*. The black on white were—"

"How old are you?" McQuinn took off his sunglasses and put them on the dash of the cruiser.

"Eighteen," I said.

"How long you had that tattoo?"

"Since I was, like, twelve. I got it after Senior Youth Camp."

McQuinn's head fell forward and he made this low sigh that sounded like a faint growl. My door clicked, and he said, "Come up. Come up here and sit in the front seat with me."

When I had, he said, "Hook up your seat belt." He rested his notepad on the steering wheel, chopped his pen at me and said, "Tell me about the 'they' that killed Theodore Sorenson."

"I don't know," I said. But I did know. Kinda. Not like I knew their names or nothing like that, but I seen 'em. "I don't know what to do," I said. "I don't have no place to go."

"Go home," said McQuinn. "Where's your family?"

"I don't have no family. Teddy and I were foster kids, ya know, like brothers but not really. And when you're eighteen, the state don't pay anymore, so you have to get out."

"Where did you spend last night?" said McQuinn. "I'll take you there."

"We were on the bus last night."

"Where did you leave your luggage?"

"We had some clothes and stuff in a grocery bag. It's checked at the bus station."

"Good!" said McQuinn. "You pick up your clothes, get on the bus, and go back where you came from. I'm sure you have friends there."

"They were Teddy's friends," I said. "And if they found out how I just let him get his head pounded in, they'd sure as like pound my head in, too."

"Buy a ticket to someplace." McQuinn shrugged. "Any place. Just get out of here. Keep moving until you feel safe."

"Teddy had all the money . . . and he had the claim ticket."

McQuinn thumbed open his notepad and clicked his ballpoint pen. "Think hard," he said. "If you're a witness, we got a whole new ball game here. They *have* to see that you get a safe place to stay. You must have heard something, seen something. Anything!"

I shook my head.

"*Smelled* something?"

"They said that if I was a witness, my name would be in the newspaper."

"Maybe," said McQuinn, "but only after the charges are filed. And that's only if somebody gives a shit. I hate to tell you this, but when somebody gets their head caved in, it ain't exactly front-page news in this town."

"It's the Mob," I said. "And if I say something, they can find out."

McQuinn wrote in his pad. When he looked up, he said, "So, how big was this mob? How many guys?"

I shook my head.

"Squirrels? Monkeys? Wombats? Give me *something*!"

"I know you, like, really *do* know what I mean," I said. "The Mafia! You probably know who all them guys are anyway."

McQuinn shook his pen at me. "I know you and your pal came to this town looking for trouble, and you found some. For openers, you started some racial crap on a bus and it went downhill till your pal turned up dead. I also know that if you don't come clean about what you saw"—McQuinn made one sideways slash with his pen—"nobody's looking to help you."

I held my face in my hands. My eyeballs felt like they would explode in my head. "I don't know what to do. I don't know. I don't—"

"You start by getting out of the car," said McQuinn.

"I don't have any place to go," I said. I could hear my pulse thumping in my ears. I swallowed hard to keep the tears from running down my face.

"If you want to be safe, you have to pull your head out of your ass. Start talking to me. Tell me what you know. What you heard. What you saw. If you're a witness, they have to help you."

"I can't."

"Get out!"

"Couldn't you just shoot me?" I said. "You got a gun. At least that will be quick."

McQuinn snapped the release on my seat belt. "Last chance. Are you riding or are you walking?"

I couldn't think fast enough to know what to do—what would be safe to say.

"Open the door!"

I didn't move. Everything stopped. I mean, I could hear him, but it sounded like a different language and like way far off. I tried to move and nothing happened. Like when they were pounding Teddy. And my feet and hands went numb and tingly, just like then.

McQuinn reached across me, pulled the door handle, and pushed the door open.

"Get out!"

I let go of my head and scrunched up my eyes a couple of times to try to see him. His face was like down this long tunnel. And that's when he smacked me, but it was like I whacked the TV and all of a sudden the picture popped on.

"What?" I said.

"Welcome back." McQuinn pinched a business card out of a flap taped to the cover of his notepad and handed it to me. It had a silver badge and his phone number on it. "Lace this into your boots," he said. "It will help identify your body. And if you maybe, *suddenly* remember something—and you ain't dead—call me."

I stepped my foot out of the car, but my leg felt like really heavy. McQuinn put his hand on my shoulder to stop me. "Listen."

"Yeah?"

"Down the street, on the other side. You see the liquor store?"

I didn't have no money or any good ID to buy liquor, but I didn't want to get smacked again, so I said, "Yeah?"

"Turn left there and walk a couple blocks. There's a mission down there—has a giant blue cross that lights up at night. Show Father Ralph that card I just gave you."

"How am I gonna know him? I mean, what's he look like?"

"Father Ralph is a monk. He wears a brown robe, looks like Friar Tuck."

It's not like I'm religious, or nothing like that. "Friar Tuck" did ring some kind of bell, but it didn't ring it loud. "Who's that?"

* * *

THE BUILDING WAS, LIKE, GI-NORMOUS. It went on up five or six stories, and all in brick, too. Above that stood two tall redbrick smoke
stacks. One stack had some white bricks in it that said "STROH."
The other chimney said "BREWERY." A giant cross in blue neon
spread its arms across the top three stories. I reckoned this had to be
the place.

"You must be John," said an old man's voice from behind me,
which was like a big surprise, 'cause I hadn't heard him walk up.

I said "Yeah" before I turned to see him—a really tall guy, maybe
seven feet, wearing a brown robe tied together with a rope. A wooden
cross dangled from the rope belt. He had white hair that stood out
from his head like quills on a pissed-off porcupine, and he wore a gray
two-day-stubble beard on a face so wrinkled that if you pulled it
straight, he'da been a foot taller.

"Father Ralph?" I said.

"No," he said, a twinkle in his eye. "I am Bartholomew. You may
call me Bart."

"Father Bart?"

"If you like. You're not baptized?" he asked.

"That's like, written on my forehead?"

"No," he said. "But you do have one message on your neck and
quite another on the side of your head."

I didn't feel like telling the story one more time, so I said, "Maybe
you can help me find Father Ralph." I pulled out the card the cop gave
me.

"Ah, Sergeant McQuinn," he said with only a glance at the card.
"Yes, he called. He could not bring you here—something about city
ordinances. Father Ralph is busy just now, so I've come to meet you."

Father Bart laughed a lot. He thought the Friar Tuck thing was
really funny, and he told me the Friar Tuck guy came like from a
movie, and not from the Bible or nothing like that. He walked me
down the sidewalk and said that the beds were already full and so we'd

go down to the rectory.

"How can this place be full?" I asked. "It's huge!"

"We use only a portion of the first floor," said Father Bart. "The loading dock is shaped like an outdoor theater, so with some old benches and folding chairs, it is our urban cathedral. The old lunchroom is, of course, our dining room."

"Is that still open?" I asked. "Can I, like, get something to eat?"

"The dining room is closed now," said Father Bart. "But there will be a sandwich and a fruit cup on a tray in the rectory."

"Really great, man!" I said. "My stomach is a little jumpy, but—"

"Ha," he said, and settled an arm around my shoulder.

"That's funny?" I said. "I think I'm going to barf, but I'm still hungry."

"I was thinking of Robin Hood and Friar Tuck." He turned me up a sidewalk that had weeds exploding from the cracks in the pavement. "This is the door here. Just grab the handle."

The door made a loud metallic bang as I pulled it open and we got peppered with gray paint chips and a cloud of red rust. With all that noise, I couldn't believe how it seemed to just glide open in my hand.

"We haven't used this door in a while," he said. "I didn't want to walk you down the hall." He stroked his neck with the tips of his fingers and shrugged. "It wouldn't do to foster excitement when we're trying to calm things down for the night."

We stepped into a wood-paneled office with a desk and a bunch of religious pictures. Just like Father Bart said, I found an orange plastic tray with a tuna sandwich, fruit cup, and a carton of milk. I sat and scooted the chair up to the desk.

Father Bart tightened up his rope belt and sat on the edge of the desk. "In the bottom drawer on the right, you'll find a medical kit. There are some capsules for the pain in your head and a very large self-adhesive bandage for your neck."

"My neck ain't hurt."

"The people who you fear are looking for your tattoo. The bandage will go smartly with the bruise on your head and cover the mark on your neck that makes you so uncomfortable."

"Just so you know," I said, shaking two generic pain capsules from a bottle I found in the blue-and-white box stashed in the bottom drawer, "I'm right comfortable with the tattoo on my skin. It's other folks—"

Father Bart laughed and struck the desk with his fist. "I'm with you," he said. "The skin is much more comfortable on than off."

I felt my neck and said, "It's only just a tattoo," but I looked him over good to see if he had a knife hid up that robe.

He shrugged. "Doing as you will is a most precious gift of God."

I peeled out the bandage and stuck it on my neck. He sat quiet-like while I ate—it sure ain't like I took my eyes off him. His eyes were closed and he seemed to be asleep, but now and then he'd smile.

When I finished, Father Bart opened his eyes, pointed to a file cabinet, and said, "In the bottom drawer you'll find a pillow and a blanket."

The pillow turned out to be kind of small, but the blanket felt big and fluffy, nice and warm, just holding it against my chest.

Father Bart slid off the desk and made a nod toward an interior door. "The beds are full, but you can stretch out on a pew. There's a mass at seven and Father Ralph sometimes says it in Latin. Maybe you'll get lucky, but come," he beckoned with a hand, "and rest for now."

He took me down a dimly lit hallway with a checkerboard tile floor.

"I don't know what to do, or where to go," I said. "You know, like, tomorrow."

"I'm an old man," he said, as he put an arm around my shoulder and we walked down the hall toward the church. He called it a sanctuary. "And I have learned that tomorrow is something that takes care of itself."

I didn't know about that, and I sure didn't believe it. "I might be here tomorrow," I said, "but what about the day after? Where am I gonna be then?"

"My son," he said. "How shall I say this? You have started a journey. You must stay till the end." He took up the cross that hung from his rope belt, held it in both of his hands and pressed it to his forehead.

After a moment, he opened his eyes and lowered his hands. He said, "You are on the road to Damascus. The map is on your neck."

I WOKE UP LIKE REALLY surprised the next morning when Father Ralph turned up, shaking me and asking me who I was and what I was doing. He looked kind of Mexican, maybe in his forties, with a goatee sporting a smidge of gray at the chin. I told him I was JD and about Sergeant McQuinn. He seemed to be up on all of that.

"Were you in my office?" he asked as he folded up the blanket, which looked all kinds of threadbare now. I didn't see how I coulda worn it out just sleeping one night.

"Well, yeah."

"How'd you get in there?"

"The door from the street," I said. My head hurt and I kept seeing little flashes of light.

He crossed himself. *"Madre mia."* He mumbled some other stuff— not in English—and then asked, "You ate my sandwich?"

I laughed.

"That's funny? You helped yourself to my dinner?" He racked the pillow and blanket under his arm.

I laughed some more and he looked, like, really angry.

"Wait a minute," I said. "Father Bart knew that was your sandwich. He's the one that played the joke and he thought it was right funny."

"Who's Father Bart?"

"Like real tall and real old," I said. "He said you were busy, so he came to meet me."

"We don't have a welcome wagon. After seven, the doors are locked."

"Well, I guess that's why he brought me down here. He said Sergeant McQuinn called."

Father Ralph threw up his free hand. "Fine! Sergeant McQuinn did call. And I told him for the hundredth time . . ." His voice trailed off and he shook his head, but he never let on about what he'd said for the hundredth time.

"Do you say mass in Latin?" I asked. "Father Bart said it was a treat, and I ain't never seen a church service."

"Father Bart?"

"Yeah."

"Real tall and real old?" said Father Ralph with a flash of his eyebrows.

I nodded.

"Sit," said Father Ralph. "You shall have your Latin mass."

Maybe five or six old ladies in head scarves filtered in through a small door between the two big roll-up doors that made up most of the church's back wall and led to the loading bay. They got to kneeling and kissing strings of beads. Father Ralph got busy lighting the candles parked on top of a big folding table covered with a fancy white tablecloth. Then he turned to face us with his arms spread and began to chant some words he knew by heart, but I sure couldn't make head nor tail of it—Latin, I guessed.

At the end of the service, they all went up and knelt at a rail in front of the loading dock's trailer bumpers and boarding plates. I went too, 'cause I didn't want to look stupid. He fed them some white chips that he dipped in a silver cup of wine. I didn't get on to anything he did, because I sure as hell don't speak Latin. When he got to me, he put his hand on my head and jabbered a couple of things. Then he made a cross on my forehead with his thumb, and asked, "Do you renounce Satan and all of his works?"

"Well, yeah," I said. I mean, how many ways can you answer that question?

"In the name of the Father, the Son, and the Holy Ghost . . ." he said, and poured some water on my head, which I guess made us even for me eatin' his sandwich.

The water felt cool and made my head feel better, so I didn't complain. It made a good joke, and it weren't like he dumped a whole bucket on me. He said, "I baptize thee John Nathan Doe, and from this moment on, you are a child of God."

* * *

BACK IN HIS OFFICE, FATHER Ralph stashed the pillow and blanket in the file drawer. I looked around and saw all the religious pictures again. He had a poster titled "The Latin Mass," but the words didn't make any sense. Another had on it, "The Road to Damascus." I asked him if he knew where to find Damascus.

"It's in the Middle East," he said.

"Dawg," I said, "I'm all the way up north here. The bus probably went through it while I was asleep."

"Syria," he said, and scooted his chair up to his desk.

"Beats me," I said. "It's my first trip out of Arkansas."

Father Ralph said he knew someone who might help me. He gave me a business card from the top drawer of his desk.

The guy's name was Raymond Kerze. Kerze was like this retired cop, with an office just across the street, like upstairs, you know. I couldn't believe my luck.

But fuck! I crossed the street and this guy pops out a door and comes down the stairs to the sidewalk. And it's the guy from the bus! The one that smacked the crap out of me and Teddy.

When he sees me, he blinks twice and sighs like a bus. "For frog's sake!" he says. "You! Today!" He looks up and down the street. "Where's your pal?"

"Teddy's dead," I said. I'm telling you, this guy is huge, and he looks like a refrigerator in a suit. And when I told him about Teddy, he looked sad a little, like maybe his burger slid off his plate and fell in the mud.

He had this wiry black hair with a lot of gray, and he pushed it back away from his face with both hands. "I'm sorry about your friend," he said. Then, "Take your best shot, I got shit to do this morning."

Like I'm going to jump both feet in a bear trap, right? "I didn't come here to fight," I said. "I mean, I didn't even know it was you."

But he stepped toward me with his fist coming up and his shoulder dipping down.

I said, "C'mon! Yeah, you banged our heads together and maybe you deserve a whack for that, but I weren't comin' here lookin' for a fight!"

He looked at me and bent his head like a dog studying a worm on a wet sidewalk. "What then?"

"Father Ralph," I said, and pointed across the street. "From the mission. He said maybe you could help me."

He kind of like deflated with a groan and closed his eyes. After what seemed like a long time, he whined, "Couldn't you just hit me? I really am in kind of a hurry this morning."

So I took my swing—got my shoulder behind it and followed through with my hip—but he ducked his face down so my fist hit him square on the top of his head, which was like punching a tombstone, and my hand hurt so bad when I shook it that I had to hold it against my chest and jump my whole body up and down, and then the bastard looked up and smiled.

"There." He gave my shoulder a shake as he walked past. "Tell Father Ralph that you feel better about the whole thing now."

"That's not it," I said.

Then he's walking backward, spreading his empty hands out, and says, "Aw, c'mon!"

"Just—just one thing."

"You wanna talk," he said, "you gotta walk. I don't like to be late."

It's hard to walk fast when you're holding your hand against your chest and wondering if you broke it, but I caught up.

He said, "Okay, what?"

"Why didn't ya—I mean, I asked ya—why didn't ya tell the Mob guys that it wasn't us, me and Teddy, that done that Marty guy?"

"The Mob guys know it wasn't you," he said.

"They pounded his brains out."

"Wasn't the Mob," he said.

"Why?"

"Too much work," he said. "They leave the body?"

"Yeah," I said.

"Wasn't the Mob," he said. "Civilians disappear. They only leave their own lying around, and that's only when they're trying to make a point."

"So, I don't have to worry about that?"

He stopped walking and turned to look at me. "Who do the cops think did it?"

"They said, the detectives, you know, they didn't say nothin'."

"Maybe you better come with me," he said.

"Where we going?"

"Genie's Wienies, up on Conant, but I got something to do first."

I HAD TO SIT IN the hallway, on the floor, 'cause they said I couldn't come in the room, but I could hear them talking all the same. They all started out saying pretty much the same stuff. So did Kerze, when I heard him.

"My name is Ray, and I'm an alcoholic. I had my last drink yesterday. I was a cop for twenty years and they said drinking ruined my career. But being a cop for twenty years is like standing neck deep in a cesspool for twenty years. How do you screw that up? After a while it's hard to tell where you end and the cesspool begins, so that ain't . . ."

The elevator dinged and the door screeched open. It sounded like whatever the door slid on had worn out or needed oil real bad. A fat black woman wearing a blue cotton uniform dress with white buttons and a white collar bumped a housekeeping cart out of the elevator—she had to lift the cart, because the elevator stopped below the floor. Her hair had been straightened and dyed copper red. She looked at me and asked, "Sugar, are you all right?"

Teddy yelled in my ear. *"Rip that bandage off. Tell that black bitch—"*

I looked around. "How'd you get here? The cops said you was dead! They scooped—"

I didn't see Teddy.

I rubbed my eyes and leaned to the side to see if maybe Teddy was on the elevator.

"I come up that elevator," said the woman. "I come up here to mop and clean, and I sure hope that don't include no scoopin'. And if they's cops, they most likely lookin' for you."

"No, I—"

"What is you doin' sittin' on the floor?"

"I'm waitin'. They said I couldn't go inside."

"Then you lucky there, Sugar," she said, with wide eyes and a nod. "You look like you need ta *start* drinkin', not quit."

"I'm sorry—"

"Race traitor!" I could hear my foster mother's voice—like she was hollering at me and standing in the hallway, right there, with us—and I touched my fingertips to my face. I could feel the sting of where she cut my cheek with her hickory switch when she caught me talking to the gas-meter reader. I was six, so the scar is mostly faded, kind of a white line, but just now I could feel it, sharp, like it just happened.

"Sugar, I don't think you're all right. Somebody done rung your bell good. You gots all the colors o' da rainbow in that bruise."

"I'm just waiting for Ray Kerze," I said.

Her eyebrows rocketed up like her face might explode and she said, "Raymond Kerze is in that AA meeting?"

"He was talking, but I think he's done," I said.

She jammed her fists onto her hips and said, "Damn, white boy. Jesus *is* comin'! And we gonna see what color he is."

I laughed.

"You go on down to the lunch counter, in the drugstore downstairs, and tell Mr. Chin that Yolonda done sent you." She pulled a beat-up straw broom out of her cart. "He'll give you something to drink. I'll tell Ray where to find you."

"How come you're bein' nice to me?" I said.

"I just need to clean this hallway, Sugar. And you underfoot." She pushed on my boot with the business end of her broom. "Now git, and was I you I'd roll down them pant legs over your boots and put them braces in you pocket 'fore somebody else welcomes you to the Motor City. Again!"

"I LIKE REALLY NEED TO know who killed Teddy," I said, leaning left and trying to keep the lunch counter's stool from wiggling back and forth under my butt.

Kerze had this watery look in his eyes. He said, "Excuse me," snatched the napkin from under my silverware, swiveled his back to the counter, and sneezed into the napkin. After a giant honk into the napkin, he said, "You, *like really*, need to know where you're gonna put your head down tonight." After another honk, he wiped his eyes, spun back to face the counter, and said, "You have a cat in your pocket?"

"Me and Teddy stayed at the white water camp, like the night before we left. Man, there's all kinda cats, because of the mice and stuff."

"White water camp?"

"Yeah, like rafts and canoes, y'know."

"And you left that to come *here*?" said Kerze.

"It's like a kids summer camp. They didn't have, like, room for us in the barracks. So, y'know, we had to go."

Kerze waved at Mr. Chin. "Give us a couple of those cheese, ham, and egg sandwiches. And some fries."

Mr. Chin looked, like, fucking ancient. He had to be like sixty or something. He wore this white paper hat cocked low over one eye, and when he turned away from the grill, he waved his spatula at Kerze. He said, "Afa' eleven o'clock, no more fucking egg sandwich."

Kerze held up his watch and pecked the face with his finger. "Ten o'clock."

"You fucking watch all the time ten o'clock. You don't eat. You take your money, buy watch, so you know—eleven o'clock, no more egg sandwich."

Kerze waved and said, "Okay, Hao. Just give us a couple egg sandwiches and fries instead. I want some coffee."

Mr. Chin launched into shouting and banging the grill with his spatula. I didn't get what he said, because it sounded like Chinese cussing or something.

"So," said Kerze, "your pals have barracks and a kids summer camp. Call 'em up, tell 'em this town is a bust and you need money for a ticket out."

I laughed. Guys like Kerze didn't understand the Struggle. "You send *them* money," I said. "They don't send *you* money."

"Didn't they send you here?" said Kerze. "At the police station, you said you were going to start a new chapter, something like that—I didn't think you two were writing a book."

"They sanctioned the mission, but it was all like Teddy's deal. Teddy had a sponsor. He sent Teddy the ticket. Teddy used his meal money to buy my ticket."

"So, this sponsor person didn't know you were coming?" asked Kerze.

Mr. Chin slid our plates on the counter. Egg sandwiches with potato chips. He said, "French fry machine turned off. They clean the hood so this place no burn up."

He reached under the counter, yanked out two white coffee mugs, banged them down next to our plates, and filled them from a pot he snatched from the back bar.

Kerze leaned to the side and fumbled a hand into his pants pocket. "So, what was this dude's name? The sponsor guy."

Mr. Chin pointed his finger at Kerze. "You money no fucking good here, asshole!"

"Thank you, Hao," said Kerze, who had this silly looking smile. Mr. Chin gave Kerze a wink and walked off mumbling something in Chinese.

"I don't know the sponsor's name," I said, but I did. Wayne West, Teddy called him Waynie—like they was old-time chums or something—but I never met him, and Teddy and I grew up in the same house. Well, we had bunk beds in the same garage since I was five, and I sure as hell don't know no fucking Waynie.

"It was like a secret," I added. "Struggle business, y'know. Teddy never said."

Kerze passed me the sugar.

"I drink it black," I said. "Mostly we didn't get coffee when I was growing up, and we sure as hell didn't have no damn sugar."

"I drink it with a shot of Kessler's," said Kerze. He dumped a long fat ivory column of sugar into his coffee. "Just not today," he said, and stirred. "So, this sponsor guy, whatever his name was, didn't know you were coming?"

"No, but Teddy said it would be okay. But like, that's why he went up to meet the guy alone, and when he came back, he had a set of car keys the guy gave us. He said it was a brand new car, man."

Kerze took a big bite of his sandwich and nodded while he chewed. He waved the sandwich at me, his cheek full like a chipmunk, and asked, "Then you went to get the car?"

"Teddy told me to wait for him while he got it. It was, like, seven or eight stories up there. He said we had to drive to Chicago, and the guy was going to meet him at the car with a box we had to deliver to the Chicago chapter. He said I should wait for him and be looking for a brand new Camaro. Man! A *brand new* Chevy Camaro!"

"But Teddy didn't bring the car down?"

"I waited for like ten minutes, but you know, I'm thinking like, 'Wow, man, a brand new Chevy.' Teddy and me finally got a break. Hell, we could even, like, *live* in a brand new Chevy."

Kerze took a slug of his coffee and chewed it. He looked a little sad, and made kind of a sigh and said, "What was in the box?"

"I don't know," I said.

Shit, I mentioned the goddamn box. Teddy was right. I am stupid! But I never saw the box and, like, the guys that killed Teddy didn't have the box either, so it had to be in the car. But the cops didn't have it, so I didn't have to tell. "Teddy didn't say."

Kerze nodded and didn't look at me. "So, you got tired of waiting and went to catch up with Teddy?"

Whew, that was like "Oh My God" close.

"Yeah, Teddy said it would be all right, so what difference did it make? The sponsor was going to meet me anyway. And my stomach was going off thinking about the car. I mean, we didn't have money to eat nothing, but still."

"Then what?" Kerze asked. He kept eating and didn't look at me.

"I'm like walking up the ramps and I hear some yelling and then I heard Teddy screaming."

"What where they yelling?"

"First, Teddy. He, like, yelled he didn't have it."

"What 'it?' The box?"

"No, I didn't see any box. I don't know what they wanted."

"What did you do?"

"I ran to help Teddy."

"But you didn't help Teddy?"

"I got to where I could see over the ramp, and there were three big guys. White guys. And they were pounding him with bats and cursing and Teddy was laying on the cement and they were just pounding away."

"Exactly what did they say?"

"I don't know what," I said. "They were cursing, y'know, like Mr. Chin just now. I mean, I didn't know the language and like that, but I mean, I know it was cursing."

"Try to eat your breakfast," said Kerze. "Sometimes when we see something awful, our mind blanks out the really bad stuff. It's not that you don't want to remember, right?"

"Yeah, that's probably it," I said.

"On the other hand," said Kerze, "my clients always lie to me. For absolute certain, they leave off the details that don't pass the smell test. In your case, I'm pretty sure you're not a coward, but you *are* a bad liar."

I started cryin' and my face fell into my hands.

"Generally, when I try to flush the truth out of a pack of lies, not too much takes wing," Kerze said. "But maybe in this case, it doesn't matter that you won't tell me what Teddy said was in the box, because there wasn't any box. The box was a lie. The truth was the men with the ball bats were waiting for Teddy to show up with the keys to that nice new Chevy."

"All I know is they wanted to kill Teddy, and they cussed him and they beat him and they took their time. They made him scream and beg, and they just pounded, pounded, pounded."

"They took their time," said Kerze. "They wanted the 'it.' They asked for the 'it' in English. What did they want?"

"I—Don't!—Know!"

They wanted the hard drive, but it was in the bus locker, and it was Struggle business, and the cops have it, but maybe they don't know what it is, and Teddy wouldn't give it up, and now they're gonna kill me for it, and I don't even have it and if I did have it I'd really get pounded, but I'm a big chicken and I'd give it up—I'd be a coward and a race traitor. "All Teddy said was that there was like guns in the box."

"Too bad there wasn't ever a box," said Kerze. "Teddy sure as hell needed a gun."

"YOU SAID WE WERE GOING to some 'wienies' place," I said, trying to keep up as Kerze paced up one city block and down another.

"Genie's Wienies up on Conant," said Kerze. "It's a Mob joint." He shrugged and made a wag of his head. "One that makes a damn fine coney dog, but they don't change the oil in the fryer often enough."

"So, we ain't going there," I said, hoping, "'cause of the French fries?"

"We're taking the scenic route. And it wasn't the Mob that killed Teddy," said Kerze. "And if you don't quit pickin' at that, it ain't gonna heal. It's not like you want their undivided attention, anyway."

We rounded a corner and—oh my God—we were there, on the street where it happened, in front of the building next to the parking deck. Genie's Wienies my ass. Kerze had tricked me into going back to the scene.

"I really don't want to see this," I said. Kerze shoved me into the revolving door. "I wasn't in here, man. I don't know where Teddy went."

The door spit me out and I heard a man speaking with that accent the guys had. I looked, and it was him, one of the guys that killed Teddy, just standing at the Starbucks kiosk, covered in blood and ordering coffee like nothing had happened and he wasn't a murdering asshole.

I stopped and turned around. Kerze stepped out, the door shushing past behind him, and he banged into me. It knocked me back a step—just a bump, but I got a sharp pain, like, right behind my eyes.

"Sorry," said Kerze. He pulled his head back and squinted his eyes. "What's the matter? You're white as a sheet." He waggled a hand and said, "No pun intended. Sorry."

"One of the guys—he's at the coffee bar. That's one of the guys." My heart hammered my ribs and I could like hear my pulse rushing in my ears—it sounded like a finger scratching on the wall.

"Guys? Who?" said Kerze. He straight-armed me out of the way of the spinning door that puked people out in a gush.

"That killed Teddy." I pointed at the Starbucks.

Kerze pulled my arm down and looked toward the coffee bar. "Which one?"

"Are you like fucking blind?" I said. "The blond guy ordering coffee—the one that's covered with blood."

"In the blue suit?"

"Yeah, the blue suit with blood on it," I said. "The one with blood on his face and hands, by the wacky broad behind the counter who's taking his money with blood on it and acting like she don't even notice, man."

"You see blood?" Kerze asked.

"Call the cops," I said. "I don't really care now. They can fucking kill me. I don't give a shit. They killed Teddy and they're gonna fucking pay!"

"That's the guy? The one with the Russian accent?"

"Yeah! That's Russian?"

"Pretty sure," said Kerze. "That and all the tattoos on his neck and hands—I'd say Russian Mafia."

"You said it wasn't the Mob."

"Visiting team," said Kerze with a shake of his head, "not the Italian Mob—not the Partnership."

"Screw it, I don't care."

I should have like fucking known it was Russians. Most of the Struggle computer cash cows were on Russian servers. "And screw the cops! I'll kill the bastard myself!"

"C'mon over here," said Kerze, tugging on my arm. We sat next to a humongous fake potted plant on a gray cement bench.

"I can't see him," I said, standing.

Kerze hauled me back down by the arm he'd never let go of, and said, "Guy's got to go one way or the other. We'll see him."

"We're like gonna just fucking sit here?"

"We're going to follow him."

"I don't want to lose him! Let's call the cops. I got that big Irish cop's card laced into my boot." I started hauling up my pants leg to get to the top of my boot, but the guy walked past with one of those cardboard trays loaded with three coffees.

"Let's go," said Kerze, his hand clamped on my sleeve. "Couple of things that you need to know: One, there's no death penalty in this state. He and his pals can tell the judge, 'We pounded Teddy's walnut-sized brains into a quart of pudding, and laughed while we did it,' and they're going to get twenty-five to life. They'll be out in five to seven years—three, if they wring their hands and tell the judge, 'Oh, we're so sorry.' The second thing is, that guy doesn't have any blood on him."

We trailed the asshole down a hallway toward a whole bank of elevators. Blood was, like, running down his neck onto his suit. "Are you like, blind, man?"

"I didn't say you don't see it," said Kerze. "But if we point this guy out and tell the cops that story, he's not going to miss his tee time and you're going to the psych ward at Receiving Hospital for observation. You can say hi to Misty while you're there."

"Misty's there?"

"Last I heard," said Kerze.

My head throbbed and I put my hand on the bruise. It felt hot. The killer asshole stopped and turned to stare at the elevator door. He pushed the call button with his elbow on account of he was balancing the cardboard tray with the coffee. "God, I wish she didn't never ask to see my knife."

"That's not why I banged your heads together," said Kerze.

"Whatever," I said. "But, if she didn't ask, I'd like still have my knife, and I sure could use it right fucking now."

Kerze pushed me into the men's room and pointed his finger at me. "You *like fucking* stay here till I get back. Lock yourself in a stall. Don't talk to anybody. Just be here when I get back."

Before the door even shut, it hit. Oh man, something like ripped in my head and a flash of light drilled into my eyeballs like a dentist, so I couldn't look in the mirror to check out the hatchet that *had* to be parked in my skull. I had to hold on to the sink because the floor wandered around and tried to hide from my feet. Lucky for me, the stalls were downhill from the sinks, so I managed to twirl and glide into a stall before I threw up.

Wedging myself between the wall and the crapper slowed down the Tilt-A-Whirl, and the tile felt cool on my bruise and made the pain go away. I felt myself, like, drifting off. And this woman had her arms around me, and I didn't know who she was, but I knew she loved me. She said *shhh* like a leaky valve, and she stroked my head, and it was finally dark and I felt like really relieved about every fucking thing in the whole damn world.

The Third of
Many Stories

Satin Doll

S O WHAT IS IT NEXT time?" said my mother, speaking to me but playing up to the nurse at the desk. "Break a nail, and you stick your head in the oven?" She'd worn her mint green salon uniform, I guess to set off her new hair-do—sort of a fake-blond helmet.

I had a long answer. *No Mom, just when my rotten ex-boyfriend lies that he gave me HIV and skips out on the bail I had to borrow from a mobster. A mobster who wanted to turn me out as a prostitute.* I shortened it to, "No, Mom," and pulled together the edges of the hospital gown I wore backwards as a robe to cover the second hospital gown under it and all its airy openness to the rear.

Since my aborted high-dive from the bridge to Canada, this was the first time I'd been allowed outside Door Number One—the locked door of the wacky ward—to go to the nurse's station, and they weren't going to give me any clothes until dear old Mom signed the release papers.

The nurse—her name tag said *Helen* but I didn't know her because she never worked inside the ward—made a small throat-clearing cough and rolled her eyes up to my mother.

"Mrs. Lake," she said.

It was Miss Lake, but I let that pass.

Nurse Helen said, "Misty—"

"There is no Misty!" said my mother. "Her name is Mora."

Short for Mornica. Which gin bottle did you pour that out of, Mom?

I said, "Please, Mom, let's just do this."

"Well, really!" said my mother as she spun around to face me. "Misty Lake! That sounds like a stripper or some porn star. What are people going to think?"

I don't know as much about strippers and porn stars as you do.

"I don't know, Mom. Maybe it's not important right now."

"Well, it is important," said the nurse. "If we change the name, this paperwork has to go back over to Recorders Court."

"I thought this was a hospital," said my mother, turning back to the counter with her fists on her hips.

"Yes," said the nurse, "but Judge Howell placed your daughter here for observation. He will want you to appear in court to explain the change. Is there some place you can spend a day or two here in town?"

How about Door Number Two, the rubber room at the end of the hall?

"Oh, all right!" said my mother, throwing up her hands. "*Misty* it is, if we can get this done!"

"Very well," said the nurse, with just a flash of a mean smile. "Misty has no meds or scripts, but she has a follow-up session with Dr. Mambar in two days, on Wednesday."

"Two days? What's the point of checking her out at all if she has to be back in two days?" Mom replanted her hands on her hips and knuckled down hard enough to leave bruises. She huffed, "We're not driving all the way back down here from Bad Axe over this silliness. Not in two days."

"Mom!" I tried to get her to focus on me, and not the nurse.

The nurse said, "A follow-up is usually not this soon after the discharge. It's just the way the scheduling turned out. If you don't sign her out, *Misty* will have to stay here until the session, after which she may be able to sign her own self out."

"Just let me sign," said my mother. "I only had fifty cents for the meter, and Beatie's old pick-up isn't worth the price of a parking ticket."

We called it the Flintstone Mobile. The driver's feet were safe on the gas, the clutch, and the brake. But on the passenger side, drop a

Twinkie and *splat*—street pizza.

"You understand that when you sign this, you are responsible for Misty. If she fails to report for the session with Dr. Mambar, Judge Howell will issue a warrant for *your* appearance in court, Mrs. Lake."

"Don't worry," said my mother. She flashed me a glance through narrowed eyelids. "This young lady is going to start toeing the mark. She's coming back to work in my sister's hair salon. She's going to beauty school like I told her and she didn't listen. Like I told her that that guy was a bum." Mom folded her hands under her chin and fluttered her eyelids. "But she fell *in love*. Show her some baby blues, a cleft chin, and a hot pair of buns, and she goes completely gaga."

I cut my eyes across at her. "What were you doing looking at Jeffrey's buns?"

The nurse looked at me. Mom looked at me too, but her stare reminded me of the glowing metal rods at the bottom of an oven.

Mom looked back at the nurse. "You see what I have to put up with? Now, things are going to *get real*, real fast. And so is she!" She snapped an *Aunt Beatie's Hair Salon* pen out of her pocket and clicked it to business. "Where do I sign?"

"YOU'RE AWFUL FEISTY NOW THAT I've signed you out," said Mom.

She shoved a brown paper Piggly Wiggly bag of clothes at me. Her signature had rendered me officially "maybe" sane, and so I wasn't allowed back behind the locked "Door Number One," as my inpatient friends had called it.

"Crazy ain't the same as stupid, Mom," I said. "Aunt Beatie may be using you, but she's not going to use me." I took the bag of clothes from my mother. "We can go down to the restroom. I'll change there."

"Your aunt gave you a place to live."

"I worked in that salon since I was ten, and she never paid me a dime. She doesn't even pay you minimum wage."

The security camera in the hall made a low hum as the lens followed our progress down the hall.

"I have my tips, and we don't pay rent, water, or electricity."

"We lived in one room! You cook on a hot plate—I can't exactly stick my head in *that*!"

"So what have you got now? *Misty!* Miss Rock Star. You think you're royalty. You're just another thankless little brat from Bad Axe."

I stirred up the contents of the bag and pulled out slacks and a sweater. "Oh my God," I said. I shook them at her. "I wore this stuff in junior high."

"You took most of your clothes when you left."

"You couldn't find the pinafore you made me wear till fifth grade?"

"You looked precious."

"It was hell," I said. I shoved the clothes back in the bag. "They called me 'Hairy Mary' and 'sasquatch' because you wouldn't let me shave my legs."

"I knew what was best for you. Besides, you always wore knee socks with the little satin bows and Mary Janes." She dug a pack of menthols out of her purse.

"If you want to smoke that, you'll have to go outside." I backed into the restroom door, one hand taken up with the Piggly Wiggly bag and the other with the sealed plastic mesh bag they'd stuffed my property into when I got admitted.

"They won't care," she said, the cigarette levering up and down as she spoke.

"This ain't Bad Axe, Mom. There are smoke detectors. They'll escort you out of the building."

"Oh, all right! I'll smoke in the bathroom while you're changing. A cigarette won't set off the smoke detector."

"Not a good plan," I said. *It's more like a cigarette detector—think airplane bathrooms.* "Just go down and wait for me outside, by the door."

"I'm not letting you out of my sight." She fished a pink plastic lighter out of her purse. "I had to sign, and you better believe I'm in charge." She lit up, took a deep drag, and vented a long plume of smoke from her smug face. Then she followed me into the restroom.

I took my packages to the end stall and stood on the commode. The two hundred bucks Meat Hook Marty had given Ray Kerze for me had stayed in my clutch bag—I was stunned. My black satin dress needed a trip to the dry cleaner, but it had been folded neatly and not just crammed into the bag. The feather boa looked like it had gotten the short end of a tag-team match with my slingback pumps and clutch bag.

The restroom door squeaked and a male voice said, "Ma'am, you can't smoke in here. You'll have to put that out."

"You can't come in here," said my mother. "This is the ladies' room."

"Put it out," said the male voice. "If you want to smoke, you have to go outside at least a hundred and fifty feet from the hospital. That's all the way across the street."

"Get out of here," said my mother. "I'm going to tell the administrator that their rent-a-cops are Peeping Toms."

"Ma'am," said the voice, now a little weary. "Please, put out the cigarette."

"Look," said my mother, "I only have a couple of drags left, and I have to wait for my daughter to get dressed."

The cleats on the guard's heels clacked up and down the row of stalls. I heard a door swing open here and there, but not mine. I held my breath, to be as quiet as possible.

The guard said two things: "There's no one here but you," and, "Are you going to put out the cigarette?"

"I certainly am not," said my mother. "Just who do you think you are?"

"Ma'am, you're under arrest for violation of city ordinance 1369."

I heard a scuffle, and Mom screamed, "Help! Help! Police!" She hit the floor with a yip.

The guard said, "I am the police, ma'am. I'm a sworn officer."

"You're a pervert. What do you think you're going to do with those?"

I heard the handcuffs ratchet down.

"You push an old woman to the floor? You think your mother is proud of you? I'm old enough to be your mother and *I* would have taught you some manners!"

"All right, ma'am," said the guard, "we're going to stand you up now."

"Mora! Mora, tell 'em you're here."

No one here named Mora, Mom.

My mother's loud bitching faded down the hallway and I stepped down off the commode. All she'd put in the bag for underwear was a white ribbed vest and cotton Barbie underpants flecked with yellow flowers. I dropped the black satin dress over my head, fluffed and wrapped the battered boa, and stepped into the black slingback pumps. The rest of the stuff went into the trash can, although I did circle back for the Barbies—a little wedgy, but at least I wasn't traveling "naughty."

Dr. Mambar and I had talked about the problems in my life, and while I didn't agree with all that he said, he had been right about one thing. Sometimes you *can* get more done by saying nothing.

RAYMOND KERZE HAD SPENT MY last eleven dollars on a pint of whiskey and some lottery tickets, but he was the only person in my life who hadn't tried to use me. Big and scruffy and in bad need of a run through the rinse cycle, Ray nevertheless impressed me as a sweet guy. So, as I stepped off the bus in front of the liquor store on Grand Boulevard, I felt like I was just a short walk away from being safe.

Clouds, stacked like dirty gray pillows, darkened the sky. The perpetual line at the liquor store had vanished and the street lay silent but for the clack of my heels echoing in a dry gulch of vacant and boarded-up buildings.

Two blocks down, I could see a stream of vagrants filtering across the street from the mission. They all headed up the side street where stairs led up to Ray's second-floor office.

The occasional raindrop warned of more to come, but I had to walk slowly—I didn't want to break a heel. About a block away from Ray's building, I heard a crowd yelling, but I couldn't make out the voices. Finally, before I turned the corner, I heard Ray yell, "I got this, guys! This ain't gonna help me and it's just gonna to get you into trouble."

I rounded the corner and saw twenty, twenty-five people rocking a tan unmarked police car higher and higher. Their jeers and cursing filled the air with every lift and I could feel the sound on my face like waves pounding a beach. The open rear door banged the curb with every lurch and, while it kept the car from rolling, it had been battered enough to hang loose on the hinge.

I kept looking around for something gory like the Rodney King beating, but I saw only Ray on the sidewalk—handcuffed and standing between two detectives—right where I would have landed if I'd jumped out his window. He was right. Even with the cement sidewalk, it might not have been high enough to get the job done.

The guys I'd seen walking from the mission were lined up on the sidewalks, craning their necks to see. I saw the guy Ray had introduced me to as Jimmy Crates—the fellow whose long red hair and gray streaked beard almost covered his entire face—and I walked over.

"Jimmy!" I yelled.

He looked at me. "Misty! You better go inside."

"What's going on?"

"They're arresting Ray," Jimmy said, and spat on the sidewalk. I jumped so it wouldn't hit my shoes. "Arresting him for nothing!"

I waved my arm at the people around the car and the rubberneckers on the sidewalk. "All this because Ray's getting arrested?"

Jimmy gave me a sideways look. "You're not from this kind of neighborhood, are you?"

The two detectives pulled Ray back toward the stairs. Ray shook them off and stepped up to the open back door of the cop car. The detectives stepped back even more. The crowd eased off the car and roared approval.

Ray yelled, "You know I love you guys!"

The crowd cheered.

A light sprinkle of rain began. Ray said, "Listen, the harness bulls are on the way. They're comin' fast, and they're comin' with hats and bats. I want you to go home."

Jimmy Crates climbed onto the trunk of the cop car, then stepped onto the roof. The roof buckled, and he brandished the hammer he always carried clipped to his belt.

"They ain't taking you, Ray," he said, shaking the hammer at the two detectives standing at the edge of the crowd.

"Yes, they are," said Ray. "But first they're gonna put the gas on you, and while you're puking your guts out they're gonna take their bats to your knees and elbows. Then they're gonna take me. The only question is how many of you guys are going to jail, and how many of you are going to the hospital."

"This is bullshit, Ray," said Jimmy Crates, his eyes wild with fire.

"Yes it is, Jimmy," said Ray. Sirens screamed from everywhere, some close and others blocks and maybe miles away. "That's why I can handle it. It's nothing. They think I'm grandstanding on some case they want flushed with yesterday's chili."

A titter of laughter bubbled up from the crowd.

"So they made up a froggin' bullshit charge to shut me up. But I got it. I ain't gonna shut up." Three squad cars screeched to a halt, blocking the street about half a block up. Cops exploded from the car doors, already in riot gear. "They can't shut me up as long as I got you guys here keeping a lid on things."

A mumble ran through the crowd. "You know you can count on us, Ray." "We got your back, Ray." "You know best, Ray."

The crowd began to dissipate. Jimmy Crates climbed down from the detective's car, but he smashed the sideview mirror off with his hammer as he left.

I walked up to Ray and gave him a hug as best I could; it's not like I could get my arms all the way around him.

"Misty!" he said. "What's up? They let you out?"

"The shrink showed me an old postcard just like the one I got in the mail—the one from Canada that said my ex had tested positive for HIV. He said that he bought it in a novelty shop in that same mall you and I went to for my pictures. He said he'd had it for years and that it wasn't the first time a patient had been fooled by it. We did another blood test anyway. Negative. They gave me this AIDS awareness pamphlet—"

"What's going on here?" said one of the detectives as they pushed through the thinning crowd. "This man's under arrest."

"Misty," said Ray, "this is Tony Jackson and Paul Finney."

Tony stood maybe six one or two, had a medium-brown complexion, and was a dandy dresser—down to a waistcoat and a stickpin in his tie. What Paul lacked in height he made up for in beef, but his tan suit looked like it had been handwashed in a sink and left to dry on a chair.

Paul scanned me with greedy eyes and said, "Ray, can you find me an unruly crowd of these? They can have their way with me."

"No," said Ray, "just smelly mean guys with clubs."

"No trick to that," said Tony. "I just did the same thing with a wave of my magic radio. And don't think you did us no damn favor. Occasionally a little chin music lesson for the rabble is a good thing."

"Oh, yeah?" said Ray. He put his face nose to nose with Tony. "Next time, get yourself a baton and helmet, and make sure you're right up front."

Tony's face hardened into a sneer. "You think I can't take you?" He drilled a hand into his pants pocket and pulled out a set of keys. "This drunken has-been is showboating on my case—"

Ray smiled and turned his back so that Tony could unlock his handcuffs.

Paul wedged himself between Ray and Tony before Tony could unlock the cuffs.

"You're a fine specimen of a man, Tony," said Paul, "and a natty dresser. And sometimes you say some real clever shit. But trust me, Tony," Paul made a wink and a nod, "Ray'll scarf you up in one bite"—Tony quit fooling with his keys and showed Paul knitted eyebrows and taut lips—"including your suit, badge, handcuffs, and funny meerschaum."

"In his dreams!" said Tony.

Paul put on a phony smile, and with a tilt of his head, finished with, "And pass you like a popcorn fart."

"He wants to make a hero out of some racist skinhead!" said Tony, trying to reach around Paul with his keys. Ray obliged by backing his handcuffed hands up to Tony's keys.

"No," said Paul. "Right now, I think he just wants to bend up your momma's favorite son."

"You takin' his side?" said Tony. "I kick *your* ass, muthafucka!"

"We both know better than that," said Paul, his eyes merry.

"I was a rookie back then," said Tony, aiming a finger at Paul, "and that time, you weren't talking 'bout my momma."

"Whose momma?" asked a giant Irish police sergeant as he rounded the corner of the building. He held a three-foot black club in his hand and had a helmet with a clear plastic visor tucked under his arm. "And where's the riot?"

"McQuinn, my man," said Paul. "What'd a riot be without you?"

McQuinn gave me a wink. I remembered him from when he arrested Ray for beating Meat Hook Marty, and from when he brought Ray out to the bridge to talk me out of jumping.

"Three men arguing over a beautiful woman does not a riot make," McQuinn quipped.

I ran a few steps and met him with a hug. "Thank God you're here. The mob left, but now they're going to kill each other."

"Looks like I get the girl," he said. "Guess the riot's over."

"I've taken control of this situation, Sergeant," said Tony, his voice a tone less shrill.

I looked at Tony's smug face and turned my eyes to Ray. He closed his eyes and made one negative wag of his head.

McQuinn said, "Gonna rain harder, anyway." He twisted his neck and spoke some numbers into a radio clipped to the epaulet of his uniform. Sirens went silent all around us.

"Sergeant," said Tony, "we may need you to transport us. Our vehicle has been damaged."

McQuinn shook his head. "Hell, that's in better shape than the one I drive to work. Why've you got Ray standing out here in his shirtsleeves and bracelets, anyway?"

"What are you? His lawyer?" Tony said. "I have a warrant. You gonna help us transport him or not?"

"I've got every badge still in the precinct out here, including the rubber-gun squad. We have three cars. If you can't drive this one, call a wrecker."

"We have to take the suspect in to the station," said Tony.

"Fine," said McQuinn. "You'll have to wait until I get this crew back there. The captain and the lieutenant are downtown, and I have a file clerk manning the desk, armed with a shotgun. Just wait here. I'll be back."

"Lid's on now," said Tony. "I don't know how this plays out if you guys leave."

"Not to worry," said Paul. "You can just work your charm on 'em again, and if that fails"—he held his fist in front of his chest and made a lurch of his shoulder—"try a little chin music."

"All right!" said Tony. "Put him in the car, but you're driving. You know it's outta policy to transport a prisoner in a damaged vehicle."

"You need a ride?" asked McQuinn, looking at me. "In your case, the guys will make room."

"Well—" I said.

"Misty's starting today as my secretary," said Ray. "Just give her the key to the door. It's in my right-hand pants pocket."

Tony rolled his eyes and peeled a latex glove out of the side pocket of his gray tweed suit coat. He reached into Ray's pocket and pulled out a key on a ring with a Pistons tab on it. He held it up and Ray nodded.

"Just watch the phone," he told me. "Use the desk in the front office."

Tony handed me the key. I asked Ray, "Do you want me to call a lawyer?"

Ray wagged his head. "No."

They pushed Ray into the back of the battered detective car. The door wouldn't quite close, so Tony lifted up on it and Paul stomped it shut, caving in the door panel. The rain went from a sprinkle to a downpour.

I had to push my soaked hair out of my face, but I bent forward to see Ray's face and yelled, "Why?"

Ray yelled back through the rivulets of water cascading down the rolled up window. "Open murder!"

I FOUND THE TELEPHONE. IT had been ripped out of the wall and deposited in the trash can—and left there long enough to collect dust, spider webs, and an ecosystem all its own. I wiped it off with some fast-food napkins I found stacked on the sink next to the commode in the restroom. I dusted the secretary's desk and chair and set the phone on the corner of the desk. I didn't think *this* secretary would be getting many calls, but at least now I looked the part.

The thing about satin is that it's kinda chilly, and I was wet. I folded my arms and wandered over to the window. Rain and wind ripped down the street in sheets. Walking down to the bus stop for a trip to the City Suites hotel to see Little Joe, the only friend I knew Ray had, would be out of the question for a while. Even the mailman had retreated to his little white truck, his flashers and windshield wipers fending off the onslaught.

I saw the flash and heard the thunder. The lights flickered and went out. I locked the door. Through the frosted window, I could read the sign painted on the door. It looked funny backwards, like the word "ambulance" that only looks right when you see it in your rearview mirror. My brain had to flip the letters around to read RAYMOND KERZE, and under that, PRIVATE INVESTIGATOR.

I backed away from the door, sat at the secretary's desk, and wondered if my predecessor, Ray's last real secretary, had left anything behind. I wondered who she was, why she'd left, and where she was now. If I could find her telephone number, I could get to a phone and call her. Maybe she could tell me how to help Ray.

The top drawer of the desk had been stuffed with unopened mail and stuck mostly shut. I broke a nail trying to wheedle it out a piece at a time, but I finally got the drawer open. Most of it was junk mail, which I dropped into the trash, but I did find a pair of blunt scissors and trimmed up my nail. I sorted the rest of the tortured wad of crumpled envelopes into piles and discovered five years of unopened bank statements. The telephone and electric bills had stopped three years ago. Most ominous were registered letters from the state's Department of Licensing, and from the county gun board, dated back two years.

Someone stomped up the stairs. When they rattled the door, I think I levitated a foot off the chair. All I had was the blunt scissors. I grabbed them and yelled, "Who is it?"

For an answer, I got a clot of soaking wet mail dropped through the mail slot. I waited for the steps to clomp back down the stairs before I retrieved the mail.

Discount coupons for a pizzeria—if Ray didn't want them, I did—and a bank statement so wet it made the envelope nearly transparent. I could almost read it, and I didn't so much open it as it fell apart in my hands.

I counted the numbers on my fingers and finally took the single page over to the window to see if maybe the ink had run. It had not. I looked back at the door and spoke aloud the backward words again, and this time they made sense—the really crazy people were all on this side of Door Number One.

Ray didn't own an automobile, and he'd agreed to help me for little more than the price of a pint of whiskey. He lived and ran his business out of a vacant building. His suit was literally unraveling on his back, but Raymond Kerze had a hundred and eighty-two thousand dollars in his checking account?

THE RAIN STOPPED. THE SUN tried peeking through a few clouds, but the twilight swallowed that up. The electricity was still out. Around seven, the neon cross on the mission across the street flickered on and bathed the office in blue light. Just my luck—the wrong mother, the wrong boyfriend, and now the wrong side of the street.

Watch the phone? If there was a message there, I didn't get it. The bank statement had dried to wrinkled parchment. I folded it up and stashed it in my purse. If I went to the City Suites, Little Joe might be gone for the day, but they'd know how to reach him. If he could help me find a lawyer, I could use the bank statement to get the lawyer to take the case.

And I could get something to eat while I was out.

The hallway had become a cavern of darkness. If it weren't for the light of his cigarette, I wouldn't have seen the man sitting at the top of the stairs, just outside the street door.

I hustled back into the office and locked the door. Footsteps lumbered closer, and then the door rattled.

"It's me," said a male voice, maybe a little tipsy. "Jimmy Crates. You all right?"

Goody! The maniac with the hammer. And drunk, too. Aunt Beatie's hair salon wasn't looking so bad now. My mother usually ended up loaded by sundown, but all she did was bitch about how rotten her life was and wax dramatic about what a creep my father turned out to be. I locked myself in the bathroom.

"Misty?" The office door rattled, hard, and the window glass shattered. "Ah, shit!" said Jimmy Crates.

I did a panic level survey of the bathroom. No window! No shower! No closet! No place to escape and no place to hide. I grabbed the toilet plunger.

Jimmy Crates' footsteps lumbered into the back office, Ray's private office. I took off my shoes, eased open the lock on the bathroom door, and made a break for it—still brandishing the toilet plunger. Bits of frosted glass sparkled by the door in the dim blue. After two or three steps, I slid to a halt and the lights blinked on. Jimmy Crates lurched back in through the door from the back office. I jumped back into the bathroom with a couple of long strides and locked the door.

Jimmy's footsteps, almost a shuffle, malingered up to the door of the restroom. I took the toilet plunger in both hands like a ball bat. I heard him settle to the floor with a sickly moan. Then I heard the crinkle of a paper bag, followed by the sound of him glugging something down.

He groaned and went silent, but finally measured out, "I'm sorry, Misty. I didn't mean to scare you." He belched and said, "'scuse me."

I said nothing.

"I didn't mean to break the door," he said. "I gotta fix it or Ray's gonna be pissed."

"What are you doing here?" I asked.

"I wanted you to be safe," he said. "The power's out. Or was. You know. And some of the guys don't act right."

I said nothing.

"I'm really sorry, Misty," said Jimmy. "I'll go if it will make you feel better. I'll be down on the street. I'll be by the stairs if you need me."

"Jimmy," I said, "how do I know that *you're* going to act right?"

"I guess you couldn't know that," he said. "Fair enough. I'm sorry. I'll just be down on the street."

I unlocked the door and eased it open a crack, but kept a grip on the knob.

Jimmy sat on his folded legs, cradling a forty-ounce bottle wrapped like a mummy in a paper bag on his lap. He took off his battered ball cap and adjusted the folds. When he looked up, he said, "You got some kinda toilet plunging emergency to get to?"

I snorted. I laughed. I laughed so hard I had to cross my legs to keep from tinkling my Barbies. He popped his hat back on his head and took a long pull on his beer, but he laughed and choked until beer squirted out his nose.

JIMMY WALKED ME UP TO the bus stop—he said he wanted to get to the liquor store anyway before it closed, but he stood and waited with me at the bus stop. We'd avoided the subject for two blocks, but I had to know. "So, who is it Ray is supposed to have killed?"

Jimmy did a double take. "What?"

"Oh my God," I said. "You didn't know. I thought you knew. I mean, climbing on top of the police car and all."

"If the cops were involved, it was bullshit," said Jimmy.

"This is where you tell me that Ray wouldn't kill anybody."

Jimmy twisted the paper bag tighter around his forty and pursed his lips. "Well, Ray sure wouldn't kill nobody who didn't need killin'. Unless—well, maybe—it was some terrible accident. Something like that. Shit happens, ya know."

"I don't know!"

"Well, you hired him to kill you," said Jimmy.

"Shit happens," I said.

"He likes you," said Jimmy.

"What did he say?" I felt a little rush.

"Ray don't say shit about nuthin'," said Jimmy. "But after you—you know, the thing on the bridge—He went to AA."

"For me?" I felt lightheaded.

"He didn't say," said Jimmy. "He just seemed, like, happy. For all I know, he hit the lottery."

"He told you about me!"

"Just in passing," said Jimmy. "Like it was sad you're such a pretty girl, but so unhappy you didn't want to live."

"But if I'd been ugly, he'da given me a shove?"

Jimmy made a sidelong glance and gave me a smirk. "Shit happens."

We laughed. The bus slowly rumbled down the street toward us. I asked, "So what do we do?"

"I don't know what to do," Jimmy said. "I don't know nothin' about what's goin' on, except, Ray's one of us, and he sure as hell didn't kill nobody around here."

"I'm going down to see Little Joe at the City Suites hotel. He's Ray's friend. Maybe he'll know something. Maybe he can help."

"I gotta clean up the mess at Ray's office," said Jimmy. "I know where there's a piece of plywood I can nail over the window for now. Tomorrow I can get some tools from the mission and I'll change Ray's door for one of the doors down the hall that still has glass, but I need you to be back with the key so I can swap the locks."

THE DESK CLERK PICKED AT her cornrows and gave me a vacant, wide-eyed stare. She wouldn't call the manager and claimed not to know anyone by the name of Little Joe.

"I can't remember his real name," I said. "I met him here, in the morning, a couple days ago. I came with Ray Kerze. Ray calls him Little Joe because Joe has four boys and four girls—eight the hard way, like a dice game. Joe said he might have a temporary job for a hostess in a couple of weeks because the regular girl's going on maternity leave."

A smile fractured her vacant look and she showed me some teeth. "You know Ray Kerze?"

"Yes," I said, "and he's in trouble, and that's why I have to talk to Joe."

"Chuck," she said, and picked up the telephone. "Chuck DeSimone—Ray calls him Little Joe, kind of a joke between them—I'll call him."

"Hi, this is Clare," she said. After the pleasantries, she handed me the phone.

"Chuck, it's Misty. Ray's been arrested."

Chuck laughed.

"This is serious," I said. "You're the only person I could think—"

"Misty, Ray gets arrested occasionally," said Chuck. "They go through the motions. Nothing ever comes of it. Ray takes care of the little things the police department can't really get involved in. You really don't need to worry."

"Open murder?"

Clare did a big-eyes thing and straightened her back. Her mouth fell open, but she covered it with her hand.

"Whoa!" said Chuck. "What's this about?"

"They said they had a warrant. A riot erupted outside his office."

"Holy shit! Who's Ray supposed to have killed?"

"I don't know," I said. "The guys who were rocking the police car don't know. I was hoping you knew something."

"Damn," he said. "Beats me."

"Should we get him a lawyer?"

"What did he say?" said Chuck.

"He said he didn't need a lawyer. He said they arrested him to shut him up about some case the cops were trying to cover up."

"What did the cops say?"

"They said they had a warrant. And that Ray was 'showboating' on their case."

"Wait a minute," said Chuck, and the line fell silent until I thought maybe it had been disconnected. Finally, he said, "Look, if they have enough for a warrant, they have enough to arraign him. Ray knows what he's doing. He doesn't need a lawyer to tell him to clam up. Ray ain't got the money for a lawyer, anyway. And before they take him to court, they'd have to provide him with a lawyer."

"So what do we do?" I said. No point in mentioning Ray's bank statement if he was going to get a free lawyer.

"We need to wait," said Chuck. "They'll hold him until he's arraigned and bail is set. Tomorrow, we ask around and see what we can find out."

"They'll put him in jail?"

"Trust me," said Chuck. "Ray is safe. Where are you staying?"

"I'm at Ray's office, but there's no phone and one of the local guys got a little wasted and smashed the front door—I mean, in a good way, if you can imagine that."

"Let me talk to Clare."

I handed her the telephone. She said, "Nah, it's pretty quiet. Some short stays, a half-dozen Jehovah's Witnesses on a mission, and a handful of casino types that may not be back until checkout time. Uh-huh. No problem." She handed me back the telephone.

Chuck said, "You're family. I want you to stay with us."

"I can pay," I said.

"Housekeeping will straighten up one of the short stay rooms. It's already paid for. Tomorrow we'll get our heads together, early."

I didn't know what to say. I gushed, "Thank you," and had a flash of how good a hot soak in the tub would feel. "Great!"

"See you in the morning," said Chuck.

I handed the phone back to Clare. She said, "You didn't tell me you were Ray's sister."

I wasn't really comfortable with that point, but that's how Ray had introduced me. It just seemed like this wasn't a good time to pick at the details. "We had different mothers," I said. True as far as it went.

Clare smiled and shrugged. "It'll take about forty minutes."

"I really *can* pay," I said.

"Sugar," said Clare, "that room goes for eight hundred a night. A city councilwoman and her hot young stud of an aide, Eduardo—and he is one hot Latin hunk—rent that room twice a week. Official business!" Clare mangled a *tsk* with a laugh. "The city picks up the tab, and they don't use it maybe an hour or two. Damn if Eduardo'd be done that quick if I got up there with him, baby."

"Wow!"

"Not to worry, honey," said Clare. "That bill's paid. Nobody gonna ask no questions. Just hang tight, we only have one housekeeper at night and Juanita's on break. You can wait here and dish with me, girlfriend. We closed the restaurant when the power went out." Clare reached across the counter and gave my hand one good solid pat. "You're so lucky to have a brother like Ray. I've got three, and not one of them is worth a damn. Not when I need some help. The only one to come and help me, when I needed it, was Ray."

Rude not to ask. "Really?"

"I caught my ex stepping around, so I broke it off. But he wouldn't let me be. He was like stalking me—leaving flowers on my car and then threatening notes. He started calling me and sayin' mean-ass shit on my machine. Then he slashed my tires."

"Oh my God! What happened?"

Clare rolled her eyes to top off a mean smile, and leaned forward to conspire with me. "Well, you know what a good explainer Ray is."

"So, your ex hasn't been any more trouble?"

Clare raised her hands even with her ears and snapped her fingers. "Not another peep outta that creep. And him gonna 'bitch-slap the black off me.'"

We laughed.

"And when he got outta the hospital, he came 'round here, on my day off, and left me money for the tires he ruined."

"Wow," I said. "Fantastic!"

"Honey," she said, "when Ray's on your side, you're on the side of the angels."

"We need some of those angels working for Ray now," I said.

"You know that's right," said Clare.

"In the meantime, is there someplace close where I can get something to eat?"

"'Bout two blocks down and turn right. There's a White Castle that stays open. But you're kinda overdressed. You know, you being alone and all."

"Maybe I can get a pizza delivered?"

Clare made taut lips and shook her head. "At night, don't nuthin' get delivered 'round here but trouble."

TINY HAMBURGERS STEAMED IN ONIONS and served on dinner rolls—I sure didn't get any of that at the hospital. I could smell them before I crossed the parking lot. I had to wade through pimped-out sedans and an ocean of sweet mack, but when I got to the counter, I ordered four of them with extra pickles and a jumbo onion chips.

"You want a drink with that?" asked the counter girl, who had sleepy eyes, a hair net, and a name tag that read *Elle*.

"I want an Orange Crush, and fill the cup with ice."

"Hey, sweet thing," said a man behind me. "You so sweet, you make my teeth hurt, baby."

The man wore a Russian-style fur hat and a full-length black leather trench coat over a flame-orange suit. He had a tan complexion, two gold teeth, and a zigzag scar that careened across his forehead until it divided his left eyebrow.

"I don't be seein' you 'round here," he said. "Who you be sportin' for?"

I ignored him and dropped one of the hundreds Ray gave me into the stainless steel tray that curved under the bulletproof partition that protected the public from the restaurant crew.

"Shhheeeow, sweet thing," he said. "Your man know you bustin' his Benjamins?"

Elle asked for a smaller bill.

"That's all I have," I said.

"You know that be right, sweet baby."

"We don't keep that much change in the register," said Elle.

"I'd like to speak to the manager," I said.

The man in the fur hat dropped a crisp twenty dollar bill in the tray. I snapped it up and handed it back. "That's very kind," I said. "I just don't know what kind."

"You got to keep your strength up, baby. Dey's a whole world full o' men what needs dey hearts broke."

"I'll pay for my own meal, thank you."

"Why can't you just let de P-Jelly be sweet to you?"

"Your name is P-Jelly?"

"You heard o' me?" he said, flashing the gold teeth. "Maybe you come here lookin' for me."

"Old family name?" I asked. Someone pecked on the partition and I turned back to the counter. A heavyset black woman with her hair tied in a do-rag showed me the hundred dollar bill I'd dropped in the tray. She had a black marker in her hand and she had drawn a large black X on the bill.

"This your money?" she said with a nod and a curl of her lip.

"Yes."

She pointed across her body at the *X* and held the bill a little higher. "You *sure* this your money?"

"Yes," I said. "I got another one just like it."

She nodded and flashed me her eyebrows over a tight jaw. "Sure you do, honey. Who gave you this bill?"

"Ray Kerze," I said, hoping that I'd found yet another of his friends.

"I know Raymond," she said. "He eats here. And he pays for his food with small change and pocket lint."

I shrugged.

"Just have a seat," she said. "Elle will get you your tray. I got to call someone to get some change."

P-Jelly said, "C'mon, we gots to go, *now*." He grabbed my arm. "I can gets you clear."

"I came here to eat," I said. "And let go of my arm."

"You knows what dat *X* mean?" he asked. "Dat *X* mean we gots to get it, *raht now*! Dat *X* mean dat *money* is *funny*." He gave a pull on my arm. "Dat *X* mean she done called the poe-leese!"

I spun my arm in a big circle and broke his grip. "Let go of me," I said, "or if she didn't call the police, I will."

Elle put my order on the pass-thru drawer. I picked up the tray and sat at a table. P-Jelly sat across from me and occasionally looked out the front window while I ate.

Two burgers and a half order of onion chips later, he said, "How be dat burger?"

"Fine!"

"How be de orange pop?"

I took a sip. "Good."

"Cool," said P-Jelly. "I comes back in three to five. Y'all can tell me how the cops was." He stood and tipped his hat and said, "On accounta dey be here, *raht now*."

"That's a good thing," I said, "because I'd rather go to jail with them than anywhere with you. Not to put too fine a point on it, Mr. P-Jelly, but fuck off. *Please*."

P-Jelly made long strides for the door. He trailed off with, "I tried to do raht by you, sweet thing."

I finished my meal, stood up, and shook out my dress. After brushing a few crumbs off my black satin, I looked out into the parking lot. No P-Jelly, but, for real, a police cruiser had shown up.

At the counter, I asked if they had my change yet. The manager and two policemen stepped out through a door that looked like just another panel in the white wall.

"Miss!" said the policeman in the lead, "did you offer this bill in payment?"

"Yes I did, Officer," I said. His name tag read *Conklin*. He stood over six feet and wore his blond hair cut in a flattop, like in the military. He had ice blue eyes and an angular jaw—kinda cute. "And I want my change. And I don't care what she doodled on it." And maybe he'd ask me out.

"Ma'am, this bill is counterfeit."

"What?" I said. "Just 'cause she wrote on it?"

He motioned at the table and said, "Please, have a seat." I did and he sat next to me. His partner—tagged Wilson, with a crooked nose and cornrows—stood behind me. I glanced back and saw him looking toward the door and fluoroscoping the other patrons with his eyes.

"That's how the pen works," said Conklin. He had great teeth and muscular hands with bulging blue veins. "This is an iodine pen. Money is printed on rag paper." He leaned to the side, pulled out his wallet, and flipped a dollar bill onto the table. He wasn't wearing a ring.

Instruct me!

"Some counterfeit money is printed on pulp paper," said Conklin. "Pulp paper has starch in it, and if you remember your elementary school science, iodine indicates starch by turning brown, blue, or black."

And damp in the Barbies indicates WOW!

He scribbled a circle about as big as a wedding ring on the bill he'd taken from his wallet. It looked yellow, but faded to nothing. "Now, I understand you have another bill like the one you tendered for payment?"

"Yes," I said.

And if you take it, I'll have no place to go, and no money, and I'll have to go home with you.

I took the bill out of my purse and laid it on the table.

He held it up in the light and said, "Humm," but when he wrote on it, the circle turned black.

He glanced sideways at me and said, "So?"

Yes! Yes, yes, yes.

"Where did you get these bills? Did someone tell you to come in here and pass them?"

"I don't know the guy's real name," I said. Things weren't going quite the way I wanted.

Conklin's face went stern. "That's not what you told the manager."

"What did you say your first name was?" I stared into his eyes, reached toward him, and patted the table with my hand.

"*Officer,*" said Conklin, his voice now brusque. "First name, Officer, last name, Conklin. Who gave you the counterfeit bills?"

"Ray Kerze," I said.

Conklin closed his eyes and exhaled a sigh.

"But they weren't his."

Conklin's eyes popped open and his face brightened.

"Some guy by the name of Meat Hook Marty? Anyway, he gave the money to Ray to give to me as part payment of a debt."

"Well, Miss . . . ?" said Conklin as he wrote in his notepad.

"Misty," I said. "Misty Lake."

Conklin cleared his throat as he stood. "Miss Lake," he said as he picked up his dollar bill and my hundred. "This bill is evidence. I'll be taking it and the one you gave the cashier." He ripped a page out of his notebook and gave it to me. "This is a receipt." He handed me a business card that had his name, a silver badge, and a phone number. "That's how you can reach me. I need your address and telephone number."

"I don't have a phone," I said. *But I could call you a couple times a day. We could have dinner.* "I'll be at the City Suites tonight." *Terribly alone.* "After that, you can reach me at Ray Kerze's office until I get settled." *And soon, please. Just call me. And if you like, we can play with your handcuffs.*

"Yes, ma'am," said Conklin. "Thank you for your help." He stashed the notepad and bills in the breast pocket of his uniform.

The manager said, "Officer, someone's got to pay for this woman's food. I only gave it to her 'cause the 911 operator said to."

"You'll have to work it out with Miss Lake," said Officer Wilson as the officers exited through the front door. "Or you can file a claim at City Hall."

The manager watched the police officers walk out with heat in her eyes. When they switched on their headlights, she parked her fists on her hips and turned her hot glare on me.

"Well, Sugar," she said, menace in her voice, "maybe you can bat them brown eyes at the cops, but me, you got to pay." She stuck out her palm face up. "That's five dollars, thirty-seven cents."

A tattooed arm reached around from behind me and dropped a ten dollar bill into the manager's open palm. I recognized the art work.

"Can't be," I said, and turned around.

He had green eyes, short curly dirty-blond hair, and a lantern jaw. It was Jeff. Jeffrey "The World's Biggest Asshole" Enwright. My ex.

I SCOOCHED MY BUTT DOWN and raised my knees. Hot water rolled up to my chin and I felt the best I'd felt all day. The tension in my body vibrated out into the tub. I couldn't believe I'd found Jeff. I held the ice pack to the three stitches that held my swollen lip together.

Also, I couldn't believe that P-Jelly—a pimp in a pink Cadillac with mink upholstery, who I'd treated like pond scum—had been the only one to help me. He threw his coat over my shoulders, hustled me to his car, and drove me to the free clinic where they sewed up my lip and asked no questions.

Mostly, I couldn't believe that Jeff lay naked in my bed waiting for me to get out of the tub. But here we were—me in the tub with an icepack, and him in the bed with a hard-on.

P-Jelly had wanted me to go back to his place. I told him I'd do that when hell froze exactly solid. Then he'd apologized and said, "Nah, I just pimpin' ya, baby. Dat's what I do. Dat's how I roll. But a sportin' man goes to school on hows to be patient." He'd dropped me at the City Suites and left me with, "P-Jelly, sweet thang, you knows how to find me."

Clare'd met me at the desk, her face a mask of horror when she saw my mouth. "What on earth?"

I'd almost lied. I mean, where do you start? P-Jelly? Officer Conklin? Jeff? I'd almost told her I got mugged, but instead I'd just held my mouth and shook my head.

Clare gave my hand a pat and shook her head. "Welcome to the Motor City."

The card key she gave me was for a suite on the tenth floor. I wish I'd taken the stairs. Jeff had been waiting at the elevator.

"I'm so sorry, Misty," he'd said. He put his arms around me and, just for a moment, it felt so right—like I'd been deep underwater and struggling for the surface and he was that first gulp of air. I pushed him away.

"You know I love you. I'm so sorry. I had to come back for you. I can't live without you."

I didn't want to make a scene in the hall. Clare had been so kind to me, and Little Joe—maybe I'd better learn to call him Chuck, like the rest of the help—might actually have a job for me. I grabbed Jeff by the arm and pulled him into the elevator. Maybe there'd be something heavy to hit him with in the room.

The ride in the elevator turned into a wrestling match with him groping my boobs and me shoving and elbowing him off while I kept telling him to stop. I could smell the cheap vodka on his breath.

"C'mon, Misty, you know you want it," he said. "I saw you with that cop at the White Castle. I thought you were going to crawl under the table and blow him."

If I'd known you were watching, I might have. "You are such a moron. Is that all the respect you have for me?"

We stepped off the elevator. The room number was 1010. I followed the arrows.

"You're the one hanging out with that pimp."

"I never met him until I walked into that restaurant. Are you trying to pick a fight or get laid?"

"I'm just sayin' what it looked like, with you in that hot dress—"

"If you were watching close, you would've seen him treating me with more respect in ten minutes than you did in the entire year we were together." I swiped the keycard in the door lock.

"Oh my God," he said when we got into the room, which was actually a suite with a bedroom, sitting room, and small kitchenette that included a well-stocked bar. The bathroom had a huge claw-foot tub and a glass shower stall with four showerheads. "I could learn to live like this."

I pulled my dress over my head, stuffed it in the dry-cleaning bag, and dropped it out the door. The bag said *24-Hour One-Hour Service*. I started to laugh, but it hurt my face. You couldn't get a meal without getting hustled, arrested, or beat up. But dry cleaning? No sweat!

Jeff came up behind me and ran his hand down my back, following the tattoo of a chain of daisies I had that ran from just below my neck to the base of my spine. I gotta admit, it gave me chills. Then he wrapped his arms around me from behind. "Oh, Misty baby, you are so hot. I love the panties."

I struggled loose, turned around, pointed at my lip, and gave him a shove.

"C'mon, Misssstyyyy! Don't still be mad. I got something to show you."

He pulled off the hoodie sweatshirt he'd worn with the hood up, which is how I missed him at the White Castle. He turned around to show me the new tattoo on his back—MISTY, with an angel at either shoulder blade.

"See, baby, when I met you, your name was Mora. But I made up Misty for you, and it fits you, and you'll always be under my skin and in my heart."

I wish I'd been wearing ice skates and had kicked him square in the ass. But I wasn't, and I didn't. And now he was *here*. I ran my hand across the tattoo and put my cheek against his back. I could hear his heartbeat, and tears started down my face as I remembered the good times and how wonderful it was to be held and loved and to be the special person in someone's life.

THE WATER COOLED, BUT I waited until I heard him snoring to get out of the tub. I used the time to remember the hurts—the mean things he said and the nasty things he did—and when I looked in the mirror, they were written large on my face. With my hand-washed underwear drying on the towel rack, I wrapped up in one of the big fluffy robes emblazoned *City Suites* and slept on the sofa.

Jeff kissed me on the forehead, and I opened my eyes to gray rain and a morning still struggling against the twilight. Jeff stood there naked with his dick hard and long enough to hang laundry on. His face a pout, he asked, "Why didn't you come to bed?"

"Two reasons."

"C'mon, Misty, I said I was sorry. It was an accident." He shrugged. "I was half in the bag. You knew that. I never could fool you."

"It's always an accident."

"You threw the change in my face." He showed me his palms. "I put my hand up and you walked into it. Besides, you were going to hit me with your purse."

"I was not!"

"You hit me all the time."

Just little love pats. "I do not! And if I do, I don't wind up my fist and try to knock you out. I don't split your lip or give you a black eye."

"Sometimes you just make me crazy. But it's your fault, because you make me love you so much." He knelt beside the sofa, rubbed his face on my shoulder like a kitten, and mewed, "You know if I didn't care, I wouldn't hardly get mad."

"We ain't hardly gonna have sex, because you have HIV."

"Oh!" he said. He straightened and looked at me through squinted eyes until some revelation released his pinched face. "No, I don't!"

"What do you mean, 'Oh!'?"

"I mean, 'Oh, no I don't!' That's what I said."

"Really? I got this card in the mail. From Canada. Said you tested positive for HIV."

"See there, I ain't never been in Canada," he said with a backhand wave. "I went to Chicago, to my cousin, but his wife got pregnant and they needed more room for the new baby on the way, and I just couldn't make it without you. So I came back, but you weren't at our place anymore. So I went to hang around at the White Castle, 'cause they're open all night."

"I wasn't at our place because you skipped out on your bail, and the judge took it, and the bloodsucker I borrowed it from took all my money. But that didn't matter, because when you left, I died inside. I lived one breath to the next, and when I got that card, I ran out of air."

"Aw, baby." He snuggled his forehead into my neck. "I begged you to go with me."

I pushed him back. "What, so we could do a threesome with your cousin's wife?"

"Now, that ain't true." He waggled a finger at me. "I got that all set right before I left Chicago."

"How many women have you been with since you ran out on me like a weasel?"

"Well, how many men have you been with?"

"None," I said. "You gave me HIV! Remember?"

"I ain't been to Canada." He tried to look indignant. "And I don't know nothin' about that damn card."

"How. Many?"

"Some. A few, I guess," he said, begging the admission by mewing like a kitten again. "But it was just sex. I closed my eyes and I was with you the whole time."

"You want to really be with me?"

"Oh, Misty. More than anything."

"You go and get tested. You get tested for HIV. *You* go through all that mess and wait and worry. And you get tested for warts, clap, and syphilis. And you bring me the paperwork, and I'll call the doctor, and if you ain't lying, as usual, I'll think about it. Until then, you don't get so much as a wet kiss."

Menace blossomed on his face. "I could make you," he said. "You'd like—"

"You could make the biggest mistake of your life."

"You got a rich boyfriend now, so you're all uppity."

"You got into my purse?"

"Well, I had to see if you had any money, and you were asleep," he said with a shrug.

"I suppose you were going to *put* money in my purse?"

"Just the money I picked up after you threw it at me. I put it in your purse. It's all I had."

"Ray Kerze is not my boyfriend."

"Suppose you could get that money for us, then?"

"What money?" I said.

"The tons of money he's got. He's not your boyfriend. What do you care? We'd have a fresh start."

"Are you nuts? Ray's a private detective and a retired cop. You know, the people you're hiding from? The cops?"

Jeff grabbed my shoulder. "Listen—"

"No, you listen. Ray is already pissed at you for what you did. He could twist your head off like a bottle cap. And when he sees my mouth, you might need to catch the next rocket off the planet."

"You told him about us?"

"I was sitting on the rail of the bridge to Canada, planning to jump."

Jeff collapsed onto me and tucked his arm around my back. "Misty, I'm so sorry. I did a lot of stupid things. When I don't have you to help me, I don't know what to do."

"You know what to do now," I said. "Get your clothes on and get out of here."

Jeff got back to his feet, his hard-on among the missing, and returned to the bedroom. I wondered if I should lock myself in the bathroom or just run down the hall screaming for help in my bathrobe.

I listened to him get dressed. I could see it in my head. He always pulled on his pants before he shrugged into his shirt. I heard the clasp on my purse open.

I sat up with a start and said, "Get out of my purse, you creep." *Get out of my life.*

He walked to the door and said, "I got the address off that bank statement so I know how to find you. I'll do what you said. I love you."

"Yeah! And look for my pimp. He knows where there's a free clinic." I collapsed into a ball on the sofa and choked on my tears until I knew he was gone and couldn't hear me.

The Fourth of Many Stories

The Iron Butterfly

MY ARMS LOOKED LIKE THEY ended in stumps, on accounta the French cuffs that lapped over my hands. I stuck my arms out like a zombie, scrunched my face, and lurched at my wife.

"AAAhhlllice," I moaned. "Neeeeed hellllp."

"That's 'Asari, could you please help me?'" my wife replied. She'd changed her name from Alice Mitchell Jackson to Asari Murphy when she ran for city council. She kept her hair straightened, but then put it up in rollers every night. In the mornings, she looked like a cellphone tower in a bathrobe.

"Why dohn you jus buy me shirts wid a button on da sleeve?"

"Well I declare, Massah Tony," Alice said, in a falsetto voice and doing a little wiggle dance, "I dohn buy yoh shirts, my secatary do."

She folded one heavily-starched cuff and gave me The Look. I was in for The Lecture.

"So," she said, "did that look good on me?"

"No," I said. It was kinda funny, but I knew better than to let off a smirk.

"Well, it doesn't look good on you, either," Alice said. "I won't have you lapsing into that street talk. It's not good for your career."

"I'm a detective," I said. "My job be on da street. I gots to talk ta my peeps."

"I ain't one of your damn 'peeps.'"

"Ebonics," I said in my professor voice. "A proud and defining part of our heritage and culture."

"Now see," she said, "that was good. That's the first thing they say . . . right after you step out of the room." She closed her eyes and wagged her head to deliver "'He's so well spoken,'" in a mocking tone.

She straightened my collar and patted my cheek. "And they best be talking about you! If they are, you'll be Lieutenant Jackson after the boards are posted."

"You want me to talk all honkey?" I said. "They'd laugh me outta the squad room. Hard enough to keep it real, wearing shirts like this."

Her brown eyes blossomed into coals—like they might set her eyebrows on fire. "The whole *point* is to get you out of the squad room. The squad room is where your ass is hanging out a mile. If I can get you off the tile and onto the carpet, I can grease the wheels for you up to inspector before I have to run for re-election."

"Nobody moves up like that." I'd heard of guys helping others up the ladder, but I wasn't happy about *her* being my "rabbi." She'd look like hell in a beard anyway.

"You ain't 'nobody,' baby. You're married to the city councilwoman chairing the Public Safety Committee."

"Dohn they gets tired o' you frontin' me all da time?"

"Now you're just screwing with me," she said.

"Don't they get tired of you fronting for me all the time?"

"They have their little projects, I have mine. Now," she said, as she folded the other cuff, "I want you to wear the gold Masonic cufflinks with this shirt and the charcoal Brooks Brothers suit. You can wear the white tie, if you want to look like a TV preacher. I prefer the red and blue diagonal stripes."

"I haven't been down to the temple in over a year."

"Don't matter what degree Mason you are, as long as you got the handshake down. You need to keep your evenings clear anyway. Inspector Falon retired, and I've arranged for you to be appointed to his seat on the Minority Equity Council."

"Oh, c'mon," I said.

"You know I need to have regular staff meetings at night," said Alice. "This will keep you out of the titty bars your partner likes, and once you're on the Equity Council, the Lieutenant's Board will just be a formality."

"I'm sick of your damn politics. You think I can't get anything on my own?"

"My politics pay for this University Park house and that BMW you drive. My politics are going to make you chief of police." She showed me the arched eyebrows. "That is *if*—and only if—you can avoid stepping in dog shit and tracking it all over the police department."

"That's all you think of me? I ought to knock you on your ass."

"You already did that once, didn't you?" Alice put her fists on her hips and closed in for the kill.

"That was us," I said. "I would never do something—"

"That wasn't *us* yet," Alice said with curled lip. She delivered the rest with her head and torso swaying like a cobra. "I wonder what the shooflies would think of you bangin' a suspect an' then drivin' her home. And you thought *you* was doin' *me*?"

"You was the one all open like a 7-Eleven. 'I gots to have you right now.' Pulling off your panties and rubbin' yourself."

"Baby, you was easy. As soon as your jammy was in my yammy, I owned your narrow little ass. You're damn lucky I didn't decide to throw you back. Could be, I still might."

"Alice, baby, c'mon." I tried to wrap my arms around her.

She pushed me off and shook her finger at me. "That's *Asari*! Alice Mitchell is just a faded memory in the back of your patrol car."

"I'm sorry, baby! I done told you a thousand times. What I have to do?"

"Mr. Tony, who likes to be a cop, should remember that I can drop him like a pair of dirty socks. All it takes is one phone call."

"All right," I said. "But you'll always be Alice to me."

"'Asari' is Nigerian," she said, touching the rollers in her hair. "It's for my base constituents."

I fingered through my cufflinks in the jewelry box, trying not to smile, 'cause I was cribbin' the three-point shot. I tried to make it look like a revelation and said, "Maybe you oughta shave your head," and snagged the rebound with, "now *that* would be Nigerian."

Her face went blank, and she actually looked like she might be considering the idea. After a moment, she said, "There's a difference between honoring and impersonating."

"Maybe you could wrap up your head in one of them big scarf things, 'cause right now you look just like a Georgia peach with honkey hair."

She snapped her back straight, drilled one fist into her hip, and whittled at me with her finger. "And the police piper wears a skirt, but everybody knows there's a package under the hem."

"Yeah, well, I still say that Murphy part is bullshit. Ain't nobody gonna think you're Irish."

"Rocking chair Democrats, baby. They're too blind to read the newspaper and too deaf to hear the radio, but they vote Irish every time." She rolled her eyes. "If you don't get it, sugar, it's too late for me to explain. Just remember, 'say nothing, and you say nothing wrong. Do nothing, and you do nothing wrong.'"

"Ain't doin' nothin' doin' somethin' wrong?" I said, mocking her head-weaving routine.

"Not when a man is as tall and pretty as you, baby. We ain't sellin' da steak, sugar," she said in her falsetto voice. She touched the end of my nose with her middle finger and said in her normal voice, "But we *are*, however, selling the sizzle."

I DISPATCHED ROSA, OUR MAID, to check the freezer for the lobster that I knew had been delivered yesterday. Before she came back, I scooped Alice's juice glass into an evidence bag.

"Well, Ms. Sizzle," I said to the glass, "I got this job before I knew you, and I passed the lieutenant's exam without your politics." I held the bag up to the light and admired a large clear thumbprint on the glass. "And I scored in the top ten."

I stashed the evidence bag in the side pocket of my suit coat. "Statute of limitations, baby. You no longer own my narrow little ass—not that you had much of a case once I married you. Now we find out why I never met nobody from your family. And why, after eight years, you don't get so much as a Christmas card."

"*Si*, the lobsters," said Rosa, her dark Latin eyes a little accusatory as she stepped back into the kitchen from the pantry. "They *are* where I put them yesterday." She scanned her gaze around the kitchen, a question on her face. "I heard you talking. Someone is here?"

"I was on my cellphone," I said as I patted the evidence bag in the side pocket of my suit jacket. "Doesn't your son work for my wife?"

"*Si*, Eduardo. He loves your wife so much. He is a hard worker. Your wife gives him a good job. Even when he works late, he does not complain."

THERE BE SOMETHIN' JUST WRONG about a honkey in a do-rag—not so much if it be scooter trash or like that, but a real live gardener that drives in from the suburbs to dig around my bushes? I'm just sayin'. I got him to push a wheelbarrow full of mulch off the drive to let me by—tall, skinny white dude, maybe thirty. And it ain't like I saw that much get done, neither.

I climbed into the Beemer and drove off.

Marked patrol cars and plain-wrapper detective cars sat double- and triple-parked in front of the granite steps of police headquarters, downtown at 1300 Barbour Street—even a couple stopped in the oncoming lane. One of them had a caved-in roof and a side-view mirror dangling by a cable. Paul Finney, my partner, had already been to the precinct and picked up our car. What the fuck he be doing downtown?

The building stacked fourteen stories. Maybe he was up working on his retirement papers—you couldn't shut him up about the subject. Forensics was on six, and maybe I could get in and out without him running into me. I flogged my whip around the corner to the Greektown

Casino and flashed my platter to the parking valet. I wasn't about to park my ride anywhere near all that activity.

I walked back across the street and eased up to the corner. The beat-up dick car still sat blocking the oncoming lane. I made all casual-like, took the stairs to the sixth floor, and ran smack into Paul Finney stepping out of Forensics.

"Tony!" he said, like it was music and I wasn't supposed to notice his pasty white face or wonder what he was really thinking.

"Hey," I said. "Saw the car, thought you'd be upstairs getting set to retire."

"Nah," said Paul. "I had 'em park my papers. The Lieutenant Board roster is out. We're both on it." He stuck his fist out. I bumped his knuckles. Dumb bastard!

"So, you make lieutenant," I said, "and you catch a big bump in your retirement?"

"There's that," he said with a shrug. "But only if I don't like being a lieutenant."

I wanted to shake my head. Ain't nobody walkin' off that board with a gold badge and a pasty white face. I managed a nod, but said, "Paul, you're a fuckin' dinosaur. What you gonna do as a lieutenant? Make a big loud *gronk* and Godzilla y'ass through the vacant buildings downtown?"

"I remember when those buildings weren't vacant," said Paul with a nod and a wistful tone.

"What's that supposed to mean?"

"It means I remember when those buildings had people and businesses in them," he said with his face all blanched white innocence.

Just some more racist crap. But I guess you get a thick skin. I let it go.

"If it comes down to you or me—" he said.

"You hope it's you."

He smiled and said, "A howdy."

"So, what you got to drop off?" I said. "Long as you're still my partner."

"The cigarette butts the shooter dropped at the pawnshop robbery."

"They ain't going to mean shit," I said. "Even if the dude's in the database, he be layin' dead in a dope house before we hear from the Feds."

"I gotta log 'em in today," he said. "They're on the fives from yesterday. What brings you down here?"

"Evidence," I said, brushing past Paul. "Different case. I'll meet you back at the squad." I gave him a wave and pointed my finger at him. "Clock me in."

"Already clocked you in," said Paul with a shrug.

"Ain't like I'm ridin' in that rolling wreckage you left out in the street," I said. "You shoulda left the keys in it to save the tow bill."

"Nuthin' in the garage until Inspector Falon retires," said Paul.

"We gonna get Falon's car?"

"Get real," said Paul. "We're gonna get whatever's cast off by the guy that gets Falon's car."

"I gotta drive myself back anyway," I said. "This here just take a minute. I'll meet you at the precinct. Really!"

"Why are you trying to get rid of me?" Paul asked.

I stepped up to the desk. "Fuckin' stay," I said, waving my hand at the space next to me. "Knock yourself out. Take root!"

A Chink evidence tech, dressed in hospital scrubs with reading glasses perched on the top of his head, stepped up to the counter and picked up the evidence bag with Alice's juice glass in it.

"What?" he said, his basset-hound face oozing annoyance.

"Need you to lift the print and run it," I said.

He flipped the glasses down to examine the receipt tag and said, "I need a file number."

"No file number, yet."

"Gimme the case name and a code," he said and clicked his pen.

"John Doe," I said. "One eighty-seven."

"I got that number for ya," said Paul. He dug his notepad from the inside breast pocket of his suit coat. After thumbing some pages, he read the number aloud. The tech scribbled it on the tag, tore off the receipt, and handed it to me. We left.

We didn't get five steps before Paul lit on me like stink on shit. "I didn't see that glass on the fives." "I was with you all day." "Where did *we* pick up the glass?" "I'm only asking the questions we have to answer in court." He kept it up all the way down the elevator and through the door to the stone steps where he wrapped it up with, "Dammit, I'm your partner, Tony."

"I don't want you to have to lie," I said.

"If it's just testimony, what do I care?" He waved a backhand at me. "We're just crossing the t's and dotting the i's here."

"It's personal," I said.

"Wrong answer." He grabbed my arm.

I stopped and turned to face him. "It don't matter," I said. "We both know that case is never going to trial."

"I thought when we arrested an ex-cop and started a riot, it had to matter a lot!"

"It matters a whole fuckin' bunch, Paul," I said. "It's about the Teddy Sorenson case. The FBI took a copy of the fives."

"Nobody told me that."

"Command didn't tell me neither. My wife told me. She's on the Public Safety Committee. She let it slip. She didn't even know I'm workin' the case."

"What do they care?"

"Two cracker skinhead racists get off the bus, and twenty-four hours later they both on a slab in the morgue?"

"*Cracker* skinheads?"

"Yeah! You know any skinheads that ain't crackers?"

"I think we have some local skinhead types." He dug a flip-top pack of cigarettes out of his inside coat pocket and pointed up the street with it. "I read something about the northern suburbs."

"They's wannabe crackers."

Paul shook me loose a square. I took it. It takes twenty minutes of screwing around to get two drags off the meerschaum Alice makes me carry.

"Hadn't thought of it in that light," Paul said.

"You know the FBI is all up in our ass." I hammered the filter end of the cigarette on my left thumbnail to tamp down the tobacco so I wouldn't burn my suit. "The whole damn department—hell, the chief's gotta call Washington to get permission to take a leak."

"Then the FBI's got nothin', 'cause we got nothin'," said Paul, still searching his suit. He never had a light, but he was fun to watch.

"Kerze got something," I said and aimed my cigarette at him. "He stepped in it good, and he's gonna track it all over you and me and the squad."

"Now that we arrested him, he wouldn't say shit if he had a mouthful."

"Ya think?" I stuck the cigarette between my lips and raised my chin, expecting a light.

Paul narrowed his eyes as he exhaled a sigh that was part grunt and part growl.

He said, "I wondered how you got the warrant." He gave his pockets a last pat down. "We ain't even got the autopsy yet. Fuckin' asshole could have dropped dead from a heart attack." He made a shrug and showed me empty palms. "Ain't got a light."

"My money's on the closed head injury the EMT talked about." I pulled out my electric windproof butane lighter. I lit his cigarette.

"No," said Paul. He took a deep drag and held it thoughtfully until he exhaled. "I think the kid was more scared of the perps than the police."

"Maybe he shoulda been afraid of Kerze." I fired up my cigarette.

"Maybe if we'd done more for the kid, he wouldn't have gone looking for help," said Paul. "If you keep pushing the Kerze case, at some point the department might have to explain why we didn't take the kid to Receiving to get his head injury examined after the bus incident."

"We got a witness saw Kerze shove the kid into the restroom." I turned to make sure the wind was blowing the ash and sparks away from me. "My working theory is that Kerze went back and finished him off." I reached out to arm's length to tap the ashes off my cigarette.

"Kerze is the one that called 911," said Paul.

"Kerze is the last one saw him alive. The next time anyone saw him, he be dead."

Paul shook his head. "Not enough, though 'last one to see him alive' is a good court argument." He studied the cherry red end of his cigarette, rolled his eyes up to me, and finished with, "We both know that people having a medical meltdown frequently head for the bathroom and then die there."

"Kerze was a cop," I said, plugging the obvious before getting to the point. "He was covering. He knew there had to be witnesses."

Paul made taut lips and gave me a head shake. "We still don't have a motive." He took a drag and then aimed his cigarette at me like a chalkboard pointer. "What's the upside for Kerze to whack this kid out?"

"We got to find the broad that was on the bus with him," I said. "That's where all the crap started. I req'ed Sergeant McQuinn's report and any patrol contact cards."

"I got a call on the way over. We got some guy waiting on us back at the squad. Charles DeSimone, manages the City Suites hotel. He says Kerze works for him part time and he wants to talk about the case."

I RODE BACK TO THE precinct in the rolling wreckage with Paul. Since he'd already clocked me in, it wouldn't do to show up in separate cars.

"You drive," I said, "I'll ride in the back like a suspect. I'd rather look disgusted than ridiculous."

"You want I should cuff you up?" asked Paul.

We found Lieutenant Gilbert standing in the door to his office with his arms folded. A red bow tie underlined his ebony jaw and an expression so malevolent, it would have panicked the Sphinx offa Giza. He said, "Jackson, my office! Finney, talk to the motel manager in the hallway."

He stepped back from the doorway and made a sweep of his arm toward his desk. "Have a seat."

I pulled out the straight-back chair.

"No, no," said the lieutenant, "my chair!" He waved an open palm at his desk chair. "Have a seat."

"Lieutenant?"

"Sit!" he said. His eyeballs looked like they might pop out of his skull.

I sat.

"Comfy?"

I rocked the chair back. "Nice chair."

"How 'bout the carpet?"

I straightened up in the chair and looked at the floor. "This is tile."

The lieutenant planted his hands on the desk and leaned over it, crouching so that his eyes came level with mine. His upper lip curled into his mustache, and he said, "Maybe you could have your wife send someone over to measure."

I looked around the room, mostly so I wouldn't have to look at Lieutenant Gilbert. Was I a dog, I coulda just curled my tail between my legs and slunk to a neutral corner. Truth be told, I was tired of my old lady's bullshit politics too, but I couldn't sink low enough to make myself say it, so I said, "I'm thinking red plush and pile, Lieutenant. And drapes. Those blinds are so last year."

Lieutenant Gilbert rose like a bear. His right arm shot out and he beckoned with his fingers. "Gimme your notepad."

"Lieutenant?" I started out of the chair.

"Sit," he said in an almost friendly tone, but then he barked, "Notepad!" a whole lot meaner, while still waggling his fingers.

I gave it to him, and he smelled it over a page at a time like a stray dog working a fire hydrant. Finally, he flopped it on top of a short stack of file folders piled on the desk blotter.

He said, "Nothing in there on the Theodore Sorenson case."

"The scene was a parking structure," I said. "No one to canvass. The car involved had been rented on a stolen credit card. The only witness was dead. It was all in the daily fives. There *is* nothing else."

"News flash, Beau Brummell," said Lieutenant Gilbert. "Witness ain't dead."

"Raymond Kerze ain't a witness."

"Skinhead John Doe ain't dead. FBI has him," said the lieutenant, like a meow. "He's in protective custody."

"Man was dead."

"*Doctor* Jackson, is it now? I didn't know you had a medical degree, and I reviewed all of your personnel jacket just yesterday."

"Robbery Homicide," I said. "Seen a whole buncha dead mother-fuckers. That motherfucker was a *dead* motherfucker."

"Yeah?" said the lieutenant. "Me too, but the motherfucker in question sat up on his motherfucking gurney and bitched about how motherfucking cold it was in the motherfucking morgue."

I had to run his words by my brain twice before they sunk in, and when they did, the best I could come up with was a lame-ass, "Holy shit!"

"Could be," said Lieutenant Gilbert. A mist of a smile dissipated on his face. "But I'm not the homicide detective that started a riot arresting a retired cop for killing a dead motherfucker who ain't dead."

"You sent me to pick up the warrant!"

"Your *wife* had the associate in the prosecutor's office cook up the warrant for his pal, Judge Levant, to sign," said the lieutenant, smug and pleased with himself. "So who else would I send to go down and sign that affidavit? Personally, I like to see the postmortem before I sign an affidavit." He scratched his neck with the back of his index finger and finished with, "Maybe do a little investigating, too. Just in case."

"Prosecutor said 'sign,'" I said. "I mean, he's a fucking lawyer. And you sent me."

"Yeah, he's a lawyer," said the lieutenant, adding a taut-lipped nod. He passed a casual gaze around his tiny cluttered office. "I was busy," he said, in feigned innocence, "so, I sent you."

My gut twitched somewhere between anger and confusion. "So what the fuck is going on? How the hell did my wife get involved?

What's the deal with the FBI? All homicides are local!"

"I've heard that said about politics," said the lieutenant. "As to your wife? Well,"—he shrugged—"politics and strange bedfellows."

"Just a damn minute," I said. "My wife and my marriage is none of your business."

"Your wife is nothing *but* my business," he said. "To start with, I know you snaked me out of Falon's seat on the Minority Equity Council. That's your wife's doing. I got stepped over two other bureau chiefs to take Falon's inspector slot, so that the chair you have your ass planted on would be available for you. Your wife's fingers are all up in that pie, too."

When you're busted, you're busted. But when there's a little breeze, and you're busted and the dye pack is blowing orange all over your Brooks Brothers, it's best to say nothing—or at least change the subject, so I said, "What's all that got to do with the FBI?"

"I have no idea what the FBI is up to, but my guess is that whatever game they're playing started long before Theodore Sorenson and his pal, John Doe, boarded the bus en route to our fair city."

"So Ray Kerze has been released?"

"No."

I felt myself shrug. I threw up my hands and said, "What?"

"He's in the jail ward at Receiving Hospital."

"What, because he's a retired cop?"

"Because he's an alcoholic," said the lieutenant.

"County jail is full of alcoholics."

"The county jail is not full of alcoholic material witnesses."

"Kerze ain't even a casual witness," I said. "He wasn't there and he can't testify to what John Doe told him because it's hearsay. John Doe is the material witness, and he's already in protective custody."

"As you say, all murders are local, and your job, Mr. Phelps, is to discover the real connection between Kerze and John Doe, as regards to the murder of Theodore Sorenson."

"Who's Mr. Phelps?"

"Mr. Phelps's notepad is on the stack of files and contact cards that he ordered and will take with him when he leaves."

The lieutenant wagged a finger at me. "A brief summary," he ticked off on his fingers. "One, Kerze was on the bus with a woman named Misty Lake when he assaulted John Doe. Two, Misty Lake was on the scene when you arrested Kerze, but you failed to interview her. And three, Misty Lake was briefly detained last night for attempting to pass a counterfeit hundred that she said Kerze gave her. Ms. Lake gave her residence as the City Suites hotel where Kerze is said to be an employee. And last but not least, the manager of the City Suites was kind enough to hang around my hallway this morning while you and your partner were out fucking around."

"We had to take some evidence down to the lab," I said.

"Both of you?"

"Chain of custody!"

"A good thing you're minding your P's and Q's," said Lieutenant Gilbert. "Because my goodwill, such as it is, will self-destruct as soon as you peel your sorry ass off, what is for now, still *my* chair. Either you're going to screw up and I *will* catch you, or you have screwed up already and I *will* find out. And when I do, I'll plow your ass under like an acre of weevil-infested Mississippi cotton."

"DAMN, YOU LOOK PALE," SAID Paul, looking up from stirring his coffee.

I slammed the files onto my desk. "Not funny."

"No, really," he said. "You don't look well."

"I'm as good as I'm gonna get," I said. "You got the motel guy in the interview room?"

"Nah," said Paul. "I told him and he left."

"Told him what?"

"It's an ongoing case and we couldn't discuss it with him."

"Sheee-it!"

"What?" said Paul.

"John Doe ain't dead. That's what!"

"Bullshit! I seen a lotta dead motherfuckers and—"

"Don't start. I been there. Even if he is, *in fact*, dead, he ain't *officially* dead."

"Dead is dead," said Paul. He waved around an open palm. "The doc at Receiving Emergency pronounced him in the back of the ambulance. They didn't even wheel him in."

"We got to find out the doctor's name."

Paul smiled and showed me one finger. He peeled his notepad out of his pocket and thumbed some pages. "Doctor Patel," he read. "Mahendra." He spelled it for me.

I exhaled and deflated into my chair. "I thought I was losing my marbles."

Paul snatched up his phone and pecked out a number.

"What are you doing?" I said.

"Callin' FeeBee. See if we can set up a séance."

The FBI dicked him around on the phone for ten, fifteen minutes and I had time to read McQuinn's report and some jarhead patrolman's report. Conklin, I seen him around—skippy looks like he's still in the Corp. If Misty'd been a sister he'da run her in steada pattin' her little hand. Though maybe that was better—better than banging her in the back seat of the patrol car. Sweet Jesus! How could I ever have been *that* stupid?

Finally, Paul spoke into the telephone again. He gave his name and badge number. "Robbery Homicide," he said. "I'm working on the murder of Theodore Sorenson. I need to interview a Mr. John Doe, a man you have in protective custody. Yeah . . . I see . . . but, really—" Paul clinched his eyes and slowly wagged his head. "No . . . Listen, I can get it all done in ten minutes . . . you could bring him here . . . Fine, we'll do it that way." He picked up his pencil. "I just need your name for the fives . . . daily log report . . . I have to keep a record that I've touched base." Paul made a start and stared, astonished, at the handset.

"So who'd you talk to?" I asked.

"Special Agent Filgaflix, or maybe he just coughed into the phone and hung up."

"So what's the story?"

"Submit questions in writing through the chain of command."

"Like the lieutenant?" I said.

"Like the chief of police."

MISTY LAKE HAD THAT "ALREADY talked to" look. We found her in the pink-and-white striped continental breakfast nook at the City Suites hotel. Her left hand cradled a bruised jaw and cheek while she used a fork to mash slices of French toast into mush. Between bites, you could see the stitches in her lip.

Paul said, "Miss Lake?"

"Leave me alone," she said, her lips barely moving.

"Who did this to you?" I asked. I pulled up a chair and sat beside her.

She closed her eyes and wagged her head. Paul walked over to the buffet to tap the coffee urn.

"You lost the counterfeit hundreds and they smacked you around?"

She held her face and said through her hand, "No! Hurts to talk."

Paul set his coffee on the table, parked himself in a chair, and shook down a couple packets of sugar. "So, what's the story?"

"Not talking," I said.

"Well, it wasn't Ray Kerze," said Paul. "We still have him."

"Who—?" Misty put her hand over her mouth to cover a grimace. "Who is Ray supposed to have killed?"

"Tell me who slapped you around," I said, "then we can talk about Ray Kerze."

"Go away."

"We can't go away," said Paul. He unbuttoned his suit coat and settled into the chair across from Misty. "The bogus Benjamins are enough for us to take you in and hold you until the Secret Service figures out how to find the county jail."

"Make us believe you're trying to help us," I said. "Otherwise,"—I pointed at Paul—"he's gonna read you your rights."

"I can't move my lips," Misty exhaled in a low monotone. "I sound funny—ow!" She cradled her jaw. "Ooohh."

"My heart pumps peanut butter for ya, honey," said Paul. "Who split your lip?"

"Now, Paul," I said, "she gonna do the best she can. Jus' have to go slow." I patted her hand. "Go easy. If you need to, you can write your answers." I laid out my notepad and pen.

A single tear stuttered down her cheek and she caught it up with the heel of her hand. "Cop took my monn-ney," she breathed. "Two guys wanted to pay for my meal. They got in a fight." She pointed at her face. "And I'm the one got hit."

"You got between 'em and tried to stop the fight?" I asked.

Misty nodded, smacked her forehead with her open palm, and let it ricochet off toward the ceiling.

"So who hit you?" I asked.

"Guy with a mustache," she measured out, moving her jaw but not her lips. "Not much taller than me. Dark. Coulda been Mexican or an Arab." She shrugged. "Maybe a white guy with a good tan."

"Hair?"

"He had a hoodie sweatshirt. I couldn't see."

"Kind of a fat skinny guy and bald with long blond hair," said Paul. "Misty, you're jerking us around. You have the right to remain si-lent—"

"Wait," I said. "She be tryin'."

"He have any scars? Tattoos?"

Misty looked down at the table and shook her head.

"Who's the other guy?"

"P-Jelly," she said, looking at Paul but talking to me.

Paul rolled his head back and rocked back in his chair.

"Was he in the fight?" I said.

"He wanted to buy my dinner, but he left just before the cops came," said Misty.

"Now, *that* I believe," said Paul.

"Came in after. Took me to a free clinic. Dropped me off here."

"P-Jelly's a pimp," said Paul. "You hooking for him? He doing a sideline in funny money? Maybe he smacked you around for lifting a few samples?"

"P-Jelly pay for your room?" I asked, keeping it just short of an accusation.

"No. They let me stay. Somebody paid and left. I slept on the sofa. Bed was used, ya know?"

"That's it," said Paul. "I'm gonna talk to the manager before this bullshit gets so deep I'll need snow shoes to get over the drifts."

He knocked back his coffee and stepped out of his chair.

"Why'd they do that?" I asked.

"They know Ray," said Misty. "They were nice to meee." A second tear crashed out of the gate and galloped down her cheek.

I handed her a paper napkin that Paul had left next to his coffee cup. "P-Jelly have anything to do with the two guys that you and Ray had a fight with on the bus?"

Misty dabbed her cheek and wiped her nose. "Skinheads! Get real."

"How do you know they were skinheads?"

"Nazi tattoos."

"Like what?"

Misty put her hand on the top of her head. "Swastika. Whole top of his head. Other guy, lightning bolts." Misty brushed her neck with the back of her fingers.

"Maybe they were friends of Ray's?"

"They were on the bus. They were assholes. They said rude things to me. One guy snapped open a knife. Ray banged their heads together and threw one guy off the bus. The other guy ran away."

"So you and Ray were supposed to meet them on the bus?"

"We didn't have money for the bus. Ray spent all my money on booze. The driver stopped. The two skinheads were being assholes. The driver knew Ray would help him."

"So where'd the Benjamins come from?"

"Meat Hook Marty. I told this all. A sergeant."

"McQuinn," I said. "I read the report."

Misty dropped her face into her hands.

"My mouth hurts," she said. Her stitches started to bleed and she dabbed her mouth with a napkin. "You're just mean!"

"You gonna be over at Ray's office later?"

"Got nowhere else," she said, closing her eyes and shaking her head.

I gave her shoulder a squeeze. "Ray didn't kill nobody. He's in custody as a witness."

Misty exhaled a sob into her hands. "Oh, God."

I gave her one more pat and left her at the table. "Maybe we can talk later. When you're feeling better."

Paul lay in wait for me at the door with a trash bag in his hand and a smile on his face.

I said, "We tryin' to make a case outta nothing. I'da smacked that guy. I'm glad Ray smacked him. It was self-defense."

"Yeah," said Paul. "That's what I thought from the get-go." He dangled the trash bag in front of me. "Now I think I was wrong."

"What'd the manager say?"

"Nothin'. Still pissed about me giving him the brush this morning. But I talked to the housekeeper. She said she made the bed in that room *before* Ms. Lake went up there. She had to make it up again this morning. Misty tell you the part about how she's Ray's sister?"

"You got to be shitting me."

"We're treading bullshit," said Paul. "Maybe this is a life boat. I got an empty bottle of Cristal and two of them snap-together plastic wine glasses. Good prints on all of it."

"Could have been the people who 'left early,'" I said.

Paul gave me a single nod. "Could be we find out who she's covering for."

"I'M JUST SAYIN," I SAID as we stepped into the elevator to go up to the evidence lab, "I just don't see Misty Lake sitting around sippin' bubbly with a smashed mouth."

"Can't argue with that," said Paul, "but she either lied about being alone in the room, or she lied about sleeping on the sofa. Somebody gave her the home brewed Benjamins, and somebody punched her in the mouth."

"What has that got to do with Ray Kerze?"

"She says Ray gave her the hundreds," said Paul.

"That's a plus," I said. "But the lieutenant wants to tie Ray, the money, and the girl to the Teddy Sorenson murder."

The elevator door opened at the third floor. A couple top-floor suits got on, so we had to shut up.

I had time to think. Ray, the money, and the girl went together—no sweat. They didn't go together with the Teddy Sorenson murder unless they planned the meeting on the bus and it somehow melted down.

As we stepped off at the sixth floor, one of the suits said, "Hearing some good things aboutcha, Tony."

"Thanks," I said.

The doors slid closed. Paul asked, "Who the hell was that?"

"I have no idea."

"Don't worry," said Paul, "one 'aw shit' cancels all the attaboys."

"Ain't no boys here."

"Fuck's sake," said Paul. "The 'Hearing some good things aboutcha' *was* the 'attaboy!' That's what it's called! I didn't name it! Gimme a break."

"You still can't say 'boy' to me." I couldn't believe he said it. I usually let that kind of stuff just slide, but not today. I said, "You white. There be things you just can't say."

"We're friends," said Paul. "I don't have any reason to ride your ass."

"Yeah, we friends. If we weren't friends, I wouldn't even start tellin' you."

Paul pinched up his face and tugged at my elbow so that we walked over to the water cooler.

"All right," he said. "Since we're friends and we can do all this explaining, how 'bout this? A guy—cranky and a pain in the ass, but otherwise a decent sort—gets put on the express elevator to the upper floors. Not everyone's happy with that. Shit hits the fan, and someone uses the shit to grease the cable. Elevator goes *whoosh*, and one problem takes care of the other."

"Don't the elevator have room for one more? And what's that got to do with you callin' me *boy*?"

"Not a damn thing," Paul said, his eyes wide and jaws tight. "Not a damn thing."

Paul stared at the evidence bag in his hand and didn't look up. I followed him into the evidence room and he turned it in to the technician.

"Let's take the stairs down," I said.

"May not be better than the elevators just now," Paul said. "Why do you think the hoods from upstairs are talking so nice about you if they aren't planning to drop your keister down the shaft?"

"How'd you figure?" I asked. "I played by the rules. They got the warrant. I arrested Kerze's ass. That meeting on the bus was an accident. No way any of that's tied to the Teddy Sorenson murder."

"Ray Kerze is in all of it."

"Only because they met on the bus," I said.

"So, you're starting to believe in coincidence?"

"Kerze didn't say he stumbled into our John Doe. He admits they went to the office building together. He admits the kid talked to him about the Sorenson murder. We told him to butt out, that it's an open case. We put that in the fives. FeeBee took copies of the fives and the lieutenant said he thinks the Bureau probably had an ongoing case with Sorenson and Doe before they even got on the bus to come here."

"Jeez!" Paul sneered. "Don't you see it? The FBI wants to know what John Doe told Kerze. And whoever got you the warrant knew Kerze would clam up as soon as we snapped the cuffs on him."

"FeeBee has John Doe now," I said. "They can just ask him."

"He's in a freezer," said Paul. "How hard would it be to hide a 'John Doe' body? Call any morgue you like, they got a few."

"They said he wasn't dead."

"They lied," Paul said. "God knows how much time and money

they've tied up in the case or what's at stake. If they could talk to John Doe, they wouldn't have crawled out on a limb."

"Now our department wants us to tie Kerze to the Sorenson murder so we can hold him as a material witness," I said. "And they got him in at Receiving in the alky ward where he can't have a visitor. Where anything he tells his doctor is privileged."

Paul pursed his lips and gave me a slow, knowing nod.

"Why don't they just whack him?" I asked.

Paul shrugged, turned up his empty palms, and made that void stare that he does. Finally he smiled and held up a finger. He laughed. "It's a thing," he said. "They're looking for a thing. They think Kerze knows where the thing's at. As long as they got Kerze, they got the thing—or at least Kerze can't get to the thing."

"So this goes all the way to the top?"

Paul gave my shoulder a shake. "They've been hearing good things about you!"

"You mean, before they start greasing the elevator cable with 10W-doodoo?"

"We turned in our evidence," said Paul. "Fuckin' lab techs take their sweet time—never act like they have a fire under their asses. We probably got a couple days."

"So we get a warrant to search Kerze's office?"

"No," said Paul. "We get a warrant and we let on that we know there's something to look for."

"But we don't know what it is," I said.

"I'm hopin' Kerze don't know either, but the same mountain of shit that fell on Kerze could just as well fall on us—if we start lookin' too wise."

"But we find out what it is," I said, "and we gonna know who killed Teddy Sorenson. And that makes Kerze a material witness."

"They already know that," said Paul. "That's why the lieutenant pointed you in that direction. That means he's already got a mountain of shit with our names on it."

"Maybe," I said, "the mountain of shit is addressed 'to whom it may concern.'"

"In that case, it's addressed to whoever's fingerprints are on this bottle," said Paul.

"They're just gonna say they was playing spin the bottle."

"Think about it," Paul said. "More and more, we find guys whose prints ain't in the system. They were never in the military. They never got busted. And women, same-ole, same-ole—only in spades. Good chance the prints are a dead end. And if not, they shouldn't have been up there playing spin the bottle. If they can afford eight hundred bucks to do the nasty for a couple hours, they can afford lawyers to tell 'em to clam up."

"In 'spades?'"

"Oh, for God's sake, pick a suit. Hearts? Diamonds?"

"All right," I said. Paul was always sayin' shit and then actin' all innocent. "Let's go get this done."

"Then we go over to Receiving, flash the tin, and talk to Kerze."

"Great," I said. "We read him his rights, again. He tells us to go fuck ourselves, again."

"Perfect," said Paul. "And we quote him in the fives."

But we didn't get to see Kerze that day. A break came in on the pawnshop robbery, and that ate up the rest of the afternoon and half the evening.

THE PAWNSHOP THING ALSO ATE up most of the next day. Turns out, the shop owner was fencing stolen PCs on the side. I had a message from Misty Lake on my cell, but when I called her back, she only wanted to talk about Kerze and how could she get in touch with him. I told her I'd get back to her.

Yeah. I'd get back to her after Paul and I talked to Kerze again ourselves. But when we got to Receiving Hospital, we had another surprise. They'd moved Kerze someplace else entirely. Paul bitched about that all the way back to the precinct.

Paul hung up his suit coat and plopped his backside into his desk chair. "So who figured they'd move Kerze out to Brighton? They always dry 'em out for two weeks before they get sent to the farm."

"Let it go," I said. "I don't care where they dry him out."

"It's an hour there and an hour back." Paul loosened his tie. "And we still got the fives and other shit to fill out for the pawnshop deal. We can annoy Kerze's ass tomorrow."

"Lieutenant is hard on *my* ass."

"Check out his office," Paul said. "He ain't fuckin' there."

I took a look. His office was dark.

I picked up the fives and started writing.

I ONCE SAW THE MOVIE *Lost Weekend*. Lotsa pasty white faces, but the acting itself wasn't bad. I bring it up because yesterday shoulda been called *Lost Thursday*. I swear, I couldn't get on the stand and tell a judge what happened that day. Meetings. Phone calls. Paperwork. Crap about shit that shoulda been settled months ago. It wasted the whole day.

By the time Friday afternoon showed, things had gotten back to what passed for normal. And Paul and I finally got the tech reports from the evidence we'd dropped off.

We still hadn't been out to see Kerze, but maybe the tech reports would give us some ammunition to shoot at him. The lieutenant had been by this morning to chew my ass about the lack of progress in the Teddy Sorenson investigation. Nothing I told him made a good-enough excuse.

I leaned back in my chair and thumbed back at the lieutenant's office. "Fucker sent me out to arrest Kerze for murder and there weren't no damn dead body."

Paul opened the tech report from City Suites. "Look, the guy was dead. He was a Nazi punk. Kerze hit him in the head. The whole day watch hit him in the head. We're the only two guys who ain't tuned him up."

"FBI says they got him and he ain't dead," I said. "If we don't turn

Kerze dirty, I'm cooked."

Paul smiled.

"Ain't all that funny."

Paul waved his hand. "Just hang on, Tony." He thumbed through the tech report.

I sat in my chair, but left my coat on. I said, "This better be good."

"I think we're back on the promotion list again," Paul said. "The broad at City Suites. Kerze's pal, what's her name . . . ?"

"Misty Lake," I said. "Sounds fake."

Paul nodded his head. "Mornica Lake. No wonder she changed her name. She'd been in the room like she said. What gets interesting is Juan Romars's fingerprints on the bottle of champagne. He crossed the Feds on a weapons-smuggling deal some years back. Arrest but no conviction. He may have swapped testimony for time."

"Where that happen?"

"Little Rock, Arkansas."

"That's exciting," I said. "My career is still circling the big brown grille."

"It gets better," said Paul. "Also on the same champagne bottle were the fingerprints of a woman named Ruby Harris. Ruby Harris got convicted of embezzling a quarter-million bucks from one ninety-two-year-old Alice Mitchell, a white lady in Little Rock. Harris made a deal to return the money in exchange for a lighter sentence. Instead, she escaped from the courthouse after the hearing and took the money with her."

"Fascinating," I said. "That's the same name as my wife. I don't suppose you got the want ads?"

"Ruby Harris skipped from Little Rock, Arkansas, eight years ago and is still wanted."

"Ray Kerze's fingerprints in there?"

"Not yet," said Paul, "but we got fingerprints from Misty Lake, Ruby Harris, and Juan Romars in the City Suites room. Kerze is 'employed' at the City Suites. Misty Lake was with Kerze on the bus when he assaulted the Nazi punks. They had a lot of tattoos. Misty Lake has a little tattoo as well. The Nazis came up from Arkansas."

"That's a little thin," I said, staring through clinched eyes. "Is Ruby Harris at least a Nazi, or mother of?"

Paul looked at his report. "Negro."

"I don't see it," I said. "And what's with the 'Negro' crack?"

Paul made an innocent face. "Just reading off the Little Rock police report," he said. "In this case, the money's all green. We've seen that before. And now they're fighting over the money. Works for me. Let's have a look at your own tech report. Maybe we'll still make lieutenant."

"Not gonna help," I said. "It wasn't from the City Suites anyway."

"Come on," Paul said, smiling, with a wink.

"Knock yourself out." I flipped him the file.

Paul fell back onto his seat and laughed. "You dog," he said. "You knew about Ruby Harris the whole time."

I FINALLY SLUNK OUT OF the evidence room. What gives them the right to be so damn polite, just because you're wrong? Why can't I just have my wife's neck in my fists, right now?

The tech had taken me around the counter when I didn't believe the results. I'd told him, "You must have confused my evidence with Paul Finney's City Suites bag."

I watched. The evidence on the juice cup from my kitchen was Ruby Harris's print.

I got back to my desk. Paul had departed—thank God. This made one time I couldn't complain. The lieutenant's office was closed and the lights were out. I got my hat.

When I got to the Greektown Casino parking garage, I handed the valet my stub. His face blanched white and he took his employee's uniform hat from his head. "Ah, sir, I'm sorry." He twisted his hat. "But they towed that car out of here."

I flashed my heat. I'd never really paid any attention to him. He wore a home-cut hair buzz and a blond goatee so spare that it looked like doughnut crumbs. I said, "Go get the right car. I'm a detective. Ain't like nobody gonna tow my car."

"It's a Beemer," he said, "the one you park here all the time."

"So the casino don't want to park my Beemer anymore?" I said. "Hope they don't never need nothing from me."

"Wasn't the boss," he said, shaking his head. "Was one of those big blue cop haulers. They had that yellow tape wrapped around it when they left."

I snapped my neck around, but stopped. "Wait a minute, I didn't do nothin'. What the hell is going on?"

"They didn't tell us anything," said the valet. "A cop in overalls pushed the tow order in my face and said, 'Gimme the tag and the key.'"

I clinched my eyes and grabbed my cellphone. Paul's phone didn't answer—and it always answers. Paul is a homicide detective. His phone answers—just not now. I shook my head and started to call the lieutenant, but stopped mid-dial. I called the desk sergeant instead.

"Somebody towed my car," I said.

"Did you make the payment?"

Now that pissed me off, but I needed information, so I said, "The car is paid off. It's a Beemer." I gave him my plate number.

"Stand by," he said. He took a whole damn year getting back. "Your car's at Finkle Evidence Yard."

"Some kids take it for a joyride?"

"Whatever happened, the FBI has a hold on your car."

"Holy shit."

"Anything else?" he said. "God knows I got nothing else to do."

"Ah, fuck you."

He laughed. "No, really, this is the best story I've heard all day. Got anything else?"

I hung up. I started down the stairs, not exactly worried about how I would get home, but—instead—focused fully on getting my hands around my wife's neck.

On the street, a humongous black Chevy Suburban stopped in

front of me. The front passenger door opened. The honkey who did my lawn sat in the driver's seat. And there weren't enough lawns in all of Detroit to pay for those wheels.

But I needed a ride, so I climbed in.

In the back seat, I found Raymond Kerze and the Nazi punk—not dead, but that's another story.

The Fifth of
Many Stories

The Ferryman and
the Passenger

WHEN YOU WAKE UP DEAD, it's cold. Real cold. My arms and legs felt like stiff salamis. A sheet covered my face. I managed to sit up.

"Holy shit!" said a voice, and something clattered to the floor.

"Hey, get back here," said another man, real gruff. "They sit up all the time. Get your ass back here! Help me keep it on the cart till we can get it in the cooler."

"Coooal," was all the sound I could make. It sounded like a moan.

"Holy shit, they talk, too?" said the first voice, now fading away. "Fuck it! I quit."

"Cold!" I said. I didn't want to go to any place called the cooler. My arms and legs felt asleep—numb and tingly. Lights flickered through the thin cloth. Someone pulled the sheet off my head and chest—a dark-skinned man. He wore white clothes. He had silver hair, and his teeth had a lot of gold.

I didn't have no clothes on. I asked, "Are you God?"

He stared at me with his eyes very large. After a while, he said, "I sure as hell ain't God."

"Oh," I said. *Oh shit!*

He twisted his face to one side and scrunched up his eyes.

I sighed, and my gaze fell to my lap.

The man in the white clothes laughed and shook my shoulder. When I looked at him, he pointed a finger at me and roared. I was scared shitless.

Another man in white clothes pushed open a door and edged his head through. Eyes and mouth huge, he held the door half closed as if to defend himself. "What's funny?"

"Thinks I'm God."

"He's not God."

"Whoooo," I said, unable to be silent. I lifted my hand to my head and covered my eyes.

"Go dial 911," said the not-God man. The other guy stepped out of the door.

I let my hand slide down enough to lock my eyes on the horror of the Devil and decided that he looked Mexican, short, and had a bushy black mustache. "911?"

"My name is Juan, and you're not dead. You're in the county morgue." He began wrapping me in sheets. "But you sure looked dead when they rolled you in. You would have been in the cooler, too, but we stopped for lunch. It's not like we were in a hurry." He wrapped my feet, but I couldn't feel them.

"I think I don't like it here," I said.

"You don't know the half of it," said Juan. "After lunch, the students from the medical school come over to cut body parts to study, and the morgue boss sells eyes and leg bones for medical grafts."

"Why they do that?"

"'Cuz they can," said Juan. "Your tag says *John Doe*. It means nobody is lookin' for ya. And that Nazi stuff on your neck? Shit! They'd be standing in line to carve on you."

"I'm so cold," I said. "I don't know what you're talking about."

Juan's partner stuck his head through the door. "I called, but they just called back. They want to talk to you."

Juan walked to a desk and hit the speaker phone. "What do you want? I got my hands full."

"This is Rickets. You got a stiff that's rattling around?"

"This one is alive," said Juan.

"Look," said Rickets, "they sit up all the time. Sometimes they pass gas or make a sound like a moan."

"This one is alive."

"All right," said Rickets, "what about the stiff's feet?"

"Frosty and blue."

"See?" said Rickets. "Give him a little time. No reason to haul this stiff for another ride around the block. He got jammed between the wall and the toilets. The cops left him wedged in there for more than an hour. Maybe we just need to let him sort of flatten out."

"Yeah," said Juan. "You're probably right. You explain it to him." Juan picked up the handset, pulled on the long curly cord, and handed me the phone.

SEEMED LIKE I HAD A long wait before the ambulance came to fetch me, but it wasn't like I had nothing to do. The morgue dude, Juan, pushed my cart against the wall so that they could push other carts into the cooler. He helped me get on my skivvies and my T-shirt, piled the rest of my clothes and my shoes in my lap, and told me to leave the sheet when the ambulance picked me up. Juan and his partner pushed a good number of folks past me. It seemed like dying in this town made big business.

They came for me, but it weren't like they were in a hurry. Two women in uniforms, their cart still folded down, stood there and stared at me like I was some kind of freak show.

I said, "I ain't sure I can walk out to the truck."

"We got that," said the first woman, a good-sized gal tagged Helen. Her partner—Carol on her pocket picture badge—wasn't no slouch, neither. Either one coulda snatched me outta the chicken hutch one-handed, so I figured I oughta be polite.

They snapped their cart open like a magic trick and sat me on it. The one named Carol said, "Your feet and ankles look blue. You have any feeling there?"

"Yes, ma'am," I said. "I couldn't feel nuthin' before, but now they're a little tingly."

So there I am in my skivvies, not even good ones, and they wrapped my legs in a blanket. When they were done, I felt like a roast ready for the oven. Felt nice and warm, though.

They loaded me into the truck. Helen rode in the back with me. She asked, "Why you got a Nazi tattoo on your neck? That how you got in trouble?"

I looked around, but I couldn't see because my neck and arms were wrapped pretty tight.

"I don't know what that is," I said. "I can't see it."

NOTHIN' BUT TROUBLE WHEN I got to the hospital. I'd never been to one before. They had a nurse whose whole job was to ask questions and fill out paper forms. I told them I didn't know the answers. But she kept at it until my head got tired and I just laid back on the pillow. I let out a sigh, thinking I'd have to do it all again, but she just patted my shoulder. "Just rest," she said. "We can wait until you feel better."

She left, but then I ended up in real trouble.

Men and women in white coats set to stabbin' my arms and legs and pumping out blood. I told 'em I didn't have no money. They said, "Don't worry," and then they stuck in two big wires that stayed in.

I figured I could pull 'em out when they left, but a whole new bunch showed up in ugly green pj's. They rushed me off to a room that had a big machine and they rolled me right in. They pumped cold stuff into my arms and legs while some guys hammered on the machine, but I was in there too tight to see who did all that.

I fell asleep, so I don't know how long that lasted. They pulled me out, and one guy said, "Your legs don't look good. We may have to remove them."

"Both?" I said, as if that would be better than one.

"We're going to check the blood and the films. Don't eat anything.

You should have a couple of hours in your room. Get some rest if you can."

I was sure I wouldn't be gettin' no rest around that place.

"MY FEET AIN'T NEAR AS BLUE as they was over at the morgue," I told the guy who rolled me back into my room. He slid me off the cart onto my bed.

"Don't worry," he said. "They're going to take good care of you."

"Tell 'em I don't have no money, and I didn't never ask them to bring me here."

"It will be all right," he said, tucking a blanket on me. "If you can, try to get some rest. The nurse will be in to give you something to make you feel better. We're gonna have a hoedown when the doctor gets back."

"I'm sorry," I said. "I don't mean to be so much trouble."

"That's all right," he said. "They were talking at you like you were still dead, but the doctor still has to look at the films and your lab work. They can't do anything you don't want them to do."

"That's a load off my mind," I said.

He smiled as he stepped out the door. He said, "Just don't fall asleep."

Well, that pretty much ripped it. The bed felt comfortable, but I had to move. I sat up slow. I could feel my feet on my heels, but my toes felt like they were asleep. My clothes were dropped on a chair, but my shoes were gone. Lucky they put some footies on my feet. I mean, who took my shoes?

I stood, but I stumbled on my feet, so I had to step high, racking like a show horse. I stepped out the door and looked around. The guy who wanted to chop my legs off wasn't around. He could show up with his crew any time, so I stepped into the crapper.

In the mirror, I didn't know who I was.

My head had a black-and-blue mark over my ear. Maybe that's why they shaved my head. But on my neck, I saw two long black lines with a chink in both. I didn't see no point to havin' that, so I scrubbed my neck. But I couldn't get it off at all. It went clear down to the skin through my beard.

It got hard to stand there by the wash sink, so I high-stepped over and sat on the crapper. I pulled on my clothes and started to feel real tired. I didn't want to pass out in the bathroom and get carried off to the morgue again. Not that they weren't fine fellows over there, but they damn near froze my ass off.

I rolled my hospital gown up under my arm and looked out the bathroom door. Nobody. I started down the hallway one clunk at a time. I wasn't getting anywhere fast, but I'd just about made it to the elevator when I heard it ding.

A door across the hall opened under my grip, and it turned out to be a storage room. Between a couple of racks, I made a place to hide with big cases of toilet paper. In the hallway I heard them rolling a cart up toward my room. I rolled my gown into a pillow, laid down, and fell asleep.

"SPECIAL AGENT," I HEARD THE voice announce outside the door. I opened my eyes, but the storage room remained dark.

"Yes, I saw him last night," said the doctor who wanted to saw off my legs. "I have no idea where he is now. He apparently walked out of here. He should *not* have been able to stand up."

Last night? So I'd slept all night and it was now the next day.

"He's pretty tough," said the agent. "The police thought he was dead. The emergency doc, downstairs, said he was dead. Then he signed him off and they dropped him at the morgue. That's when the shit hit the fan."

"I just take the ones they give me," said the doctor.

I wriggled my toes and feet. My feet felt good, but some of my toes felt a little hot. I didn't want to move and give up my hideaway.

"What's his name?" said the agent. "All I've got is the tag from the morgue wagon."

"I don't know," said the doctor. "Let's go to the desk. The nurses may have what you're looking for."

I heard them walk off. I wished they'd said what my name was.

The door rattled and snapped open. The storage room light clicked on. "All right, Carl," a rough voice said, "we got to park 'em last night, but today we have to put three cases on each floor. I'll stack 'em up in three piles and you load 'em on the cart and run 'em upstairs."

"Why I got to do that?" said Carl. "You could take 'em upstairs and I could stand here."

"See here on my shirt? My shirt says Ronald, Building Maintenance. Your shirt says Harold because you ain't been here long enough to get a shirt that says Carl."

"Well that shirt don't say I got to do all the totin' and haulin'."

"If you weren't my wife's nephew, I'd put the toe of my boot up the crack of your ass."

"I'd like to see . . ." said Carl, and then I heard a whack and a big thump.

"The judge gave you this last chance to work," said Ronald. "Or you can go clockin' and you'll be dead before you're twenty. It ain't nothin' to me. Maybe your momma?"

"Where do you get off dissin' me?" said Carl, and from the scuffling I guessed he was scraping himself off the floor. "I'm gettin' me a club, you mean old bastard." I heard him ring the elevator across the way.

"*You* going to get you a stick?"

"Fuck you, old bastard."

"Carry some of them boxes with you on the way up," said Ronald. He laughed and pulled out cases from above my head. He didn't see me and hurried over to the elevator carrying two cases.

"We oughta do downstairs first," Carl complained.

"What difference does it make? We have the elevator."

Carl said, "It make more sense!"

"Christ Almighty," said Ronald. "Fine. We'll do downstairs first."

The closing of the elevator door cut off their arguing.

That was close. I didn't know how long I could stay hid. I stood up and stamped my feet. They felt good. Last night, I couldn't feel 'em at all.

I wrestled my way to the door of the storage room. I wrapped my pj's around my neck to hide the lightning bolts. Then I picked up two of the cases to cover my face and stepped out into the hall—

Right behind the doctor and a cop.

I headed for the elevator.

"You seen that patient from the room on the right?" the doctor asked.

"I ain't seen nobody," I said. "Ronald said to take the cases of shit paper upstairs."

"Thanks," said the doctor. "The patient needs surgery. Gangrene will set in if it hasn't already. I don't see him walking around. If you see him, I'd appreciate the help."

"I'll ask Ronald," I said. I pushed the elevator button, keeping my back to the doctor and the cop. "What's the name of this guy you're looking for?"

"We don't have his name," said the doctor. "He came in on an ambulance." The elevator door opened. "Short hair like you. I don't think he could walk far."

"I can't believe we haven't turned him up," said the cop.

The doors closed and I rode down to the first floor. I stepped out and crashed straight into Carl from upstairs. He knocked the cases out of my hands.

"Get the fuck out of the way," said Carl.

"Where'd Ronald want these to go?"

"He's in the men's room," said Carl, hustling for the main door. "But he ain't got much to say."

I carried my two cartons to the men's room, pushed the two boxes through the swinging door, and got out of there—wasn't like I really wanted to meet Ronald.

A kid about eight or nine years old burst out of the men's room door behind me and ran past me toward the security guard near the door. Before he even got to the guard, he was already hollering, "There's a man on the floor in the bathroom and his head is all bloody!"

The Sixth of Many Stories

Paper Moon

I F YOU EVER DECIDE TO jump off a bridge, do it! If you sit on the railing and look at the river and don't do the high dive, nobody will ever shut up about it. "Misty Lake, photos at six on WTF." So now I have to go back to Dr. Mambar once a week, just so he can shrink my brain.

He had talked to me a couple of times when I first got admitted behind Door Number One. Today was the first time I'd showed up in his office voluntarily. Sort of.

As usual, he parked himself on a folding chair, wearing a battered lab coat, and read my file for ten minutes like my report card. Then he wasted a lot of time talking about my mother, before he got to anything I needed to worry about.

"I see your lip has stitches. Is there a story behind that?"

I tried to smile, but it still hurt. "I have two jobs. They're both part-time, but they help. At night, I'm a hostess at the City Suites, and during the day I'm a secretary at a detective's office."

That's two nights at the City Suites, and for the other five nights I slept at the detective's office. Best to leave out the details—Dr. Mambar could zap me back behind Door Number One whenever he wanted.

And the detective, Raymond Kerze, got arrested a couple of days ago, and no one seemed to know where he was—not even the cops.

Dr. Mambar definitely didn't need to know about that.

"Detective work can be dangerous," said Dr. Mambar. "Is that how you got hurt?"

"Hotel work is even more dangerous," I said. "They have me working in different places, wherever they need me. You know those double doors that lead to the kitchen?"

Dr. Mambar raised his eyebrows. "Yes?"

"Well, I'd just passed through those, taking up a room service order, when I realized I'd forgotten the spinach, and I turned around just as someone else was pushing through."

"Ah. And what happened then?"

"My boss told me I'd get my 'sea legs' eventually, whatever that means. He did take me to the clinic to get my lip fixed."

"So who are your bosses? For my records?"

"Ray Kerze, K-E-R-Z-E, is a retired cop. He runs the detective agency. But he's away right now on a case. My boss at City Suites is Charles DeSimone."

I'd been waiting for this. I had to be sure I didn't accidentally call him "Little Joe."

I asked, "Why do you need this?" I already knew why he wanted it, but I enjoyed putting a little "squeeze" on the "shrink."

He wrinkled his brow before coming up with, "Confirming employment is a large part of your evaluation, Misty. It lets me know when and if I can tell the court that you're competent to become unsupervised."

Dr. Mambar finished scribbling in my folder. "So you are quite busy. Have you been making any friends?"

"A few new friends," I said. Sure! *Jimmy Crates, Gimp, Cheaters and a half dozen other winos.* Aloud, I said, "Mostly where I work. Mr. DeSimone lent me his car to come here for my session." Mr. DeSimone had also lent me the car when I headed to the bridge for the swan dive, but I didn't mention that.

"So you seem to be settling in," said Dr. Mambar. "Next week!"

I stood up and asked, "How many weeks?"

Dr. Mambar's eyes made an impish twinkle. "Until I think you're fully recovered."

I beat feet. Outside his office, I exhaled. If Dr. Mambar called up the City Suites and talked to "Mr. DeSimone," Little Joe would confirm my employment. And if Dr. Mambar asked about my busted lip—unlikely but still possible—Little Joe would say, "I'm sorry, but I'm not authorized to talk about employee accidents." Again, true as far as it went. Anyway, that's how Little Joe and I had worked it out.

I should have continued holding my breath, because in the parking lot I found three men slugging it out around my boss's car.

My first thought was to leave and call the police. I practiced describing them—two black guys in scruffy gang colors and a white guy in a Stars-and-Bars T-shirt. For all the bangers' efforts, they could only land the occasional punch on the Stars-and-Bars guy, but he looked like he was running out of gas.

I fished the keys out of my purse and stood there thinking, *Oh, shit!* Then the white guy rolled one banger across the hood and I shut my eyes, thinking any second I'd hear Little Joe's windshield go *pow!*

The fight spilled over to the asphalt on the passenger side and I ran up, unlocked the door, and jumped behind the wheel.

I cranked up the car, and that's when I saw the head bruise and the lightning-bolt tattoos on the white guy's neck.

"Holy shit!" I shouted. I laid across the seat and rolled down the car window.

It was John Doe—John Doe, who was not dead. John Doe, who Raymond Kerze, detective, had *not* killed. I wouldn't have believed it in any town but this one.

"For God's sake, John," I shouted. "Get in!" I pulled the handle to open the door.

John dove headfirst into the car and I did my best impression of a getaway driver. The bangers grabbed for his legs but only got one hospital slipper.

"Thanks," he said as he got his head up and feet down. "Am I John?"

* * *

IF HE DIDN'T KNOW WHO he was, I sure did.

I took him to the breakfast bar at City Suites. He went to feed the inner man and didn't look like he would wander off. So I dug the number for Detective Jackson out of my purse. Little Joe stood at the desk as I picked up the house phone, but I didn't wait to tell him who I was calling.

I dialed, but ended up in Detective Jackson's voice mail. I began, "Detective Jackson, this is Misty at City Suites—" but Little Joe jabbed his finger on the hand-set hook and cut off the call.

"Whoa, Misty," he said. "What's this all about?"

"John Doe! I've got him in the breakfast area. Now the police can let Ray go home!"

"Where did you find John Doe?"

"Outside the hospital, when I left my appointment."

"And it's the right guy?" Joe asked.

"Needs a shave," I said, "but the bruise on his head and the tattoos are the same."

Little Joe pursed his lips and looked off into the distance. I could almost hear the gears meshing. "I think we need to talk to Ray before we do anything. Something's going on that neither of us knows about. Let me make a couple of calls. You go make sure John doesn't get itchy feet again."

I found that John had loaded the table with plates. He ate with both hands. I didn't think I could get his attention, so I got a cup of coffee.

He wore a T-shirt and ragged jeans. For shoes, he wore one hospital slipper. His other foot was bare and filthy—none of which bothered him as long as he had food on his plate. You'd think he had just *discovered* food.

"Doesn't that Nazi tattoo bother you?" I asked.

"I can't see it," John said around a mouthful of biscuit. "I didn't know I was so hungry."

"Other people see it."

John chewed and thought. "That why those guys at the hospital were so mean to me?"

"It makes you look like you hate other people. And like you think you're better than they are."

"Wonder who put that on me," said John. "I'm begging a meal and I ain't even got shoes."

"No one put it *on* you," I said. "You did. You really remember nothing?"

John shook his head.

"How about when we were on the bus? Your friend had that swastika on his head. And my friend Ray banged your heads together and threw you off the bus."

"I don't remember none o' that," said John. "There's a lot of angry folks around here, but I don't remember doin' nuthin' mean. Maybe you help me find my friend with the swastika and we can just get outta here?"

"Your friend was killed," I said. "They found him dead in a parking garage."

John sighed, closed his eyes, and shook his head. "My friend is dead and I don't even know who he was. I don't know who I am. I only call myself John because that's what you call me."

"We met on the bus," I said. "You have to remember that!"

John ate and thought. After a moment, he shook his head and said, "Nothin'."

"What's the first thing you remember?" I asked.

"Yesterday. Yesterday was really cold."

Truth can stun you down to your knees, especially when it's not what you expected. I didn't have another question, so I went with, "We've got to get you some shoes."

John said, "I don't know where to go after here."

"I can take you over to Ray's," I said. "I'd like you to stay around long enough to talk to him, before you talk to the cops."

"Didn't you call the cops while I was eating?"

"Almost," I said. But John didn't seem angry.

* * *

I WALKED BACK UP TO the desk to see if Joe had heard a word on Ray.

Joe said, "I called everybody and they said that I had to call Detective Jackson. Jackson is off somewhere."

"Maybe you can find some little job for John."

"I don't know," said Joe. "This is a business. I can't take on every stray bum. And that storm trooper crap on John's neck is going to be nothing but trouble." Little Joe drummed his fingers on the desk. "Ray would know what to do. Does John have a place to go?"

"No," I said, "but I told him he could stay at Ray's. He seems to think it's a good idea. He just doesn't know where that is."

"Maybe he won't wander around." Joe closed his eyes and shook his head. After a bit, he opened his eyes and dug some cash out of his pocket. "Take my car with John and go down to the Good Family store. There's not one close to here, but it's a straight trip. Just go right and keep going. When you get there, it's at the corner of the British Gas and a Kroger store. Get John some shoes and a shirt with a high-neck collar."

We had seventeen dollars between us. I left the desk, dragged John from the breakfast bar, and towed him to the parking deck. He was still clutching a handful of biscuits when I stuffed him into Joe's car.

GOOD FAMILY CARRIED OVERSTOCK, SALVAGE, and donated items at prices that stunned. I found a long, red, knit dress that I could wear to work. It cost three-fifty, brand new. I spied a three-tiered beaded dress. That cost eight dollars, and I didn't think it was hardly worn. I just hoped it would hang around until I got paid.

John got shoes for two bucks, three shirts for a dollar each, and a sleeping bag for five bucks.

An hour later, we were back on the road, John in his shoes and me in my new red dress.

"It's all the way over on the west side, but sure worth the drive," I said. "I'm going to drop you off at Ray's office. I have to take the boss's car back and I hostess in the restaurant tonight."

"I don't know this Ray guy," said John. "If he finds me in his office, this might not go well."

"He knows you," I said, and turned left past the liquor store. "You know him, too. You just don't remember."

"When did that happen?"

"Ray was helping you out," I said. I didn't want to admit that I talked him into pulling out his knife on the bus. I mean, maybe it wasn't my fault. Maybe Ray would have banged their heads together anyway. "Ray should talk to you about that."

"You think Ray will let me stay here for a while?"

"I'm pretty sure," I said. I parked next to the stairs that led up to Ray's office. Jimmy Crates waited at the steps like a big shepherd dog. I think he had a crush on me, but he was a good guy to have as a friend in this part of town.

Jimmy Crates opened the passenger door, screwed his bushy face into John's mug, and said, "Who the hell are you?"

The hammer from Jimmy's belt slid into his fist like a magazine into an automatic.

"Time to be nice," I said, dipping a wink at Crates. "This is John Doe and—"

"'John Doe?' You're putting me on!"

I stepped out of the car door and said the first thing I shouldn't have. "John is the guy that Ray's supposed to have killed."

John said, "What!" His eyebrows went up like Coke-bottle rockets.

"So put the hammer back in your belt," I told Jimmy.

"Holy shit," said John. He covered his head with splayed fingers.

"Don't be such a baby! I *told* you Ray went to help you after your friend got killed."

"So why would the cops think Ray killed me?" John asked. "Why would he *want* to kill me?"

I shook my head. "Ray wouldn't. The cops just got it all wrong, see?"

For a moment, no one spoke. Then Jimmy coughed. "I finished

that door swap," he said. "Got one from down the hall from Ray's office. And Sammy Vee's gonna do the window sign—once he finishes the last of his pint."

"I hope we get it done before Ray gets back," I said.

"Look, I'm just gonna get going," said John.

"Don't be such a jerk," said Jimmy, parking his hammer on his belt. "Misty is trying to help you. You got some other place to go?"

"Some place I ain't dead," said John.

"You dead now?" I said.

"No!"

"That's the point," said Jimmy.

"We need you here," I said. "We need to make sure you don't *get* dead."

Jimmy and I started up the stairs. John followed, but dragged back. We found the agency door and the glass in place, but shards still cluttered the hallway. And, there was a problem.

"The original door had frosted glass," I said.

"Wasn't another one of those," said Jimmy.

I shook my head. "Who'll want to sit in a private detective's waiting room when anyone walking down the hall can just look in and see them?"

Jimmy shifted from one foot to the other. "I can find some mini blinds, or maybe a pull shade, and mount it to the inside of the door."

Before the Second Coming? "Anytime soon?"

"Uh, sure. It's not like Ray's got people lined up to see him just now," said Jimmy.

"What about the shards?"

"I told you I'd clean that up," said Jimmy. "I just wanted the door fixed so you would be safe at night."

"Thank God we got shoes," said John. He picked his way through the glass to the door.

"I'm working tonight at the restaurant," I told Jimmy, "and I always spend the night in the City Suites."

"Nice to be rich," said Jimmy. "Maybe you can pay me to do all this work?"

"They just let me use one of the rooms after the customers have finished their business and gone home. I get to have a hot bath and wash my hair. That's hardly 'rich.'"

"But—" said Jimmy.

"*You* broke that door," I said. "And, I want the key."

"OH MY GOD," I GROANED. Little Joe, my boss, was standing on the sidewalk waiting for me to return his car. I didn't think I'd spent that much time at Good Family, or at Ray's. But maybe I had.

"Save parking it," said Little Joe as I pulled up. "Go and help Clare on the desk until you start in the restaurant."

"I didn't mean to be late," I said as I got out. "I'm so sorry!"

"You're not late," said Little Joe. "I'm going up to the cop shop. If I call about Ray, the detectives drop the telephone like it's on fire."

"So what's the point?" I said.

"The desk sergeant and I are ushers together at St. Mark's. He won't say anything on the phone, but he may help us out if he's not being recorded."

"They can't just disappear Ray," I said. "This isn't some banana republic."

Little Joe patted my shoulder and climbed into his car. He said, "I'll call you," and drove off.

I walked into the motel. I didn't see Clare anywhere. I finally found her hiding behind the front desk, pulling her hair out of cornrows. The strands stood out straight, like Clare had scuffed a carpet and loaded up on static electricity.

"Your hair on fire?" I asked.

"Eduardo will be in later with that gal from the city council. She wears her hair straight. I tried to get his attention with my braids, but it might be better to brush them out—more of a *chiquita* look."

"Better hurry. Looks like Eduardo and his secret girlfriend are coming in the door right now."

"Oh, shit," said Clare. She bent and headed for the ladies' room. "I can't let him see me like this. Just give him the key. I'll call him to come down to the counter later."

"What about the gal that's with him?" I asked.

"She goes straight to the elevator," said Clare. "Married, but not to Eduardo." Clare scuttled out of sight.

Eduardo stepped up to the counter, looking like his last name was Banderas and wearing a thousand-dollar suit.

"Why have you been cheated from my life for so long?" he oozed in a soft Latin accent sugared with just a hint of Ricardo Montalban. He took my hand in both of his.

"Why are we still here?" I asked, batting my eyes and doing some oozing of my own, though I had no intention of letting him take my hand or any other part of me away from the service desk.

He put a hand over his eyes and shook his head. "*Ay dios mio.* Alas, I must ask for the key for room 1010, Miss . . . ?"

"Misty," I said.

"Misty, darling." His eyes sparkled. "The key, and I need a split of champagne."

"Room 1010?" I said. I should have remembered that. I'd borrowed the room after Eduardo's last "conference." Well, *Jeffrey* and I had borrowed it—though Jeff had sort of bulldogged his way in. One bit of luck was that he hadn't shown his lying face since I told him to get lost and not come back until he had a clean bill of health from a doctor.

I fingered down the list. "According to this, the room's listed for a city council conference."

"That's the one." Eduardo smiled. "I need the key, and send up a bottle of champagne."

I gave him the key. "When would you want the champagne sent up?"

"Now would be fine." He took the key, flashed me another smile, and departed for the elevator.

I was just thinking it was lucky that I had worn my new red dress, and that I had my black satin dress folded in my purse. Their "conference" would be over at nine o'clock. I could hang my dress outside their room after nine. The dry cleaner would pick it up and have it back early in the morning. The city council never questioned the room bill.

Clare returned with a knotted scarf holding her hair out of her face and eyes. "Isn't Eduardo just yummy or what? If I got up there with him, I'd drain his crankcase till he squeaked and carry him home under my arm."

"Damn, girl," I said. "All I want out of the deal is a room for the night and getting my dress dry-cleaned."

"You sure about that? That red dress you're flaggin's bright enough to stop a whole lane of traffic. And I stuck my head in the restaurant yesterday, when you were wearing that slinky black thing, and all the guys were huggin' you with their eyes and checkin' out your tattoo, and that includes Arnold the busboy, and he's gay."

I felt myself blush.

"That tat of yours has 'em peepin' like schoolboys, starin' at your neck and down your back into *Mysteryland*."

"Clare—"

"Just how low does that go? Any kinky down there?"

Clare's jealousy needed dousing, and I needed her as a friend, but I'd had about enough. I said, in my sweetest honey voice, "Eduardo didn't ask."

WHEN THE RESTAURANT CLOSED AND everyone else had headed home, I walked across the lobby to the front desk where Clare sat, still staring at her hair in the mirror of her compact.

"Not happy with that do yet?" I asked.

"Eduardo didn't even notice when he dropped the key," said Clare, "but the woman he brings here is way older than me and has straight hair. I'm gonna do my hair straight, too, but I'm adding extensions."

"You go, girl," I said, reaching over to grab the key for room 1010.

"I'm going to get my dresses on the hook for the dry cleaner."

"You gonna be almost naked, child," said Clare, one eye narrow.

"All the better to wash my hair and take a nice hot bath," I said.

Clare racked her fists on her hips. "You ain't goin' up there waitin' for Eduardo, are you?"

"Come up with me. Spend the night. If Eduardo shows, he's all yours. But I get the sofa. I like to turn on the fireplace."

"That ain't a real fire," said Clare.

"I like to pretend," I said. "You could pretend Eduardo."

Clare sighed. "I got to go home," she said. "I got to make sure the cat didn't eat my daughter's parakeet."

She fetched a note from behind the service desk and slapped it on the counter. "Chuck called and left you a message. Says that Ray Kerze ain't in jail and Ray wants to talk to you. Chuck left a number for him, but you can't call until after one and before three."

I blinked. So Little Joe's trip to his policeman friend had panned out. I picked up the note, read it, and carefully folded it into my purse.

THE NEXT MORNING, I FOUND John Doe sitting on the stairs going up to Ray Kerze's office. He followed me in. The broken glass had been swept up. The new window announced, "RAYMON KERZE, PRIVATE INVESTIGATOR." Their hearts were in the right place, but I had just seen their asses lined up waiting for the liquor store to open.

I gave John a bag of food I'd brought from City Suites. "I get the French toast," I said. "Thought you would be down at the liquor store with the fellows."

John opened the white paper bag. "Wow!" he said. "I don't know if I drink. But I'm pretty sure I eat."

He sat down in one of the waiting room chairs and fished out a couple boxes of frosted cornflakes, a carton of milk, and a plastic bowl and spoon. "Do I get any of the cinnamon buns?"

"Have to share," I said. "Those are Ray's. But he won't be home today."

"That could be bad," said John. "Some suit guy came by yesterday. He left some papers on the door."

"I don't see any," I said. John worked on his cornflakes. "Do you know where they are?"

John held up one finger, took a bite of his cereal, and pulled the papers from his back pocket. At the end of his bite, he said, "Guy said everybody had to be out of this building in ten days."

"Oh, crap," I said, getting panicky. "Ray's gonna come back, find his window's been busted and his name painted wrong on the new one, and now he's gonna lose this place?"

"Jimmy Crates says that they send out a letter every few months and Ray throws them in the trash."

I stared at John. "So you just scared the hell out of me for nothing? I thought I was on my way back to the nut ward!"

I dug out some orange juice and French toast, and parked myself at the secretary's desk.

"I read the message on the back of the letter," said John as he downed a cinnamon bun.

"Seriously?"

"Really!" said John. "I read the whole thing."

I watched John's face and ate my French toast. John's face fizzled like he might explode.

"Oh, all right," I said. "Spill it!"

John smiled. "Oh, you don't want to hear it anyway."

I drank some orange juice.

"You can buy this building for one dollar," said John, smugly.

"Bullshit!"

"One dollar!"

I had a dollar and some change. I opened my purse and flipped Old George to the desk. "You fly and I'll buy. Go buy us a building."

"Well," said John.

I picked up my buck and stuffed it back in my purse. "There's always a 'well.'"

"You got to pay the current six-month tax due," said John. "Plus the dollar."

"Great," I said. "A million bucks and a dollar."

"Eight hundred fifty-eight dollars and one buck," said John, "though it might as well be a million."

I snatched the papers out of John's hand and read them repeatedly until the black-and-white squiggles sunk into my brain. "I know who has that much money. And lots more."

The Seventh of
Many Stories

No Rainbow

MY LUCK'S SO BAD THAT if a bird flew over me and shit, he wouldn't even need to aim. But today, I'm making my own luck. I set myself to be at Ray Kerze's office at seven in the morning, 'cause all the boozehounds would be off, lined up and waiting for the liquor store to open. When I got up the stairs, I found the building door unlocked and Kerze's office door broken open. I'd brought a rock along, and now I didn't need it.

I sat on Misty's chair. I could smell her perfume. It gave me a hard on. In the first drawer I found Kerze's checkbook and stuffed it in my pocket. In the back of the second drawer, I found Kerze's passport, bent and water-stained and with the edges of the pages chipped. I flipped it open and saw it still had three months to go before its ten-year life came to an end. I said, "Eh," and slipped it next to the checkbook. Nothing else was worth swinging with, but I hated to leave Misty's smell.

In the second desk, I picked up Kerze's driver's license. It was at least three years out of date, but I knew how to get that fixed. I pulled up my hoodie and headed out.

I stepped out of Kerze's office and out the door. But—my usual luck—on the stairway, two guys grabbed my ass, dragged me to the street, and tied me up in the back of a truck. They took turns pounding my chest and beating on my back until they got tired. By then I'd figured out who they were.

Marco and Tony Corrado, brothers in assholery.

"What's this about?" I tried to ask. It came out as a growl. I was still hoping they didn't remember me, or hoped at least they thought I was someone else.

Marco, the older and meaner of the two, started the truck. Tony started punching my face.

"Don't start tuning him up until we get him out of the truck," said Marco. They had put me in a laundry truck; I guess they didn't want to get my blood all over the towels.

Tony groaned, but quit punching me. "Where are we taking this piece of shit?"

"Out behind the old wash pens. Nobody goes out there anymore. Nobody to see or hear squat."

I finally got a little air and said, "What did I do to you guys?" I mean, I knew, but I just hoped they forgot maybe some of it. "If I owe ya, I'll pay ya!"

"Where do you want me to start?" said Tony. "This ain't about the four hundred in laundry service you screwed us out of at the tattoo parlor."

"I'll pay," I said.

"I already wrote that off," said Tony. "Well, I sued you, but that's just business and you never paid me anyway. But that kind of chicken-shit crap shows you have no respect."

"I was new in town," I said. "I didn't know who you were."

"Actually, I was rootin' for ya," said Marco. "You were stickin' it to the old boss."

"And I'll pay," I said.

"But when the old man was dying," Marco said, "the one thing he said, while he was checking out, was to get that rotten piece of shit that stole his money and poured sugar in the engines of our six trucks."

"I only did four trucks," I said.

"The other two trucks needed new engines," said Marco. "I put sugar in the other two for you. The insurance company picked it up anyway. But that don't matter. When you sugared up the first engine, you committed suicide."

"I'll pay for it all!"

"What? Eighty thousand dollars?" said Tony. "You ain't got eighty cents in your pocket. If you did, it don't matter. We already got paid. Now we're gonna pay you."

"Just a minute," said Marco. "Where were you going to get that kind of money?"

"I'm going to steal it," I said. "I was about to get my hands on it when you guys grabbed me."

"That's bullshit," said Tony. "And even if it's true, it don't matter. I'm still going to pound your head into a pile of crap, and it's going to take me a week to do it right."

"Hang on there," said Marco. "Eighty grand? That's forty for you and forty for me."

"You know what Daddy said," said Tony. "He made us promise."

"It's swag," said Marco. "I don't remember Daddy ever leaving a dime on the table. And if you want to cap this dirt bag, you got to pay me. You can piss on forty grand if you want, but me you got to pay."

We pulled into the old Corrado wash building and parked behind the factory. They opened the door and both were smiling, like a hundred teeth apiece.

"You said I could pay," I said.

"Oh, you're gonna pay," said Marco. "But that don't mean you ain't gonna take a beatin'." He took out a huge knife and cut the rope they'd tied me with.

"Start walkin'," he said. "If you run, you won't get three feet."

They told me to stop after just a few steps, and when I turned around they were both holding small pistols. Tony also held a black baseball bat in his left hand.

"You said I could pay. If you beat me with that, I'm dead!"

"We ain't gonna beat you," said Marco.

"You're gonna beat yourself," said Tony. "If you don't do a good job, then I get to shoot you."

Tony flipped me the bat. It turned out to be a plastic kid's toy.

"This will take a little longer," said Marco. "But you get both hands on it and swing for the home run wall."

I hit my head until I got tired, but when I slowed down Tony shot me in the foot, and I kept hitting my head until I passed out.

I DON'T KNOW HOW LONG I lay there. I was getting hosed down with water, and I hoped it was coming from a hose. My eyes wouldn't open except for a corner edge of my right eye.

It turned out to be rain—a hard rain, and colder than snow. I struggled to my feet but fell back to the ground. My foot hurt like it'd been stomped by an elephant, and my left leg folded under me when I tried to stand up. I picked up the bat, still on the ground, and used it as a cane.

I worked my way around to the front of the Corrado wash building. I couldn't find a door or a window. But it did have an overhang that I could use to keep my head dry as long as I hugged the wall.

I couldn't stand up very long. I struggled, but I kept falling. And then the wall opened and swallowed me up.

I OPENED MY EYES. THE darkness didn't go away. But I was warm, lying on a bed, and covered in blankets. And pleasantly stoned, floating on a sea of clouds.

"Cool," I said.

"Don't talk," a male voice said. "Marco and Tony are up at the truck unloading hot cigarettes from Virginia. They won't come up here unless you make a ruckus. Tony doesn't want me to see who brings the cigarettes in, but in the morning he wants me to load them into the laundry truck."

I went back to sleep.

* * *

I WOKE UP WITH A single mission. I had to pee. I kicked the covers off. I saw I had on green scrubs, and that my left foot was wrapped in white bandages. I put that foot down on the floor and screamed.

"What are you doing?" said a black man, also wearing green scrubs.

"Oh my God, what happened to my foot?" I said. "I still gotta pee."

The black man put a five-gallon paint bucket in front of me and popped off the cover. With no time for privacy, I dropped my scrub pants—none too soon.

"And when you finish, you make sure you put the cover back on," said the black man. "This is still my house."

Standing on my left foot hurt like hell. "What happened?" I asked, still thundering into the bucket.

"All I saw was the end," said the black man. "Your face looked like mush, and you'd been shot in the left foot. That part I can explain. Tony Corrado carries a .25 Junior Colt, and that's how you got shot. If he'd shot you in the head with the .25, it would have scrambled your brains like a bad omelet. So I guess you were lucky."

"He just shot me," I said. "What's the lucky part?"

"You were lucky it wasn't Marco. He carries a .32 Colt—now that would have made a mess."

"Now I remember," I said. I shook my pecker dry and pulled up my scrub pants. "That fuckin' Tony said I had to beat my head faster. And then he shot my foot." I sat down to put the lid on the paint bucket.

The black man laughed.

"Where's the guy who was here earlier?" I asked.

"You beat—" He laughed and sat on a chair. "You beat your own head."

"That's not so funny," I said. I crashed out onto the bed. My left foot had started to bleed.

"Oh, come on," he said. "What did you do to piss them off that good?"

"Nothing," I said. "They're just mean-ass."

"Yes, they're mean-asses, but they're also lazy mean-asses," he said. "If you were an ordinary pain in the ass, you'd be lying in a pile behind the laundry."

"I stole some money to marry my girlfriend," I said. "They caught me and said I had to give *them* the money."

"Swag!" he said.

"That's what they called it, him and Marco."

"I'm glad you didn't tell me that before," he said. "If I knew you had their swag when I was taking the bullet out of your left foot, I might have laughed hard enough to cut off some toes."

"You're a doctor?"

"I used to be a medic," he said. He moved his hand like a ship on the ocean. "In the navy."

"Where's the guy I talked to before?"

"Nobody here but me," he said. He wore his hair and beard bushy and natural. "I guess you weren't quite awake. I gave you a happy pill. I didn't want to have to listen to you screaming while I dug out the bullet."

I looked around. The room looked huge, maybe a thousand feet square. About a third of the room was set up as an apartment—kitchen, dining area, and a laundry room. The rest of the space looked like a lunch room. "So what is this place?"

"This is one of three of Corrado's old laundry factories. One burned down. Only one that's still open is in the city. Almost everything in this town is closed. The cops and the fire department don't come out here. When something catches fire, it burns until it finishes burning. The ambulance doesn't come out here, either."

"I guess I *was* lucky you were here," I said.

"Usually I don't open the door," he said, "but you were like a lost puppy drowning in the rain."

"So what's your name?" I said.

"Levar," he said.

"I need to sleep," I said. The window shades were closing over my eyes.

"In the morning you need to leave," said Levar. "I can't keep you safe. Tony will be here in the morning with the laundry truck. I have to help load the cigarettes. In three or four hours, he'll be back with groceries. If he's in a good mood, he helps me carry them in."

I HEARD THE TRUCK BACK into the loading dock and opened my eyes. It was six o'clock, maybe. The morning sun looked pink. I sat up. Next to the bed my clothes were washed and folded, and Kerze's stolen checkbook, passport and driver's license lay on top.

Levar left a note: "Leave the scrubs. They're the last thing we still wash for Corrado."

Screw the scrubs. I wasn't inclined to change clothes. I put my right shoe on, and then stared at my left shoe. Blood ringed a hole in the middle of the shoe, behind where my middle toe would go. I pulled the shoe onto my left foot and found I had to leave it untied. I could walk—slowly. I found the plastic bat on the floor next to the chair. I could use it to lean on.

I folded my clothes under my arm and worked my way to the door. On the way past the lunch counter, I found a clear plastic jug of maple syrup. Just right! I took it with me and eased out the door.

My scrubs felt cold on my skin. I could hear the truck, but I couldn't see it. I walked close to the building. The weeds and branches hurt my left foot.

Down by the loading dock, I heard a metallic clang and an "Okay, that's it!"

I had to hustle to the end of the building.

I peeked around the building and was stunned to find that I was only twenty feet from the truck. I never had a plan—just fill up the tank with maple syrup. So close!

Levar was closing the loading door. Tony pulled the truck past the chain link gates. He left the truck running and the driver's door open when he walked back to the gates.

I put down the bottle of syrup and started for the driver's side.

Tony pulled the gates closed and didn't see me until I'd gotten in the truck. I locked the door and stepped on the gas. I laughed all the way out to the road.

I slowed down to turn onto the highway. Tony jumped onto the driver's door, holding on to the driver's mirror and standing on the driver's foot post. He scared the shit out of me, but I stayed on the gas.

"Pull this truck over!" he said. "I'm going to beat your skull flat!"

I had gotten up to thirty and saw a tree I could use to swipe him off with. He let go with one hand and took out his pistol. He pointed it directly at me and fired. The bullet bounced off the window and ricocheted into his right eye. He looked surprised, and then he dropped outta sight.

Holy shit!

I WAS AFRAID TO KEEP driving and too afraid to park. I was afraid someone would recognize me and burn my ass to Marco, or the cops.

I'd just wanted enough money to start over and get Misty's mind right. What I got was two goons from the laundry company. If they had just left me in peace, I would've never been in this mess.

Why couldn't it've been someone else?

I finally drove to the Renaissance Center Mall, parked in the delivery court, and climbed out. Under the seat, I picked up my clothes. I also found two stuffed yellow envelopes. Both were crammed with hundred-dollar bills.

No time to count the money. I took the keys and rolled up the truck's rear door. Cases of cigarettes crammed the entire cargo area. Some fell out—Marlboros.

I hustled the keys back into the dash but left the door open. In the rear, I loaded three cases onto the truck's dolly and walked away. Anyone might have thought I was doing a delivery. I planned to park the dolly at the rear of the first business I passed. But the cases of Marlboros—and the dolly—stuck to my hands. I could get two grand from anybody just walking by.

I parked the cart by a bench and wrapped the cartons with my shirt and pants so they'd be hard to make out. I parked my ass on the bench and checked out the two yellow envelopes. I still had too much money to count, but I grinned up at the sky and said, "Oh man, am I screwed now!"

It took too much time. Kids these days are either stupid or just lazy. When I was a teenager, that truck would've been gone so fast you'da thought it had wings.

Finally, a couple of guys rolled up on their bikes and hustled off one case each. *One case.*

Nobody had the balls to swing with the whole truck. I started to think I'd have to put a sign on it: *Steal this truck!* If nobody stepped up, the cops would haul it away, and they might figure out that I was the guy.

No sooner did that thought form than a cop did show up, and I figured I was screwed for sure. I was sitting there with three hot cases of cigarettes. But the cop turned out to just be a Renaissance Center Mall security guard, alone and on foot.

He looked around, locked down the cargo door, climbed inside, and drove away. He headed out to the road and kept on rockin'. I laughed so hard my swollen face hurt.

I COULDN'T BELIEVE HOW MUCH money I'd found in the two yellow envelopes. Seven thousand five hundred dollars in each one, that's fifteen thousand dollars. And that's in addition to the fifteen hundred I made deep-discounting the cases of cigarettes to a passing street hustler. I recounted the envelope money twice—once to check the count, and the second time just to run the rhubarb through my fingers.

I had to use a couple hundred to rent a suite. Guess it takes money to make money, and I had to get out of sight. I had to make a plan. I spread the money all over the bed, took off my clothes, and took a nap. The only thing I could think of that would be better was Misty wrapped in my arms.

I woke up. My face and foot still hurt. The suite had a big tub, so I decided to dunk myself.

I stepped into the crapper and found a man with a fat, swollen, black-and-blue face staring at me. I hit him and screamed. A spider web of cracks exploded across the monster man.

My fist felt crushed. I grabbed my hand, backed up a step, and touched my chin. The man did, too. I ran my fingers over every lump and gash on my face. Damn it, it was me.

On the upside, no one else would recognize me, either.

I filled the tub to my chin and sank into the water.

FIRST THINGS FIRST, I PUT five grand in my pocket and put the rest in the room safe. I grabbed the green scrubs, dumped them in the trash can, and put my other clothes back on. I headed downstairs and over to the Renaissance Center Mall across the street. I found one of those glitzy unisex places that cuts hair for women and men too.

A lady led me to a chair. Her name tag said *Dixie*. She asked, "What the hell happened to you?"

"I got robbed," I said, "by some very bad men."

"A haircut ain't gonna make this look a whole lot better," said Dixie. "And there's a barber shop a few doors down. It would be a lot cheaper."

"I have a plan," I said. "First, we cut my hair—short, like a cop, or military. My hair is blond. We make it brown. Then we add a little gray, just around my ears."

"You're going to look older," said Dixie.

"Exactly!" I said.

Dixie slapped the plastic cape around my neck. "This is gonna be around two hundred dollars," she said.

"That's fine," I said. "I just don't want the guys who beat the hell out of me to find me again."

"I do my best work when I don't worry about getting paid," said Dixie.

I gave her two hundred bucks up front.

"My man!" she said.

Dixie worked and I listened to the radio. Mostly they had pop on, and at the hour they had news. The news got my attention. "Firefighters put out a vehicle fire at Elmwood Park this afternoon. The driver of the vehicle, a Corrado Brothers Laundry van, is missing." I held back a snicker and turned it into a lip fart. It hurt my face.

"You know the Corrado guys?" said Dixie.

"A few years ago," I said. If the security guard burned the truck, I was as good as gold. "They delivered laundry where I worked."

I had no idea what women went through to get their hair done. I spent two hours in the salon. Why didn't I think to eat before I went in there? My stomach rumbled, and my scalp stung from the brown goop she slathered on my head like tar. Dixie dunked my head in the sink and rinsed. Next, she added metal strips around my ears and painted my hair with more goop. Then she parked me off to the side, I guess to bake.

After the timer dinged, she toweled my head, blew my hair dry, and cut it short.

I wondered if this would be worth the trouble. If I didn't like my hair, I could always claim to be somebody else. I smirked and started to laugh. It still hurt. Dixie said it was time to let my brain get some air.

I finally got to see how it looked. In the mirror, from the back, I did look like Raymond Kerze. In the front, my face still looked a mess.

I COULD HAVE EATEN TWO Subway twelve-inch subs, but I was in a hurry and settled for one. I needed clothes, and I couldn't use jeans. People stared at me and whispered all the way to the food court, and the girl making the sub sort of looked past my ear. I wolfed down the ham-and-Swiss sub at the food court and took my large soda with me over to the mall directory. *Hero's Men's Finery!* I could afford some nice threads now.

My scalp still sort of itched and stung, and my face ached all over. I walked into the store and saw a salesman look over and frown. But my eyes went to this hot-looking navy blue suit on a mannequin right in the middle of the store. If Misty didn't go for that, I'd have 'em lined up for what she was missing.

I walked over and fingered the fabric. Nice. Fucking top drawer.

This lemon-faced salesman oozed over and said, "May I help you, sir?" while goggling at my face.

"Yeah, how much is this suit?" I said.

"That's our Palladium Wool Twin-Button Side Vent Suit, sir. The regular price is two thousand, one ninety-five, but you're in luck." He smiled behind little round glasses. His jowls looked like a hippo's. "To-day we have it on sale for seven sixty-eight, twenty-five."

I gave him an evil leer with my bad eye. "How soon can you have alterations done?"

I STOPPED AT A DRUGSTORE in the mall, stocked up on rolls of gauze wrap and that hospital white bandage tape, and hobbled back across the street to my hotel room. My swollen, sore foot had leaked thin red stuff all over my sock and shoe. I wrapped it in gauze, stripped down to my new silk boxers, and ordered prime rib from room service.

While I waited for it, I checked out the pay channels on the hotel television. Misty wasn't here to see, so I hammered the remote control until I found a channel with lotsa flesh tones.

The next morning, I had to be back at the mall to pick up the three suits—two Palladium Wools, one summer weight—my new shoes, some shirts and ties, and some luggage I had picked out.

My foot fucking hurt. I hated it, but I finally had to break down and go back to the drugstore for a cane. Made me look older, anyway. More like Ray.

I flagged a taxi to help me get the stuff back to my hotel room. I paid the bellboy to carry it up, all the while wondering which suit Misty would like the best.

I figured on the navy blue—girls like colors better than browns. I wrapped gauze around my head, covering up one eye, and then for good measure I wrapped one hand up, too. I counted my money: twelve thousand and change. It would be enough.

I went downstairs, dressed in my new suit, tie, and shoes, and hailed a taxi.

A toothless old black guy picked me up in a yellow-and-red cab. "Where to, man?"

"Take me to the nearest SOS." Michigan was weird. In any other state, that'd be the DMV. Here it was the Secretary of State.

I TOLD THE CAB DRIVER to wait for me and sat in the SOS lobby for about twenty minutes before they called my number. All the while, I was thinking about how to sound old.

A black girl with braids piled on top of her head and chain-link earrings that hung all the way to her shoulders said, "How can I help you?" She didn't even look up from her computer screen.

I slid Ray Kerze's old driver's license across. "I need to renew this."

The girl peered down at the driver's license, glanced at me, looked at her computer screen, then looked back at me hard. "What happened to you?"

"I got mugged. Just got out of the hospital."

"Well, we can't renew this today 'cuz you gots to take a new picture, and you all banged up like that. You gonna have to wait till you get them bandages off."

"Ah, cripes," I said. "Can't we just use the old picture? Look, I'm a retired cop, my daughter's getting married in Ann Arbor next weekend, and I need to drive there. I need to get it renewed today."

"Ain't nothing I can do about it. You gots to take a new picture."

"Is there somebody else I can talk to? A manager, maybe?"

The girl rolled her eyes and turned her back to me to wave a hand at someone. "Yo, Letitia! Can you help dis man?"

An older black lady came over. She must have been tipping the scales at three hundred and change. "How can I help you, sir?"

The girl cut in. "He want a new license today, and he need a new picture. He can't take no picture lookin' like dat!"

The fat lady crooked her finger. "Step this way, please."

I grabbed Ray's license and followed her into a plastic, white cubicle of an office. She sat behind her desk and tapped at her computer. I slid the license across the desk.

"It's like I said. I'm a retired cop, for Chrissakes. My daughter's getting married in Ann Arbor next weekend. How'm I supposed to get there? I can't spend the weekend in jail instead of giving my little girl away, can I?" I tried to rough up my voice a little so I didn't sound so young.

The fat woman smiled at me. "Okay, officer, that'll be fifty dollars. Plus the fee."

A thought hit, and I pulled Kerze's old passport from my jacket. "Can you make that an *enhanced* DL?" Michigan was one of several border states that had enhanced DLs. It would be as good as a passport for where I planned to go.

She pursed her lips at me. "Can you make that a hundred?"

I smiled back. "That'll be just fine."

AFTER ANOTHER HOUR, I WAS officially Raymond Kerze, with a Michigan enhanced driver's license that would let me cross the border into Canada, and back, if I wanted. The cab meter had rung up over fifty bucks by then, but I didn't care. I had money to burn.

"Jesus, man," said the cabbie. "I'm about to cook out here. Where we going now?"

I had him drive up Grand River Avenue and turn off on Schoolcraft Street going towards Redford. There were some good places here to find a hot ride. Last year, I dragged Misty to a car show, picturing myself in a red Corvette, but she drooled like a dog over the big luxury sedans. A gleaming white Lincoln MKS caught my eye.

"Pull off here," I said.

I hobbled out of the cab to check out the car. Blocking the sun's glare with my hands, I peered into a spotless gray interior with what looked like genuine leather seats.

"Can I help you, sir?"

I looked over to see brown eyes and freckles framed by a forest of long red curls. The girl wore a suit hemmed above the knee. It would have been a shame to cover up stems like hers. A shiny pair of black fuck-me pumps completed the vision. Her eyes traveled up and down, stopping at my bandages and bruises, then dropping to my brand new suit, and ending with my left hand. She held out her right hand.

"I'm Jessica Whitlow, and you are—?"

I caught myself just in time. "Ray Kerze," I said, fumbling for my "older" voice. "What can you tell me about the Lincoln here?"

"It's a 2010 MKS EcoBoost with a genuine leather interior and a brand new sound system. It only has fifty-eight thousand miles on it, and it runs like a dream," said Jessica.

The sign in the window said $12,000.

I smiled, even though it made my face hurt and my bandages itch. "Let's go for a ride."

I turned the key. The car idled so smoothly, I had to listen hard to make sure it had started. It purred out of the lot and onto Schoolcraft.

"Nice," I said.

"If you don't mind my asking," said Jessica, turning toward me and pushing one long red curl behind her ear, "what happened to you?"

"I got mugged a few days ago," I said. "Just got out of the hospital."

"You look like you're lucky to be alive," she said.

I had a vision of Tony Corrado dropping off the side of the laundry truck, one eye a bloody pulp. "No bullshit," I said.

JESSICA'S LONG HAIR FELL ALL over her face as she wrote. She looked up from her desk inside the dealership's crappy little air-conditioned trailer. "So, with the license, title, tags, and fees, that will come to twelve thousand, four hundred thirty-nine dollars. And twenty cents."

I had put ten thousand five hundred into the breast pocket of my wool suit. I pulled it out and peeled off ten grand.

"Look," I said. "Listen carefully. Ten thousand dollars is what I'll pay for it, and that's more than it's worth. This is cash; take it or leave it. It's a good deal."

"I've got to get at least eleven," said Jessica. "My boss will fire me if I take ten grand." She gave me the big brown eyes. "You wouldn't want me to lose my job, would you?"

"Of course not," I said. "Let me talk to your boss."

Jessica sat back in her desk chair. "Ten grand. Ten grand is all you've got? Cash?"

I laid out the last five hundred from the breast pocket, spread out on the desk like a fan. "Hey, look, there's car dealerships all up and down the street. If you don't want this ten grand, I'm sure somebody else does."

Jessica took the deal.

I PAID UP THE CABBIE and drove my new car to Grand River Avenue, turning back toward Detroit. I pulled into the first Central Fidelity Bank location I saw, walked in as Ray, and opened a new checking account. Then I drove a little farther to the Dominion Bank branch closest to Ray Kerze's office.

I walked in to the usual scripted chorus of, "Welcome to Dominion Bank!" Several of the tellers jerked their heads up and looked at me twice.

I leaned on my cane, and a manager in a suit and tie hurried over. "Can I help you, sir?"

I remembered my Ray Kerze voice. "Yes, I need to arrange for a regular monthly transfer."

The manager helped me to a small office and sat down behind a glass-topped desk. I sank into the plush chair in front of it and handed him my new driver's license and Ray's account number. "I just got robbed. Can you tell me how much is in this account?"

"I'm sorry to hear that, sir," said the manager, tapping his keyboard. "Looks like you really took a beating." He wrote a number on a piece of paper and slid it across the desk.

"Yeah, I really did," I said, and read the paper.

Cha-ching! I tried to keep the smile off my face. One hundred and eighty-two thousand dollars!

"I'd like to withdraw forty thousand of that, please," I said. "In cash."

The manager glanced up at me. "Will that be all in hundreds, sir?"

"Yes," I said. "And one more thing." I reached in my pocket and pulled out my new checking account number at Central Fidelity. "This is my new account. I want forty thousand transferred to it immediately, and forty a month transferred on the first of every month, until there's nothing left in here."

"We could put this in a CD for you instead," the manager suggested. "We're offering 1.8 percent on a sixty to seventy month CD."

"Why bother?" I said.

The manager made a sour face and got up. "I'll just go to the vault and get your cash, sir."

He counted the money in front of me and placed the stacks of hundreds into a paper bag.

"Thank you very much." I turned to go.

"Oh, sir?" the manager called. I turned around. "Did the robber steal your wallet? Do you need us to cancel your credit card and debit card numbers? Issue you a new debit card, perhaps?"

"Oh, I took care of that on the phone," I said. "Thanks."

I DROVE BACK TO MY hotel to get out of my itchy bandages, check out, and pick up all my stuff. One more thing to do, and then back to Kerze's office and Misty. I stared at myself in the mirror. Maybe if I told her that I whaled on P-Jelly for trying to pimp her out, it would score me some points.

I headed out to Corrado Brothers Laundry. Marco sat alone in an office with two desks, foggy behind layers of cigar smoke that almost made me gag. When he saw me, his eyes popped open like golf balls on tees.

"Holy shmoly," he said, and put his cigar in an ashtray. "I guess you did a better job than we thought. Nice threads. Where'dja get those?"

"Stole 'em," I said. "Same place I got this." I opened the bag and showed him the money. "This is your forty. I didn't bring Tony's. I didn't want to have to beat myself shitless again."

"Lemme count that," said Marco. He lifted the stacks of hundreds out and counted, grinning like a loon and trying not to drool.

"So you got your money," I said. "We're all set."

Marco peered at me through the curling smoke. "You clean up pretty good. I think you could do some work for us."

Yeah, I thought, *until they find Tony in the bushes with one eye shot out.*

Marco said, "Come back when you don't look beat to shit. We can do some business."

ONE GOOD THING ABOUT DETROIT is that when you need to leave town, all you have to do is cross a bridge and you're in a whole different country. Well, if you have the right ID. One thing's for sure: I didn't want to be anywhere around Corrado Brothers Laundry when Tony finally turned up. But I had one person I didn't want to leave behind.

I drove back to Kerze's office off Grand Boulevard, imagining Misty in that slinky black dress. Imagining her taking off that slinky black dress. Maybe I could take her to dinner, someplace really nice. I checked my teeth in the rearview mirror, and that was when I realized I'd have to say something to explain not only my face, but especially my hair. Something that would make her want to come back. I pulled up at Kerze's office, parked at the curb, and went in.

Inside, footsteps came up behind me, and I heard, "Ray!"

I turned around. A Grizzly Adams-looking mountain man with huge biceps and a hammer on his belt stood there in the hallway like Sasquatch. He said, "You're not Ray."

"No, I'm not," I said. "I'm looking for Misty Lake. She works up here, right?"

The Sasquatch pulled the hammer off his belt and crossed his big arms in front of him. "Who the hell are you, and why are you looking for her?"

"I'm Jeff," I said. "I'm her boyfriend."

Sasquatch said, "She ain't never said nothing about no boyfriend, especially not one all beaten to shit like you are."

"Misty got into some trouble the other night. I had to fight off the other guy. You can ask her."

Sasquatch tilted his head to one side. When he narrowed his eyes, they almost disappeared into a mat of head hair and curly beard. Finally, he said, "Well, Misty ain't here now."

"Do you know where she is, man?" I asked. "I can meet her, surprise her. I got a car; I can take her someplace nice."

Sasquatch squinted again, like what I said had to travel 'round his cranium by way of Poughkeepsie before it registered.

"I don't know where she is," he said. "I'll think about telling her you stopped by. I'll think real hard." He waggled the hammer like an annoyed tomcat flicking his tail.

I couldn't see the point of getting into a fight with the guy, so I turned to leave. Figured it was the smart thing to do. Besides, I could try finding Misty at the City Suites. Course, avoiding a scene there might be hard.

If not getting into a fight with Sasquatch was smart, not paying attention to my bad left foot was stupid. I stepped off the curb rough, and a sharp stab flashed from my toes straight to my hip.

Shit.

I bet the damn foot had started to bleed again. I hobbled my way around the car and dropped myself into the driver's seat. I thought for a moment and wasn't happy with the conclusion. I'd have to check myself into the hotel again, for one more day, and Misty would have to wait until tomorrow. Shit.

* * *

THE NEXT DAY, I DIDN'T get up until after noon. I'd checked back into the hotel the previous evening, and I could tell the staff was thrilled to see my ugly mug again. They still had no problem being happy with my money, of course. I'd soaked my foot, ordered dinner in, and had a couple of stiff ones to wrap up the night. The combination of food, booze, and twelve hours' sleep helped more than I'd imagined it would. When I awoke, I almost felt human, and a few of my bruises had begun turning green. A good sign.

I hustled to check out before the two-o'clock deadline and got all my stuff crammed into the trunk of the Lincoln. Again. I drove around a while, trying to figure out a way to approach Misty at the City Suites that wouldn't start a riot. I saw a florist shop on the way and stopped for flowers. A bouquet made-to-order. That had to be at least Right Step Number One.

I'd wandered away some in my driving, so it took me a bit to get back to the City Suites. I drove around the block a few times, still trying to get a plan together, when I saw Misty step up into a city bus. One more trip around the block and I would've missed her altogether.

But now I'd have to poke behind a bus, waiting for her to get off and sucking up diesel in the meantime.

She took the bus way out. Way out. Got off in a business area that still had some life and stepped into a second-hand goods place called Good Family.

I parked outside the Good Family store, screwed up my courage, and went in holding the flowers over my face. I wandered the aisles looking for Misty. She was the hottest thing in the store, standing there in a red knit dress talking to a saleswoman in a blue smock. She stopped mid-sentence and stared at me in my stylin' blue suit with the flowers in front of my face. Her mouth opened and no sound came out.

I pulled the flowers to one side so she could see me.

She said, "What the—oh my God. Jeff?"

I said, "Misty, baby. You look great."

She spluttered. "You look—what happened to you? And what did you do to your hair? I didn't even recognize you!"

"I went to leave the hotel the other morning and that P-Jelly guy was there hanging around, and we got into it. I couldn't have him hassling you. It's dangerous."

"He was there? At the hotel? Well, he was really nice to me," she said, frowning.

"He said you were going to be working for him, and I know you got a job someplace else," I said. "Do you know what kind of guy that is? You don't need him hanging around."

"Jeff," Misty said, "I don't know what to say."

I held out the flowers. "Say you'll come out to dinner with me. I'm celebrating."

"Celebrating what?"

"Things are looking up for us, baby. I've got a new job." I patted my hair. "New distinguished haircut. New car! I've got a great new car. Come outside—you're going to love it."

She frowned some more. "How did you manage that, when the police are still looking for you for skipping bail? Last I saw you, you didn't mention any job, and you were wearing clothes I know you had in high school."

I was still holding the flowers at arm's length. She'd take them, I knew, eventually.

"I came out here because I had a job interview," I said. "I didn't want to say anything, in case I didn't get the job. But I did get it, and it's a good job, and we're going to be okay now. I wouldn't come back out here after you if I couldn't take care of you."

I watched her face change. I expected her to look confused, but the corners of her mouth went down, too, and she looked sort of sad for a second. I didn't know what that was about. She sort of looked at the floor, and then back up at me.

I held the flowers out again. "I did this all for you, babe. Look, I know things got bad there for a while. But I owe you a lot. You stuck with me through all that shit I pulled, and you didn't deserve it. And I want to make it up to you, baby. I want to take care of you. I love you."

Misty stood there. She didn't say anything.

I said, "Come on out and see the car, at least. Let me treat you to dinner."

Misty shrugged. "Well, I am hungry."

We walked outside and she stopped when she saw where I was walking. "This is your car?"

I held up the keys. "Yup."

I opened the passenger door like a gentleman.

Misty passed by me and gave me a dirty look as she slid in.

"What?" I said.

"Who are you and what did you do with the real Jeffrey Enwright?"

"You gonna let me make it up to you, or what?" I said. "One dinner."

I held out the flowers again. Her look softened, but she sat back in her seat, still not taking the flowers. I closed her door and started around the car to my side. Her door opened and shut again.

I opened my door and got in, sticking the flowers between the armrests. "What was that about?" I asked.

"Just making sure I can get out of here," she said. "Last time we were together, I really whaled on you."

"I deserved it," I said. "Forget about it."

I drove and made some turns. She squealed when I pulled onto I-75. "Jeff! Where are you taking me?"

I smiled. "Just relax. This is going to be a dinner you'll never forget."

"Where are we going?"

I just smiled. Misty held on to the armrests as if she were riding a roller coaster. I pretended not to notice.

"Jeff. You can't drive any farther than I can get home by myself."

I fished my wallet out of my back pocket and peeled out two hundred-dollar bills.

"Here," I said, and tucked them into her hand. "If you're not happy, you can take a taxi back."

Misty sat back and folded her arms and glowered. "Fine."

When I turned into the restaurant parking lot, her eyebrows shot up so high they almost met the headliner and her mouth made a big round O. "Adolphe's Steak House? We're eating here?"

I grinned even though it made my mouth hurt. This had to be Right Step Number Two.

Misty twisted her head all around to look as we walked in the door. I took her arm and walked her in like a lady.

The hostess blinked as she took us both in—me with my face and Misty with her lip—but she didn't miss a beat. "Welcome! Do you have reservations with us tonight?"

"No, we don't," I said.

"We still have two places open tonight for our cocktail dinner. You can sample five of our finest drinks along with a five-course meal."

I looked at Misty. I didn't know clever, unpronounceable food. I hoped the hostess wouldn't reel off loads of gobbledygook that sounded French.

Misty asked, "What's the main course?"

"Filet mignon and crab cakes with sweet potato casserole," said the hostess. "There's also a light, wonderful melon salad, and scallops for the third course."

Misty's eyes blazed with hunger and delight as she looked over at me. For the first time, I thought I might have a real chance.

"What do you think, Jeff?" she said.

"If you want it, you got it."

I didn't drink much myself, although the cocktails slid down my throat like silk sweetness over a dry gully. Instead, I waited for the liquor to soften Misty up. The first course had a name with too many vowels and not enough consonants, and it barely covered the pattern on the plate. Misty grilled me all the way through it. I spent the first course and the salad making up a job at a car dealership in Canada, and telling her that I had sold some high-dollar, late-model luxmobiles to get all this cash.

Halfway through the best seafood I'd ever eaten, Misty slipped the hundred-dollar bills from her purse and murmured, "You sure you won't need these?"

I slipped my billfold back out and showed her what I had left. Misty's eyes popped.

I formulated a plan. All I had to do was get her across the border. After that, she'd be sure to stay.

"I haven't found a place yet," I said. "I'm staying in a hotel close to work. I've got money for a security deposit on an apartment—a real apartment, not like that dump we were staying in. Come and help me look for a place."

The waiter arrived with our steaks—tall, fragrant filets swimming in butter. Just the smell would make you faint. Misty sat back and folded her arms as the waiter put her steak in front of her, but I knew she wasn't just making room.

She waited for the waiter to put all our plates down, pick up our salad plates, and leave. Then she said, "Look, Jeff, we just aren't right for each other. You hit me. I hit you. All that shit that went down—I just don't know if I can get over that. You had me thinking I had HIV! I borrowed money to bail you out, and you split! You expect me to just forget all that?"

Now was the time to turn it on—real romance-novel stuff.

"Misty," I said, looking down at my plate. I kept my eyes down a while, like it was real hard for me to say. Then I looked up, right into her eyes. "Misty, I've always loved you." I tried to put a little cry into my voice. "I never knew how to before, but now I do. I don't care how much things are looking up for me, it's nothing without you. If you don't come with me, I don't know how I can ever be happy again."

Misty glanced sideways across the room, and I saw a hint of tears. She brushed one away with her hand. "I just don't know if I trust you," she said, with a real cry in her voice. "This all sounds really good, but . . . I don't know if I trust myself, either."

I saw the waiter coming with drinks and waved him away. I said, "Look, we both had shitty lives and a lot of bad luck. I got whaled on at home. You got whaled on at home. We don't really want to whale on each other, and we both know that. And what have you got? I guess you're working, but you got two dresses to your name. Come on, Misty. Help me pick out an apartment, at least."

She rolled her eyes, and I had to smile. We both knew that last one was a lie.

She stared at me. A tear rolled down her cheek.

I signaled the waiter over. He put two short, jewel-colored drinks in front of us and took a breath, about to explain what they were. I held up an index finger and indicated Misty with my eyes. She sat there, brushing the tear away. The waiter nodded and left.

"Misty, let's make a deal right now. A secret deal, just between us," I said. "No more hitting."

She looked up at me with her eyes, her chin down. "No more other women," she said. "And don't you ever make me bail you out of jail again."

"That's a deal," I said, and picked up my glass. *Bingo*. Right Step Number Three.

DURING THE WEEK, THE LINE through customs on the Ambassador Bridge isn't too long, at least not at seven-thirty at night. But this was Friday, and the line crawled. I sat behind the wheel, thinking of what kind of hotel I'd check Misty and me into—and what would happen after. We inched up to the customs booth. I was glad it had gotten dark. I couldn't give them my own license 'cause it wasn't enhanced and because of the outstanding warrant.

The crusty old guy in the booth, wearing a blue customs uniform, asked, "Citizenship?"

"American," I told him.

"Need your identifications," he said.

Misty handed me her NEXUS card. I'd always been jealous of that— her being able to go to Canada and back when I couldn't. She told me once that she'd gotten it during a time when her mom and her would trip to Canada to get second-hand salon equipment for that bitch of an aunt of hers, Aunt Beatie. I slipped Kerze's ID under hers and passed them over.

As he scanned their cards, he asked, "When was your last visit to Canada?"

Oh, shit. I thought fast—Kerze hadn't renewed his driver's license in three years, so I doubted he'd been to Canada recently, if at all.

"It's been so long, I can't even remember," I said. At that, Misty's head turned and she stared at me. I ignored her.

"What's your destination?"

"Windsor," I said. "I'm looking for an apartment."

"You got a place in mind?"

"No," I said. "Just looking."

"Do you have any tobacco products, firearms, or ammunition?"

"No guns or ammo, and neither of us smokes."

The guard squinted at Kerze's license and moved it toward and away from his nose. A pair of reading glasses hung at his uniform collar. He pulled them out and put them on. He gave Misty's passcard a quick glance and focused on my ID.

"How do you pronounce that?" he asked. "Kurz? Kurzey?"

Shit. "Kurz," I said.

"Have a pleasant stay, Mr. Kerze, Miss Lake," the guard said. "Good luck apartment hunting."

I took our IDs back, my throat tight. "Thanks."

Misty's mouth opened and her throat clicked, but she grabbed her ID and said nothing. She was going to cover for me! I put the window up, stepped on the gas, and we inched forward.

"Thanks, babe," I said.

I heard a click and Misty's seat belt retracted. Then the passenger side door opened, and she was gone. I turned to look. The passenger side mirror reflected her back to me, in her long red dress, stumbling down the ramp.

The car behind us honked. I leaned as far toward her open door as I could. "Misty!" I yelled. "Misty, come back here!"

She didn't turn around. I heard her babbling something.

"Misty!" I shouted. "I can explain!"

Now several cars honked. I couldn't see her in the mirror anymore. I turned around and looked. She had dropped to her knees on the pavement.

Another border guard strolled up, carrying a big flashlight in the twilight. He leaned over Misty. "What's the problem, Miss? Are you okay?"

Between the blaring of car horns, I heard her speak. She said, "He lied! He lied again!"

The Eighth of
Many Stories

I'll Be in the Bar

LOOKED AT THE CLOCK hanging from the wall of the dayroom in my corner of Brighton's alky ward. "Frog!"

"What the hell does that even mean?" A young white guy wearing coveralls and a do-rag walked in waving an FBI badge. "Raymond Kerze," he said, "get your stuff together. We got shit to do."

"We going to a costume party?"

"Yeah, a frog party."

"*Frog* means I've been sitting, waiting for a phone call," I said. "It means you ain't got a frog's chance of jumping me out of here until I get my phone call. You guys made me miss my call yesterday."

"How'd we do that?"

"You had me glued to a chair in some moldy conference room and asked me the same twenty questions about thirty times."

"That wasn't me."

"Doesn't matter. Until I get my call today, I'm not going anywhere."

"We got to go!"

"Am I under arrest?"

"You're a witness," he said, "but I'll be glad to arrest you and let a judge sort it out."

The phone in the dayroom rang. "I'm pretty sure you don't want to piss me off. Go get a coffee. When you come back, I'll go anyplace you want as long as it ain't here."

The FBI agent in the do-rag left, throwing his arms out like he was shooing bees away from his head. I answered the phone.

Misty said, "Ray, is that you?"

Hearing Misty's voice felt good all over, like fresh air after a night of poker in a cloud of cigar blue. I said, "Misty! You're still working for Joe, or you wouldn't be calling me."

"I tried calling you yesterday. When somebody did pick up, they didn't know who you were."

"Long story. I was tied up. How's work?"

"Fine," said Misty, "but what's more important is what's in your office."

She seemed to be all right, and that lifted a weight from my chest. "What's in the office?"

"That John Doe guy."

"He's there? I heard he cheated the ferryman and made it back to this side of the Styx, but— He's *there*?" I paused to fill in the picture. "Misty, if that guy is giving you trouble, get Jimmy Crates—"

"I'm actually more afraid of Jimmy," said Misty. "But listen, here's the problem. I left John Doe watching the office. Some brown-suited city guy gave him a paper thing that said we have to be out of the building by the end of the month."

"Not to worry," I told her. "I get one of those every few months and I just pitch 'em."

"That's what Jimmy said," said Misty. "But John read the paper and on the back of it, it says you can buy the building for a dollar as long as you pay the taxes, which is like eight or nine hundred every six months."

That broke my heart. This was one short romance. "Misty," I said, "I don't have any money."

"Ray, you have a hundred and eighty thousand in your checking account."

"Oh my God," I said, and laughed. "Who told you that?"

"You told me to clean up the secretary's desk. The bank statements were on top—years of them."

"I know," I said. "I haven't looked at them since I ripped the phone out of the wall and dropped it in the trash."

"What's that got to do with your bank statements?"

"My stepsons," I said. "Just before my wife died, she asked me to see that her sons went to college."

"*Her* sons?"

"We weren't very close," I said. "After she passed, both of them went to live with her sister. All I ever heard about was college bills. After I had to retire, I didn't have any more money, so they sent me school loan papers. They were both in medical school."

Misty went quiet. At last, she said, "So your wife just married you to shovel the walks and occasionally plunge the toilet?"

"That's not really fair," I said, though I wondered if Misty hadn't just nailed the onion to the pegboard. "Anyway—to get to the point—the boys' loan payments cleaned out my retirement until one of those banks overdrew it all and wouldn't return the money. The other bank called and they added finance charges. They just kept calling me. I finally ripped the phone out of the wall, and I sure didn't want to read the crap they sent in the mail. They sent a collector out once."

"Oh great. What happened?"

"Great big guy," I said. "He fell down the stairs. The ambulances won't come out that way and I didn't have a car, so I had to order him a taxi. He never came back."

Misty's voice turned dry. "Fancy that."

"Don't be mean," I said. "The guy had a *bona fide* accident. But, the point is, there ain't no money."

"The day you got arrested for John Doe's 'murder,' it rained buckets. Your mail was soaked. I could read your bank statement without opening it. It fell apart and I had to lay it out to dry. It said you have a hundred and eighty thousand dollars. Just check it—for grins. If I'm right, you can always buy me a White Castle and some fries."

* * *

THE FBI AGENT IN THE do-rag and coveralls collected me from the day-room and liberated me past the gate and to the curb, where he stuffed me into a black, four-door Chevy Suburban. He pulled us out onto the state expressway and set the cruise control.

"So are you mostly mowing lawns," I asked, "and just part-timing as a FeeBee?"

He gave me a dirty look. "You really think there's an upside to pissing me off?"

"So what was your name?"

"You forgot?"

"I'm old," I said, "and you flashed your Popeye's coupon at me so fast I didn't get the name."

"So why did you come with me?"

"I don't care where we're going," I said, "long as it ain't mind-numbingly-boring Back There."

"We have to go and find John Doe. Since he ain't dead anymore, he's taken to wandering around. They said he beat up some cleaning orderly and the guy died."

"Shit," I said. "I know where he's at."

"How can you possibly know where he's at?"

"Unlike you," I said, "I really *am* a detective."

He dug out his creds and dropped them on my lap. They said, "Charles Hartcan, Special Agent."

"So should I call you *Chuck*?"

"Special Agent Hartcan will be just fine," he said. "So where is John Doe?"

"When we get into town, take the first left and there's a bank on the right side." I gave Chuck back his creds.

"He's at the bank?"

"No," I said, "I want to go to the bank."

"Why would I take you to the bank?"

"You want to buy my lunch?"

* * *

SHARON BOLSNI HAD HER BUSINESS cards on the corner of her desk. I took one and waited for her to come and talk to me. When she strolled in—short hair, pantsuit, and all business—I asked her what Bolsni was short for.

"That's all we ever had," she said. "How can I be of service to you?"

I gave her an old check that I had carried in my wallet for five years. She said that check was from two business mergers ago.

"Is the account still good?"

Sharon checked the computer to see if I had anything and then smiled with a banker's shine. "Still quite good," she said.

"Enough to take out twenty?"

She hesitated. "I think I'm going to have to see some ID. All things considered. You understand."

I pulled out my wallet. My SOS ID was expired, so no good after the Patriot Act, and sitting in my office desk anyway, but I still had my retirement ID, and that had a picture on it *and* was still good. She accepted that.

"Mr. Kerze, you have one hundred and two thousand dollars," she said, starting to warm up to me. "We have several CDs that are a good opportunity."

"I didn't know I had that much money in there," I said. "Where did this money come from?"

She tapped on the keyboard, and we went back-and-forth with questions and matched the account activity with my more-or-less ancient history. At last she said, "When your sons went into the military, it looks like the army paid off their school loans. So your retirement has been accruing for nearly five years. Two more years, and the state would have taken the money under the dormant account escheat rules. That's why I thought you took out the money, to give yourself another seven years."

"When did I take this money out?" I said. "I've been out of town."

"Only yesterday," she said. "At one of our other branches."

"Where did I send this money?"

"Forty thousand went in cash. Forty went to Central Fidelity

Bank."

"Eighty thousand dollars . . ."

"Also," she said, "the rest of the money is to be transferred in installments of forty thousand dollars on the first of every month until it closes this account."

"We can't be doing that," I said, "what with all these important CDs hanging around."

She did a double take and had to wipe her mouth to keep from drooling on the desk.

I said, "Let's stop the transfers. Call Central Fidelity and ask them to close the account and send back any balance."

I found it hard to believe that Misty would take the money and then send me over to check the account. And I couldn't imagine the usual suspects having the moxie for something this clever. Well—there's John Doe, but he hasn't got a phone, doesn't know where things are, and has no way to travel. Just the same, thinking Misty was a thief felt like breathing razors.

"I can stop the transfers," she said, "and I can call Central and have them freeze the account as 'Ownership in Dispute,' but you'll have to go over and talk to the manager yourself."

"You can count on that," I said.

FBI CHUCK AND I FOUND John Doe staring out the window of my office. He should've run when he saw me getting out of the vehicle, but he acted as if he didn't know me. When we got to the office, we parked him in my office chair and began grilling him.

"I didn't kill anybody," said John Doe, wagging his head between FBI Chuck and me. "I got in a fistfight with two guys. Misty let me in her car and drove me out of the parking lot."

"Did you arrange for Misty to pick you up?" asked FBI Chuck.

"I didn't know her, but I was happy for the ride," said John.

"You didn't know her?" I said.

"I don't remember nobody from before I woke up freezing my ass off in the morgue," said John.

"So who did you forget?" asked FBI Chuck.

"I didn't forget," said John. "I remember everything, it just starts three days ago."

"Maybe you just forgot that you caved in the skull of Ronald, the building maintenance supervisor," said FBI Chuck.

"I do remember that I didn't kill anybody," said John.

"So who killed the maintenance supervisor?" I asked.

"I didn't know he was dead," said John.

"Where's the last place you saw him alive?" said FBI Chuck.

"I never saw him," said John. "I just heard him arguing with Carl, his nephew."

"Ba-rumb pumb, drum roll please," I said. FBI Chuck laughed.

John made a face. "What?"

"Don't stop now," I said. "You're on a roll."

FBI Chuck shook my shoulder. "Show me where the crapper is."

Just pick a door in the waiting room. If there's no crapper, you're in the hallway. But I didn't say that. Instead, I went with, "Hang on for a minute, I'll show you."

In the waiting room, FBI Chuck whispered, "What is up with you?"

"He's a ringer," I said. "But, by God, you guys are good."

"What?"

"He looks like him," I said. "His voice is the same. You even mocked up a helluva bruise. But, he's not the rube."

"This is the same guy," said FBI Chuck. "*Same.* Dead, reheated, and no bullshit."

"God swapped him?"

"Let's just talk to him," said FBI Chuck.

We stepped back into the office. John sat with his chin on his palm. FBI Chuck said, "Just tell us the story from the beginning, or until your story puts me to sleep."

* * *

JOHN WAS STILL TALKING. "So the doors close and I ride the elevator down to the first floor. I step out and crash straight into Carl from upstairs. He knocks the cases out of my hands and cusses me out. I could tell it was Carl 'cause I recognized his voice.

"I asked him where Ronald wanted the toilet paper, and he said something like, 'He's in the crapper, but he ain't got much to say.'

"So I pushed my two cartons into the men's room and turned to get out of there. Wasn't like I really wanted to meet Ronald, y'know? And then a kid about eight years old runs out of the men's room door behind me, screaming that a guy's on the floor with a bloody head."

At that point, FBI Chuck opened his eyes.

"I thought you really were asleep," I said.

"I just listen carefully," said FBI Chuck. "After you set down the boxes, you never went into the restroom?"

"No. After the kid started screaming, I hustled out of there and saw Carl in the parking lot. He and some guy were talking, but Carl saw me as I walked past. Carl told me I better keep my mouth shut. I asked him what happened. Then one kicked me and they both started swingin'. I ran farther out into the lot and, lucky for me, Misty picked me up."

"Misty was waiting for you?" asked FBI Chuck.

"I didn't know Misty or why she was there," said John. "She didn't tell me. I didn't care. I was getting my ass kicked."

"Just one last thing," said FBI Chuck. "When you and the guy you came with, Teddy Sorenson, arrived here on the bus from Little Rock, where did you put your bags?"

"I don't know who that is," said John.

"Guess you better stay with Ray and me for a while," said FBI Chuck. "The police want to arrest you for the death of the supervisor at the hospital. There are also some Russian Mob guys who will ask you what I just asked you—only they'll ask really hard."

FBI CHUCK HAD ME RIDE in the back seat with John. John liked to ride in the big black Suburban and didn't look like he'd be jumping out at the next stop light. We couldn't open the doors anyway.

"So, who broke my office door?" I asked him.

"Don't know," said John. "Jimmy Crates said he swapped the door from an office down the hall. One of the guys from the homeless shelter across the road came over to paint the sign."

"I just wish he had spelled my name right," I said. "Maybe when Misty buys the building, she can fix my door."

John laughed. "Misty ain't got no money. She just said she knew somebody who had money."

"And who was that?" I said.

"Didn't tell me," said John.

"But she said you read the letter," I said. "I thought you would know something about the money."

"The suit from the city said you had to leave in ten days," said John. "But the back of the letter said you could buy the building for one dollar, if you paid the six-month taxes. I just read it because the suit from the city was so snooty. I told Misty, you know, as a joke. We didn't have a dollar between us."

"But she never talked to you about that before?" I said.

"No," said John.

FBI Chuck turned past police headquarters and stopped in front of the Greektown Casino. Detective Jackson stood in front of the casino taxi stand, styling in his thousand-dollar blue suit and matching hundred-dollar Fedora, his goatee so pencil-thin he could deny wearing it. FBI Chuck opened the passenger door.

Detective Jackson, molten lava in his eyes, growled, "What the hell are *you* doin' here?"

"Need to talk to you, Detective."

"Cool," said Jackson. "Give me a lift to my house. Some asshole stole my ride."

He stepped into the Suburban and saw me and John smiling, sitting in the back seat. He pulled his weapon, leaned across the seat, and said, "You under arrest."

"Who, me?" I said.

"You and John Doe," said Detective Jackson.

"You going to arrest me for not killing John?" I asked. "Or John for not being dead?"

"We're going to my office, we're going to talk about this, and then you're both going to jail."

"FBI," said Chuck, flashing his badge on Detective Jackson.

"Holy shit," said Jackson. He laughed. "You *all* goin' to jail." He turned to FBI Chuck. "You know somebody that can do my lawn while you in the slammer for flashin' fake creds?"

"Better take another gander at my badge," said FBI Chuck.

"You been doing my lawn for the last three years," said Jackson. He took the FBI badge and studied it.

"Yes," said FBI Chuck, "and I'm the one who had your car seized."

"What kind of bullshit is this?" Jackson said, as he returned the badge to FBI Chuck.

"You need to holster your weapon," said FBI Chuck. A black sedan pulled up alongside us. "Your ride just arrived, and the crew gets all excited if they see a lot of guns flashing around."

"I'm going home," said Jackson.

"Ain't as simple as it was a couple days ago," said FBI Chuck. "A couple of days ago, Ray Kerze was a drunk, John Doe was a corpse, and you were married to Alice Mitchell."

"Just a fuckin' minute—" said Jackson.

"Put the gun *away*," said FBI Chuck. *"Now."*

Jackson blinked twice and slowly holstered his gun.

"We need to talk someplace private," said FBI Chuck.

"Put the bums out of the truck," said Jackson.

I notched up my tie. "I'm ready!"

"If I unlock the door," said FBI Chuck, "I'll have to spend the rest of the day looking for these guys."

"I'll be in the bar," I said. "I'll take John with me." John spread on a grin.

Jackson turned to stare at me in the back seat. I guess he thought that John and I looked too happy. "Just tell me," he said.

FBI Chuck said, "You ain't gonna like this story."

"I ain't gonna like hearin' nothin' neither!"

"Any time you want me to stop—"

"Get started!"

"You found out today that your wife's name is not Alice Mitchell."

"That crazy woman changes her name like shoes."

"You found out today that her name is Ruby Harris."

Jackson shook a finger. "I don't blame her. She needed an ethnic name to run for office."

"You *didn't* learn this morning that Alice Mitchell is a deceased ninety-two year old white woman from Little Rock, Arkansas?"

"Ain't no law against being dead."

"But," said FBI Chuck, "the story gets better. Ruby Harris worked as Alice's nursing assistant. When Alice died, her lawyer discovered the checkbook short a quarter million dollars."

"That don't mean my wife did it," said Jackson.

"Ruby admitted the theft. She told the judge that she would return the money, and he gave her a suspended sentence."

"Well, then it's a sad story, but—"

"Not so fast," said FBI Chuck. "The judge let Ruby make a quick visit to the restroom. She left the bailiff at the door, went out the window, and neither she nor the quarter million has been seen since."

"Whatever else is true," said Detective Jackson, "the judge gave Ruby a suspended sentence."

"That's true," said FBI Chuck, "and it was seven years ago. And the judge is retired. Unless Ruby Harris rushes back to Arkansas, runs to the courthouse, and demands due punishment, no one in law enforcement is going to look for her." FBI Chuck hesitated. "Of course, the estate's lawyer would want to squeeze her for whatever he could get."

"She's still my wife," said Jackson.

"That's not quite all the story," said FBI Chuck.

"You in so much trouble. My wife is a councilwoman!"

"Twelve years ago, Ruby Harris married Juan Eduardo Romars in

Little Rock, Arkansas. And, they're *still* married."

Detective Jackson's mouth snapped open. After a moment, he turned a shattered face to FBI Chuck. "Juan that works for my wife?"

"*Sí.*"

Jackson's eyes glared. "I'll spike his ass on a traffic cone!" But when he stepped out of the door, he fell right into the hands of four burly FeeBees.

"What the hell you doin'?" Jackson shouted. "I'm a cop!"

One burly FeeBee pulled Jackson's weapon. Another grabbed the backup from Jackson's ankle. The third nearly got Jackson's elbow for dinner. The fourth tried to play nice. "Sir, you have to come with us."

"I ain't got to do jack shit! I got rights! Slavery ended with the Thirteenth Amendment! You don't own me!"

The four FeeBees stuffed Detective Jackson into the back of the black sedan. The last words I heard were, "Fourth Amendment, you pasty-faced white crackers!"

And then the door slammed shut.

I HAD NO IDEA WHERE we were going. No one said a word. Finally, FBI Chuck parked at the curb across from the precinct. A few seconds later, a new chaperone FBI car pulled up behind us and parked.

John spoke first. "Why did you arrest Detective Jackson?"

FBI Chuck looked at John. "Detective Jackson hasn't been arrested. He's in protective custody."

"For just right now," I said, "there ain't a hell of a lot of difference."

"It's a big difference," said FBI Chuck. "But we have to keep him out of the way tonight."

"Do we get to know why?" I said.

"No."

I leaned back in the car seat. "So what are we doing here?"

FBI Chuck seemed to be struggling with a decision.

"If I go in there, it'll start a riot," said FBI Chuck. "Just show John Doe in there and have them return his property. We need the bus claim ticket that they found in his pocket when they thought he was dead."

"How do you know it's there?" I said.

"So far it isn't anywhere else," said FBI Chuck. "I searched in the morgue and the wagon they delivered John in. Detroit police didn't find any claim ticket among Teddy's personal effects. Now, John did tell Sergeant McQuinn that Teddy had the claim ticket, but—"

John said, "I don't remember—"

"—any of that," FBI Chuck finished. "Yes, we know. At that time, John was either lying to McQuinn, or Teddy managed to slip the claim ticket to John without John knowing, as some kind of safety play. As it turned out, Teddy still wasn't safe."

"Okay," I said, "but aren't you forgetting a teensie-weensie detail? Like, the arrest warrant out for John Doe for offing Ronald the maintenance man?"

FBI Chuck sucked in his breath. "Shit. I may have to do this ugly after all."

I said, "Who's got the Ronald case?"

FBI Chuck checked his notes. "Some pair named Elgin and Something-opolis."

"Ari Papadopolis?"

"That's what my scribble looks like."

I closed my eyes, trying to dredge up old memories. Eventually, the dredge hauled up a body.

"Tell you what," I said. "You and John take a break in the other FeeBeemobile, and I'll make a phone call. This could be your lucky day."

"I can't leave you alone," said FBI Chuck.

"So take your keys. I'm not going to hot-wire this thing."

FBI Chuck knew he was out of good options. "C'mon, John," he said, popping the door, "I'll introduce you to the B Team."

I coughed.

"What?"

"Need a phone."

FBI Chuck reached into his jacket and pulled out a smart phone. Then he put the smart phone back in his jacket, rummaged around, and pulled out a flip cellphone.

I said, "I don't qualify for the free upgrade?"

"This one doesn't have interesting telephone numbers on it," said FBI Chuck. "And I want it back." He tossed me the phone, then got out and opened the back door for John. We weren't kids, but those child locks worked just the same. The back doors had to be opened from outside.

After they got out of the car, I tapped a number on the cellphone. A couple of false starts later, I got who I wanted.

"Ari," I said, "this is a Voice from Your Past."

A quiet two seconds later, I heard, "Jesus Christ, Kerze. You still alive? What the hell happen—the Devil not want you?"

"I love you too, Ari. I have a tip, and I want a favor."

"I'll take the tip. Why the hell should I do you a favor?"

"I'll answer the second question first. Remember when Dickie the Grifter got fished out of the Detroit?"

This time the silence lasted a good ten seconds. "Yeah, so what?"

"I caught that case. Funny thing about Dickie. He never went tech. He loved the old ways. When we went through Dickie's things, back in his home, I found your brother's name in his Rolodex. I never said anything to anyone."

"Which means you can't say shit to anyone now, Kerze. Nobody'd believe you. They'd think it was one of your drunken hallucinations."

I ignored the aspersion. "Funny thing about Rolodexes. You can pull out a single card and nobody notices. If you pull the card out carefully, you preserve the prints of the person who last touched the card. Then you put the card in an envelope and wait until you might need a favor."

"The statute of limitations has passed on my brother's indiscretions."

"It'd still look ugly."

Papadopolis sighed. "What the hell do you want, Kerze?"

"Ronald the maintenance man."

"What? That's the case you're interested in? What about it?"

"Carl, the nephew, did it."

"And how the hell do you know that?"

"I have good sources."

"You have cheap booze."

"If you don't pull in your claws, I might just slip the card to IA out of spite."

"Fuck you, Kerze. All right, we'll check out the nephew. What do you want?"

"I want you to pull the warrant on John Doe."

"You're crazy. What am I supposed to go to the judge with?"

"Do a quick check on the nephew. Call me back." I closed the phone.

Three minutes later, Papadopolis called back. "This guy, Carl Demster, is a piece of work. He's got the initiative of a slime mold and the temper of a badger with jock itch. He's also on parole. We can squeeze him. You sure about your sources?"

"Real sure. The warrant?"

"All right. But it may take an hour or two. I'll call you." He hung up.

I took a look out the rear window. Nobody from the B Team seemed particularly antsy just yet, so I dialed the City Suites, looking for Misty. She picked up right away, like she had been waiting for the telephone to ring.

"Ray!" she said. Her voice rang clear and cool. "I was afraid you wouldn't call."

"Of course I was going to call—I'm just busy right now."

"So what did you find out?"

"Found out that you were right," I said. "I'm shocked. I couldn't believe how much money there was."

"Did you think about taking over the building?" she said, but it sounded more like, "Can I have a pony?"

"I haven't had time to think about it," I said.

"I have," said Misty. "John and I walked all over the building. On the third floor there's three apartments marked out. And I thought we could open a secondhand clothes store on the first . . ." She rattled on like it was the only chance she would get to make her case. I just had to let her run out of gas.

When I got a word in edgewise, I said, "I'm looking forward to working with you." I didn't risk asking her if she'd lost her mind. I could see her dangling her legs from the bridge to Canada again. "Just for right now, I want you to pick up a futon bed, so you don't have to sleep at the secretary's desk."

"Don't have any money," said Misty. "Well, I've got enough to get a cute little three-tiered beaded number I saw at Good Family, but that's about it."

I said, "There's a checkbook in the secretary's desk."

"Didn't look for that," she said. "I'm real sure I couldn't write a check on your book anyway."

"Right," I said. That was good news and bad news. So Misty wasn't in on blessing my bank account for eighty large. But now I had no clue at all. "Right! Tomorrow we'll go down and get you on the account."

Misty said, "Cool."

I said, "Do you know who broke my office door?"

"Jimmy Crates. An accident, honestly. I was there."

"Do I want to know the details?"

"Only that Jimmy wasn't feeling any pain when he did it. And he sweated getting it all fixed before you got back."

Knowing Jimmy, that sounded about right. It also explained Misty's reluctance to trust the guy.

I said to Misty, "I got to go. Will you be at work, or are you on the way to the office?"

"My shift's almost over. I'm going for a quick run to Good Family in a minute. Then I'll sleep here later tonight." Misty added, "C'mon over in the morning for the continental breakfast with me."

I closed the phone, leaned into the front of the car, and managed to reach the window controls. I unlocked the back windows and stuck my hand out and waved to the other sedan. FBI Chuck and John Doe returned to the car.

"I fixed things with Papadopolis," I said. "But it may take a couple of hours to clear the warrant. He'll call me."

FBI Chuck looked at me. "What are we supposed to do in the meantime? Sit around with our thumbs up our asses?"

"You could take me to the nearest Central Fidelity Bank," I said, leaning back into the seat.

"Another bank? What for?"

I leaned back in the seat. "Just consolidating accounts."

A LITTLE OVER AN HOUR later, I had my forty thousand back in hand, along with the seed money that my impostor had used to open up the phony Kerze account in the first place. I figured it was only fair. The bank also let me have a copy of the photocopy they took of the fake Mr. Kerze's SOS ID. Totally nuts. No SOS/DMV on the planet would permit a photo like that. Still, if the bandages were legit, this guy had already been worked over. Wouldn't keep me from doing a re-run on him, of course, if and when I caught his ass.

Ari Papadopolis called a few minutes later.

"Kerze," said Papadopolis, "you are one lucky son of a bitch. Elgin and I went out to question Carl Demster, and the first time I mention Ronald's name, this idiot cold-cocks Elgin and makes a run for it. I had a couple of uniforms with me who ran him down. He screamed all the way about Ronald bein' a POS and how he'd gotten what he'd deserved. Totally nuts. I think Demster's into steroids, myself. The uniforms had to tase him twice before he even felt it."

"'Good sources can be an asset to the dedicated investigator,'" I said in my best Academy Instructor voice.

"Bite my ass, Kerze. Give me another half hour and I'll have the warrant for John Doe cleared. And one more thing."

"Yes?"

"That item in the envelope is a good-for-one-time-only coupon. You use it again, I'll get six of my relatives to pound your ass. I expect to hear you say you burned it and stirred the ashes. *Soon.*"

"Consider it done, Ari. Thanks for the help." I put the phone away and nodded to FBI Chuck. "We can make our way back to the precinct. Before we go in, we check that the warrant's been cleared."

FBI Chuck coughed.

"What?"

"Phone," said FBI Chuck, holding out his hand.

I sighed. "Hoped I could use it for a while." I tossed him the phone.

As FBI Chuck pulled out of the bank's parking lot, I thought back on Dickie the Grifter and his Rolodex. I had found Papadopolis' brother's name there all right, and I had saved it as I said, because at that time, Papadopolis had been a son of a bitch to do business with and I figured sooner or later I'd have to use it. But when I retired, I put my small bag of "favor coupons" to the match. What Papadopolis was worried about hadn't existed in years.

Soon, FBI Chuck, John, myself, and our shadow FeeBeemobile arrived at the precinct for the second time that day. A check through one of FBI Chuck's sources verified that the warrant for John Doe was "no longer current."

I led John Doe in the front door—strange for me, the cops usually take me in the back door with handcuffs—and walked him up to the sergeant's desk. He wasn't anybody I knew.

I said, "I'm here with John Doe to pick up his property."

He said, "Some reason he can't pick up his own property?"

Right there I knew things were going downhill. "He doesn't remember his name," I said.

The desk sergeant still hadn't looked up from his perch. "Why doesn't he know his name?"

"Because he was dead," I said, "and now he doesn't remember anything."

Now we had his attention. In a motion as fluid as a practiced salute, the sergeant pulled out his weapon, guided it around his fifty-inch girth, and put it in John's face. "You're under arrest. Don't move."

I coughed. "Arrest warrant's been cleared."

"Arrest warrant was new this morning," said the sergeant.

"Just check it," I said. "Save yourself embarrassment. Pick up the phone."

His eyes didn't move, but his free hand found the phone on his desk. He also dialed the extension without taking his eyes off us. I wondered if he practiced that.

A minute later, after a couple of *No Shit!*'s and *When?*'s, he put the phone down and the gun away.

"Sorry about that," said the sergeant. "But until this is straight, you two sit in the chairs by the wall."

"Need to use the restroom," I said.

The desk sergeant stared at me deadpan and drew a long breath. At last he said, "Left, past the telephone. Don't get lost. And make sure *he* doesn't get lost."

On the return trip I saw John napping in his chair. I placed my butt in an old stuffed chair next to him and leaned back.

The desk sergeant shook my shoulder. I guess I'd dozed off as well. He said, "I told you to watch him, not snore with him." His belly nearly covered his gun belt, making his earlier fast-draw even more impressive. "This guy you brought has no ID."

"That's because you guys thought he was dead and the dicks picked up his pocket crap to take to the evidence room. He's alive again, so now he needs it back."

The desk sergeant's eyes widened. "I heard about that. So this is the guy? Looks pretty good for a dead guy."

"Yeah, he does," I said. "Now how about his stuff so we can get out of here?"

The sergeant got a look like he had an argument to make, but must've thought better of it, because he just nodded and said, "Fine, but wake him up. Don't want anyone to think I'm lettin' the homeless crash here."

* * *

JOHN DOE DUMPED THE BAG from the police lockup onto a corner table in the National Coney Island diner. I fingered out a yellow plastic ticket that tumbled out and passed it to FBI Chuck. "It doesn't look like a bus locker key card."

"It's a ticket, and it has a number stamped on it," said FBI Chuck. "Whaddya you think this is, John? It says D-47."

John unzipped a wallet made of plastic supposed to look like tooled leather. "I have no idea," he said. "I've never seen any of this stuff."

I peered over his shoulder. Five plastic windows started with an ID page, John's picture with "John Doe" in a child's scrawl. The address had been scratched out.

"Do you remember now?" asked FBI Chuck. "Where does this ticket go?"

John opened the cash fold and found what looked like a twenty-dollar bill. "I don't know about the ticket, but if this is my wallet, this must be my twenty bucks!" He pulled it out with a smile, but saw that it was just a religious tract folded to look like a bill.

"Well, that was mean," he said.

I said, "Pretty sure he doesn't recall any of this. He doesn't even talk the same."

"John," said FBI Chuck, "at some point you have *got* to remember. Take this ticket and hold it in your hand. Rub it with your fingers, taste it. This is a billion dollars!" He pursed his lips and looked away.

Hyperbole! You never hear that from the FBI. I asked, "How much of that is bullshit?"

The waitress interrupted my question with our dinner—three orders of French fries and three plates of coney dogs on one arm, leaving the other arm free to deliver the drinks.

"Leave a tip on the table and I'll remember you forever," she said. She laid out the food like a blackjack dealer. "Leave *that* on the table," she said, pointing to the fake twenty-tract, "and I'll *really* remember you forever."

After the waitress left, I said, "So what's the deal?"

"First thing is to get whatever the ticket leads to," said FBI Chuck.

"We have about two hours. After that, it's all in the crapper. I hoped that John would remember."

"Before he died and forgot everything," I said, "he said that he and his pal had stashed their clothes at the bus station, just a couple of paper bags."

"You didn't think that was important?" said FBI Chuck.

"He said it was just a couple of grocery bags," I said. "Christ, they didn't even own a suitcase."

"They probably didn't know what they had," said FBI Chuck. "Let's get to the bus station."

FBI Chuck and I each stuffed a couple of mouthfuls down our guts before we stood up to go. I made Chuck leave the waitress a tip.

John took his coneys with him.

OUTSIDE, I DISCOVERED THAT OUR Suburban had attracted a second chaperone sedan. Eight men—four for each sedan—milled around wearing their blue FBI jackets. One of them called to FBI Chuck.

Chuck said to us, "Climb in, this'll just take a minute and we're on the way." He left to talk with the FBI agents.

"What's with all the cops?" said John. "That's, like, more FBI guys than I ever seen outside TV." He added, "I mean, I guess."

"Chuck might tell us," I said, "but don't hold your breath. This shit is deeper than I thought. FBI Chuck is being pretty catty."

"He keeps asking me to remember stuff that happened before I woke up at the morgue."

"He's hoping that your light will flash on," I said. Like FBI Chuck, I wondered how much of John's story was bullshit. But on the other hand, he had been bona fide dead.

"You think it will flash on?" John gave me that puppy-dog eyes look.

"Maybe. I knock heads—I don't shrink them. I'm not the expert here. Sometimes thinking too hard about remembering isn't the best thing. Sometimes thinking *really hard*, when you're under the gun, will make you remember." I tried to recall what little I knew about trauma-induced amnesia. "You haven't had any moments at all when you've felt like you were just about to break through to your past, to realize something just out of reach?"

John's eyelids fell to half-staff. "A couple times, when I was walkin' up the stairs of your office building, I thought I was walkin' up a whole 'nother flight of stairs. But just for a moment. Then, *pfft*, it was, like, *gone*."

FBI Chuck opened the driver's door and climbed in. He had his notepad held open between his thumb and finger. He looked at me and said, "When you saw John at the bus station, what was he carrying?"

"I never said that," I said. "The first time I saw him was with his pal on the bus." I was getting a little pissed. "You know I told you that!"

FBI Chuck closed his eyes and waved a hand at me. Still, a moment passed before my brain turned on. We were talking to a listener in one of the other cars. I nodded.

"All right," said FBI Chuck, "just take it from the top. I have to check notes."

"Misty and I were walking down to the City Suites hotel to get breakfast," I said. "The bus stopped right beside us. We got on and saw two guys dressed up as skinheads who were making trouble. They made an off-color comment to Misty. One of them showed a knife. I banged their heads together and hustled John's pal—I never knew his name—out of the bus."

"Was the door open?" said FBI Chuck.

"Yeah," I said. "I'm pretty sure the driver thought somebody was about to be leaving. I went back to get John, but he was already hoofing his way out. I just got out of the way."

"So you and Misty got on the bus planning to meet John and his friend?" said FBI Chuck.

"No," I said, "and quit tryin' to put crap in my mouth. We didn't go to meet them. We didn't *want* to meet them. I didn't have enough money for the bus, anyway. The bus driver, Henry Lee, who is a friend, stopped the bus because he needed help to deal with the skinheads."

"So, John," said FBI Chuck, "that what you remember?"

"I don't remember anything about that," said John.

"We have to get going," said FBI Chuck. "But I have just one more question. Why didn't you drive up to City Suites?"

"Because I don't own an automobile," I said. FBI Chuck put his notepad away.

"Sure about that?" said FBI Chuck.

"I have a '57 T-Bird in the left middle drawer of my desk," I said, and put an edge on it. "Die-cast. Still in the *original* packaging!"

FBI Chuck gave me a dirty look but pulled into traffic. And we were lucky. One more inane question, and I'd've started a fistfight, right there, going down the road.

We pulled into the bus station and climbed out. We now had four sedans. I wondered if anybody in the city *didn't* know the heat was on.

The bus station no longer had lockers. We walked up to the ticket counter and FBI Chuck flashed his badge. He said, "John Doe is here to pick up his luggage."

He shoved John's yellow tag between the sales clerk and a GI buying a ticket.

The sales clerk, whose tag said *Regina*, didn't much care for the interruption and said, "You want to get in line?"

"You want to go to jail?" said FBI Chuck.

She pointed to her right. "Through the door."

"That's the manager?" said FBI Chuck.

"No, that's where you go to get the luggage. But if you're as rude with them as you are with me, all you're likely to get is some American Sign Language."

FBI Chuck handed the yellow tag to John and we went through the door. No one else stood in line, so John had his stuff in a couple of minutes.

That's when the shit hit the fan.

The sealed white plastic bags, revealing two grocery bags, had a pretty big price on them. Apparently it cost two dollars for two hours to check in a bag. And it had been seven days.

"Holy shit!" said John. "It's just two bags."

The gal on the counter rang it up. "One hundred and sixty-eight dollars."

"That's ridiculous," I said.

"I could have rang this up as two different packages," she said. "That would be three hundred and thirty-six dollars."

"I don't care how much you charge," said FBI Chuck. He held up his badge. "The bags are going with me." He pulled out his badge and slid out his business card.

"You can't just take this," she said.

A security guard, a very tall black fellow, walked up and growled, "All right, what's up here?"

FBI Chuck had to dance between his own annoyance, public relations, and exigent law-enforcement circumstances, but in the end, the gal on the counter had to be happy with his FBI business card and the number for the FBI claims section.

A minute later, we were on our way out the door with John's sacks. One was marked "Teddy," the other "JD." Both looked equally worthless.

Back in the Suburban, FBI Chuck had me sit in the front and had John climb in the back. He handed the sealed plastic sacks to John and said, "Well, does this belong to you?"

A FeeBee sedan pulled up on either side of us.

"I never seen any of this stuff before in my life," said John.

"Did you ever see John with these bags?" said FBI Chuck to me.

"Already asked and answered," I said. "So who is Teddy?"

"Yes," said FBI Chuck. "Who is Teddy, John?"

"I don't know," said John. "I never saw any of it, you know, until we got here."

"Let's open them up," said FBI Chuck. "Just dump 'em out on the seat."

The first bag spilled out shorts, T-shirts, and shaving gear. A head hair shaver tumbled out.

"Not much discovered for one hundred and sixty-eight tax dollars," I said.

The second sack revealed more clothing and a cigar box. John opened the box and spilled plastic packing peanuts all over the seat. A computer hard drive lay nestled in the box.

"Bingo!" said FBI Chuck. "Tell me what that is."

John scratched his neck and shook his head. "I have no idea."

"How about you, Ray?"

"It's a hard drive," I said, "but it's like a billion others. All my business is hand-to-hand. Cash. I don't have a computer."

FBI Chuck's phone rang. He said, "Hold that thought," and brought the phone to his ear. Several *Really?*'s and *No Kidding*'s later, he put his phone away and gave me a stare.

"How about your secretary?" said FBI Chuck. "She showed up the same time as the skinheads. Immediately showed up at the City Suites hotel."

"I tried to get her a job there," I said.

"Misty Lake works for you," said FBI Chuck.

"A real job," I said. "Not just to get out of the rain."

"Really?" said FBI Chuck. "Did you know that she and her boyfriend, Jeff, just got arrested in your car trying to escape to Canada?"

"I don't own a car," I said.

"The white Lincoln," said FBI Chuck.

"The last car I owned was a beat-up Chevy. The transmission crapped out and I gave the car to Mother Waddles. I quit driving when I turned in my badge and decided to drink full-time."

"Jimmy Crates said that Jeff dude showed up at the office," said John. "He said he just bought that Lincoln and wanted to show it off to Misty."

I stared at John. "You didn't think you should tell me that?"

"I didn't think it should be me," said John.

"That little bastard is the one that stole my retirement money," I said.

"Jeff Enwright is in custody on an old open warrant," said FBI Chuck. "Your car's on the way to the impound lot to join Detective

Jackson's BMW. And Misty Lake is looking at a long night of questions and bad coffee."

The door opened behind me.

FBI Chuck said, "You're in protective custody."

"What about John?" I said.

"He's got to go with me," said FBI Chuck.

"You know John doesn't know shit about any of this, or what is going on."

"He knew it when he arrived in town. He knew it when you cold-cocked him and his pal Teddy on the bus. Forgetting what you had planned *then* doesn't make you innocent *now*."

"How about you?" I said. A couple of FBI types started pulling on my arms. "For three years you watch all these creeps destroying this town." I hauled on the back seat. "All you do is take notes? Detective Jackson shakes a little light loose"—I couldn't hold on any longer and they dragged me out—"and *now* it's time to clean up this town?"

The Ninth of Many Stories

Just in Case I'm Dead

ARE YOU REALLY GOING TO arrest me, Agent Chuck?" I asked. "I really don't remember anything about this stuff." I tried the door handle, but it wouldn't open.

"I locked the doors," said Agent Chuck, raising an eyebrow at me. I turned away and looked out into traffic.

"Let's start at the beginning," he said. "Ray Kerze can call me anything he wants. You may call me Special Agent Charles Hartcan. For short, you may call me Agent Hartcan."

"Yes, sir," I said. "Agent Hartcan. Am I still going to jail?"

"That's kind of up to you," he said. "You would need to cooperate. Frankly, I just don't believe the 'I forgot' excuse."

"I remember everything," I said.

"Cool," said Agent Hartcan. "Now we're getting somewhere. Who gave you the hard drive?"

"What's that?" I said.

"The metal thingy on the back seat!"

"Oh," I said. "Never saw that before. Just now."

"All right, you had your fun! Now you're going to jail." Agent Hartcan cranked up the car and picked up his phone.

"Wait!" I said. I pulled on his sleeve like a little kid. "Please! There has to be a way that I can help. I don't want to go to jail. I don't even know what I did!"

"Bullshit," he said.

I shut my eyes and said, "For God's sake! Tell me what I did."

Agent Hartcan put the SUV back into park. "Tell me the first thing you remember."

"It was really cold," I said. "And dark. I was under a cover."

"When was that?"

"Three days ago," I said.

"You're trying to tell me you were killed?"

"I never said I was dead. I just don't remember anything."

"Look," Agent Hartcan said, "I have to write a report. I have been on this case for over three years. I'm not going to let it go to court on the strength of witnesses who never saw any of this."

"Maybe you could help me remember," I said.

Agent Hartcan pulled out into the road and said, "Get your head out of your ass. You're in trouble. The judge will decide how long you're going to jail."

THE RADIO IN THE CAR spit, and a voice said, "Hartcan."

"Yes," Agent Hartcan answered it. "I just pulled up."

"You're a little early. Go dark until I call you," said the voice.

"Ten-four," Agent Hartcan said.

Across the street from City Suites sat a beat-up, sixteen-foot Ford step van with the name of some bakery barely visible on the side. One wiper blade held on to a stack of parking tickets. A parking boot bear-trapped the front left tire. Graffiti covered the side panels. Agent Hartcan made a U-turn, and we pulled up behind the van and parked.

"Okay," said Agent Hartcan. "This is your shot. Tell me what you remember."

"I don't remember anything," I said—again—and figured I was in for a beating. They just weren't believing me.

The radio crackled again, and the voice said, "Okay. Now." Agent Hartcan stuffed the hard drive thingy into his coat pocket, climbed out, and walked over to the passenger door.

"Get out," he said. "If you run, I'll drop you right on the street." He grabbed me by the arm and pushed me toward the back door of the trashed van. "You're going in there. You can do your waiting and thinking in there."

"I don't want to go in there!" I said, close to freaking out. I thought maybe they'd lock me in the wreck and then haul me off to the crusher. "Can't you just send me to jail?" But Agent Hartcan opened the back door of the beat-up van and pushed me through.

I saw chairs, computer screens, and two more FBI agents in the low light inside. They had their coat jackets on their chairs, their ties were hanging loose, and they had their shirt sleeves rolled to their elbows. They looked up at me from their radios, cameras, and computers.

I sucked in a breath. "Oh my God, I thought you were going to kill me!"

One of the FBI men turned off the bank of monitors.

Agent Hartcan handed the hard drive to that man and said, "I see you have a new partner."

"Agent Park," said Monitors FBI Man. "He's up on assignment from Arkansas."

Agent Park reached across his computer to shake Agent Hartcan's hand. "Love your undercover outfit," he said.

"Oh, no," said Agent Hartcan, "this is our regular outfit."

"Really?" said Agent Park. "That's the jauntiest do-rag I've seen since Quantico."

I kept looking around, feeling dumb. But as long as they were gabbing among themselves, they weren't hurting me.

"Don't you guys down in Arkansas do all your work in coveralls?" asked Agent Hartcan.

"Only if you're a real *local* Arkansas agent," said Agent Park.

Agent Hartcan groaned.

Park sat back in his chair. Monitors FBI Man looked at Agent Hartcan and said, "Now, as to John Doe. I listened to the interview over the radio. I think you pressed him pretty hard. I really believe he doesn't have a clue."

"Then he's of no use," said Agent Hartcan.

"He's perfect," said Monitors FBI Man. "They never tell the cou-
riers anything anyway, and that Nazi lightning bolt crap is perfect."
Then Monitors Man turned to me. "Just the same, I have to tell you
there's always a certain amount of danger. You don't have to do this.
You can wait here until everyone is arrested and we'll send you off with
the rest of the crooks."

I swallowed hard. "What do I have to do?"

"You've been in the City Suites across the street," said Monitors
Man. "You've been filmed in there with a woman you know as Misty
Lake."

"Misty brought me here to the breakfast bar."

"You ever go upstairs?"

"No."

"Tonight I want you to go upstairs and take the hard drive with
you," said Monitors Man. "Go to the elevator. Go up to the tenth
floor and knock on room 1010. Got that so far?"

"Tenth floor," I said. "Room 1010."

"Whoever comes to the door, you show them the hard drive. You
ask them, 'This what you want?' Ask it just like that. *Exactly* like that!"

"Is this what you want?"

"Good," said Monitors Man. "If they take the hard drive, you ask
them, 'Do you have something for me?'"

"Do you have anything for me?"

"All right," said Monitors Man. "If they say no, just bring the hard
drive back here. If they take the hard drive but don't give you anything, just come back to the truck. If they give you something, bring
it back to the truck."

"And that's it?" said John.

"In your case, that's the difference between being an informant and
being a resident in the House of Many Slamming Doors."

I reached for the hard drive, but Monitors Man picked it up and
plugged in a couple of cables.

"Not just yet. First we'll run an image-copy of the drive. But look here at these computer stills. See that heavyset older lady wearing the hat?"

I stared at the screen, and so did Agent Hartcan. Monitors Man made the picture twice as big.

"Good God," said Agent Hartcan. "What did she do? Run that hat through a wood chipper? That's a felony all by itself."

"She uses it as some kind of trademark," said Monitors Man.

"So what's she doing here?" asked Agent Hartcan.

"She's buying banking account and routing numbers from our city councilwoman Asari Murphy, better known as Alice Jackson, also Alice Mitchell, originally known as Ruby Harris. We think. We hope to learn all of her names tonight, or maybe in the morning."

Monitors Man looked at me and said, "As soon as Hat Lady leaves, you're going to do us and yourself that favor."

Agent Hartcan said, "I expect Murphy has as many lawyers as names. We should have picked her up months ago."

"She's a city councilwoman."

"What difference does it make?" said Agent Hartcan. "A crook is a crook."

"Isn't that cute?" said Monitors Man. "You still believe in the tooth fairy." Monitors Man then looked at me again and said, "John, we've got to do a little talking here, between ourselves. I want you to go sit up front in the cab for a minute. Keep your head down; we don't want to blow our cover. It'll only be a few minutes, okay?"

I didn't think I had much of a choice. "Sure. I guess."

They opened a skinny door near the front of the inside of the van and pushed me through. I sat down on the passenger seat. The windows were so grimy, I doubted anyone could see me even with a flashlight up to the glass.

Agent Hartcan said, "Don't get ambitious—the doors are locked. And remember to slouch down." Then he shut the door.

I didn't think they'd ever really done this before—putting someone up front to keep them from hearing things, because I could still hear muffled voices. I was already pretty low in the seat, so I bent to the left and pasted my ear up to the door.

Agent Park was saying, "In this case, we may have a Santa Claus. The skinheads I followed for a year have set up business on the Russians' server here . . . with city councilwoman Asari Murphy."

Agent Hartcan said, "You're shitting me."

"Black is black and white is white," said Agent Park, "but money is *green*. The skinheads have listed over five million Social Security recipients, and they've figured out how to steal from every one of them. The US Attorney can't shrug this off."

"How on earth can they steal Social Security money?" asked Monitors Man.

"A little at a time," said Agent Park. "Most Social Security recipients have Medicare. The payment is paid directly from the government. The skinheads have figured out how to skim a small amount from each payment. It's a tiny skim, but it's for over five million Social Security recipients."

"So how much does it amount to?" asked Agent Hartcan.

"Maybe two hundred thousand," said Agent Park.

"They've got to split it between three partners," said Agent Hartcan. "It doesn't seem worth the trouble."

"That's two hundred G's *every month*," said Agent Park. "And then there are the baby boomers, disabled people, and children receiving benefits. More sources to tap."

For a minute, nobody spoke. Then Agent Park said, "Do we really need John to deliver the drive? Agent Hartcan could carry the package in himself."

Monitors Man answered. "The US Attorney would run away from this case like it was shit on fire if Hartcan carried in evidence. Of course, he could just stick his badge on it. Wouldn't be entrapment then."

"Har, har," said Agent Hartcan.

It got quiet again. Then Agent Hartcan asked, "Who've we confirmed in 1010?"

Monitors Man said, "Just Asari Murphy and her husband, Juan 'Eduardo' Romars. Nobody else."

A woman and a guy. Asari and Juan. That didn't sound too bad.

"Do we have video from inside the suite?" asked Agent Hartcan.

"Outer room only," said Agent Park. "But the audio pickup is rather sensitive, so we should pick up some conversation from all parts of the suite. Anything loud, anyway."

"Oh look," Monitors Man said. "Hat Lady is leaving. Unit Two, Ratty Hat is on the move."

I heard a radio crackle, but I couldn't make out the words. A few minutes later, I heard Monitors Man say, "Hat Lady is in the bag. Time for John to earn his pay."

I pulled away from the door and got back into my slouch. A moment later, the door opened and Monitors Man motioned me in. He had me repeat everything I was to say, just to make sure I remembered. Then he unplugged the hard drive from the cables and handed it to me.

"All right, John, remember that all your business is at the door. Don't go inside. If you do go inside, you'll have no one to cover you. You'll be totally on your own. So Don't. Go. In. *Capisce?*"

I nodded vigorously.

THEY TURNED OFF THE INSIDE lights and I stepped out of the bread truck. I started across the road to the City Suites hotel, but I stopped in the middle of the street and looked back. Could those guys really help me if things got ugly?

I crossed the rest of the way but didn't go into the hotel. Bad feelings rushed up from the ground, through my legs and into my gut. For a second, the City Suites and the street vanished, and all I saw was cars, concrete, and steps. Then the street returned.

I crossed back over to the truck.

Agent Hartcan popped out of the bread truck like toast from a toaster and caught me just as I got to the truck side of the road. "You said I didn't have to do it," I said.

"That's right," said Agent Hartcan. He grabbed me by the shoulder and spun me around to look at the City Suites. I felt his fist in the small of my back and his other hand on my throat. "You still want to do this job? Or do you want to go to jail? I'd rather drag your sorry ass to the jailhouse."

"I don't want to go to jail," I said.

"*Somebody* is going to jail," said Agent Hartcan.

"All right, all right. I'll do this."

"My man," said Agent Hartcan. He patted my shoulders. "Go get 'em, tiger." I walked back across the street. As I did, I heard the door to the bread truck slam, like the trapdoor on a hangin' machine. I twitched, but I got hold of myself and entered the City Suites.

I KNOCKED ON THE DOOR of 1010. Somebody answered from inside. "Who are you? What do you want?"

"John Doe," I said. "Do you want what I've got here?"

"Back away from the door," said the voice from inside. I stepped back.

A Mexican-looking guy opened the door just a crack. I figured he had to be Juan. I held up the hard drive. Juan opened the door wide, showing a shoulder holster with a silver gun and a sharp, smooth business suit with no snags or frays. He looked up and down the hall, grabbed me by the arm and pulled me in. The door slammed.

"I'm supposed to stay in the hallway," I said.

"Who told you that?" said Juan. "I never do business in the hall-way."

I thought hard. "My mother," I said.

"Cute," said Juan. "You're more than a couple days late." He took the hard drive from my hand.

"Don't you have something to give me?" I said.

"I have to hook the hard drive to my computer," said Juan. "You going to carry a brand new Chevy home in your pocket?"

A woman walked in from the other room of the suite. Asari—I remembered her name—walked up to me, smiling. She wore a tight blouse, black slacks, and a gun belt with an automatic around her waist. I was trying to be nice, but before I knew it, she pinched my ear in her left hand and jammed her gun under my chin.

She said, "There's something wrong with this setup."

My ear hurt and I yipped.

"His hair hasn't been shaved lately," said Asari, "and he ain't wearing those shit-kicker boots. Go and get a rag to scrub on his neck tattoos. If any wipes off, this guy's a rat."

The gun in my neck made my heart pound, and I felt hot all over. The room shimmied, and the furniture shuffled around like leaves in a whirlwind.

"Oh, God," I said. "Oh, God! I remember!"

"I can hardly wait," said Asari.

I swallowed hard. The wind stopped and the furniture flew back into place. The room steadied, but the gun was still pressed to my neck.

"That's the reason we were late," I said. "Teddy, they killed him. I saw it. I couldn't help him."

"Teddy Sorenson?" Asari said. "Hold that thought."

Juan walked back with a washcloth and scrubbed my neck. Nothing rubbed off. He showed it to Asari. She let go of my ear but held the gun ready.

"Tell me about Teddy Sorenson," said Asari.

"We came up here together," said John. "We put our stuff in the bus station, including the hard drive, and went to visit the guys who were supposed to give him the brand new Chevy."

"Who?" said Asari.

"Three Russian guys. Downtown, in a real tall building, in a real tall parking garage. Teddy told me to wait until he came down, but I couldn't wait any longer and started to walk up. I got almost to the top. I could see the next floor and I saw three Russians beating on Teddy with bats. After the Russians left, I ran up to Teddy, but he was dead."

"Police?" said Asari.

"They came. I didn't know anything."

"Didn't you tell the police about the Russian guys?"

"No."

Juan began packing up equipment.

"Why?" said Asari.

"I wanted to find them myself," I said.

"Today's your lucky day." Asari holstered her pistol. "Two of them are going to be here shortly. Juan and I are leaving. Feel free to sit here and wait for Petrov and his pal."

"Just give me what you're supposed to," I said, "and I'll be on my way."

"That's the deal," said Asari. "Petrov and his partner Alexei run the Struggle's computer servers. They're the ones who arranged for the car to pay for the hard drive."

"Then I'll just go downstairs and check the car."

"There's no car because we didn't know you were going to be here," said Asari. "Of course, the last time you tried this trade, you didn't get a car that time, either. If I were you, I'd hit the streets and never look back."

"Well," I said, "I'll just go wait downstairs."

Juan opened the door and tipped his head at me. I wanted to run like hell, but forced myself to just walk into the hallway. After Juan shut the door, I hustled down the hall and around the corner. A second later, I was pounding the button to the elevator. When it arrived, I jumped in and punched the button for the ground floor. It seemed like for the first time in an hour, I could breathe.

When the elevator doors opened, I shoulda just kept my eyes to the carpet and walked out, casual-like. But I was looking straight ahead and saw the two big Russians—two of the guys who beat Teddy to death—and I couldn't keep the shock of recognition off my face.

They looked surprised, too, but not so surprised that they didn't grab me as I tried to walk between them.

"Hey!" I said. "What gives?" After all, there was no way they could recognize *me*.

But they pulled me back into the elevator with them, and Big Guy One pushed the button for the tenth floor. In a strong Russian accent, Big Guy Two said, "A skinheader shows up at meet time. Too much coincidence, I think. We must talk."

The doors closed.

I said, "I don't want to talk."

Big Guy One elbowed me in the ribs. It hurt so bad, I saw pinpoints of light.

"Why?" I asked. "I never did nothin' to you guys."

Big Guy Two elbowed me from the other side. Being nice wasn't working.

I bent over and gasped. Then I twisted my body so I could throw a kick between Big Guy One's legs. He moved and I missed, but not by much.

"Son of a bitch!" said Big Guy One, who fell back into a corner.

I backed up into Big Guy Two and tried to slam him against the wall of the elevator, but he got an arm around my neck. I was in for it now, so it didn't matter what I did. I bit the hell out of his arm, right through the suit and the shirt, until he screamed.

The bell dinged, and the elevator doors opened.

The three of us fell out into the hallway, arms and legs all tangled, like a kid's box of action figures that had been knocked over.

And just then, Juan and Asari came around the hallway corner carrying their suitcases and their computers. I was busy throwing punches and getting hit, too, and I think Juan and Asari laughed. Somehow they stepped around and over us and got into the elevator. In the elevator, Juan put down his stuff and pushed away the legs of Big Guy One—they were keeping the doors from shutting.

Big Guy One let go of me, grabbed Eduardo's ankle, and said, "Do not be thinking you are keeping the hard drive!"

Juan stomped Big Guy One's arm.

Big Guy One said, "Fuck you," drew a pistol, and shot Juan twice.

Juan gurgled and dropped to the floor.

With Big Guy One busy with Juan, I managed to land a weak fist on Big Guy Two's crotch. It wasn't much, but it doesn't take much to get results *there*. I kicked my legs and I was loose, scrambling down the hallway on my hands and knees.

As I stumbled along, I heard Asari yell, "You sick bastard!" and I heard two shots.

Big Guy One croaked back, "Cunt whore!" And then I heard more shooting, but I didn't look back.

I made it to the corner and got to my feet. I hurt like hell, probably had a few broken ribs, and one eye was closing on me. I started pounding on doors. "Let me in!"

I sucked in a breath. *Idiot!* If anyone was behind them doors, they sure as hell wouldn't open them with a gunfight going on outside.

I stumbled down to 1010. The door was locked, but I gave it a kick and got it to open. I stepped in, closed the broken door, and pushed an overstuffed chair against it. Outside, I could hear what had to be Big Guy Two cursing in Russian.

For a moment, I wondered which one was Petrov and which one was Alexei. I guessed it didn't matter now.

I pushed a sofa to back up the overstuffed chair.

Big Guy Two was starting to push on the door. "You are dead meat, skinheader!"

I'd pushed the sofa against the chair lengthwise, and that gave me an idea. The room had two chests of drawers, and I pushed the nearer one against the sofa's end. Now I had a solid wedge from the door to one wall of the room.

"Thank God," I said.

"Exactly," said Father Bart from the mission. He stood seven feet tall, wore a brown robe tied together with a rope, and had stepped out of nowhere.

"Father Bart," I said. "Why are you here?"

"I was pretty sure you'd be needing some help. Follow me. There's another way out."

The top of the door cracked. Big Guy Two had somehow gotten hold of a coffee table, maybe from another room, and was beating down the top half of the door. Police sirens screamed up from the street.

In the bedroom, Father Bart opened a set of adjoining doors to the next room. He said, "Go through this bedroom and out the door. Push the door closed and turn left. Just after the turn, there is a stairway. Take it to the first floor. You will find Agent Hartcan on your way down."

Big Guy Two splintered his way into the first room. The adjoining door slammed shut behind me.

I ran to the other hall door and stepped out. Big Guy Two was shooting up the adjoining door. I shut the hall door and turned left. I found the stairway, pushed open the door, and tried to hurry down without falling on my face.

I was down one flight when I heard the stairway door a floor up slam. I kept going, my legs feeling like they were high-stepping and not even touching the stairs. Another floor, and I heard a shot, and just ahead of my hand a bullet went splat on the metal handrail. I ducked to the outside wall of the stairwell and kept going.

Big Guy Two thundered down the steps like bad weather in an echo chamber. He fired a couple more times, but he couldn't have seen me, so he was just firing for spite. Or maybe to get lucky with a ricochet.

A big "6" on an exit door whizzed by me before I saw Agent Hartcan coming up the stairs with a shotgun. I screeched to a stop and almost fell, trying to keep from running him over. But Hartcan lowered his shotgun and caught me by the arm.

"Go," he said, "it's clear outside."

I turned to go when the thunder from above also stopped, and a shot rang out.

I heard a groan, and a thud, and Agent Hartcan sagged to the side of the stairwell. His shotgun rattled to the landing. Two more shots fired. Hartcan was fumbling for his automatic but couldn't make his fingers work.

I heard myself shout, "No!"

Father Bart bent his big, seven-foot frame quicker than I thought he could, and grabbed Agent Hartcan's automatic from him. He pointed it up the stairwell and fired until it clicked. For a long second, nothing happened. Then Big Guy Two tumbled, and two hundred pounds of bad attitude bodysurfed its way down the flight of steps.

Agent Park came out of nowhere. He pulled the automatic from my hands and said, "John, I think you just punched your own ticket . . . to anywhere you want to go."

The Last of
Many Stories

The Best Thing . . .

HE BLUE NEON LIGHT FROM the cross across the street filled my office. The cross came on at ten at night and stayed on until five in the morning. I rested my head on the pillow on my desk.

I'd bought a sofa for the front office, but I can't sleep there anymore because the workmen start so early. Most of the time, I sleep on the futon that I put in my office, but tonight Misty stayed on my mind—more than usual.

The biggest problem was that she had used the room after Asari Murphy and her husband had left for the night. She used the shower, slept on the sofa, and used the city bill to send her dresses out to get dry-cleaned. I could see why the FBI got the wrong idea.

The radio news reported that City Councilwoman Asari Murphy and her "aide" Eduardo were robbed and shot at the City Suites hotel. Councilwoman Murphy died en route to the hospital. Juan "Eduardo" Romars has been in a coma at Detroit Receiving Hospital for seven weeks.

An FBI agent got shot. I mean, it was just two in the vest and a flesh through the arm, but that's enough to keep 'em pissing for months. They held me for three weeks, and I hadn't been anywhere near the shooting.

I still wasn't sleeping. I sat up and imagined Misty's face hovering in the blue glow of the neon. Behind her, I painted the face of the guy

246 ROBERT E. BAILEY

that stared back at me every time I shaved. I didn't think it resembled the face a young woman was looking for.

I shook my head and the images vanished.

I got up, slipped my pistol on my hip, and walked over to the window. I pulled the edge of the blinds open. The white Lincoln, which Jeffrey Enwright had bought with the money stolen from my bank account, sat at the curb. Jeff sat in jail. The judge said I could take the car or wait for Jeff to get out and pay me back. Since I'd quit drinking, I went ahead and got a driver's license.

Little Joe had stopped by this morning to ask after Misty. The FBI had finally rolled up the yellow police tape and had given up trying to arrest somebody—anybody.

"We're going to get the City Suites open next week," Little Joe said, "and we hoped Misty would come back."

I told him I didn't know where Misty was. I didn't know if she was out of protective custody or still being held as a witness. Little Joe told me that the John Doe guy with the tattoo on his neck had stopped by the day before yesterday. He was looking for Misty too, like the rest of us. But he just wanted to tell her that he was on his way to New York to attend the Catholic seminary.

That made for a future for John Doe that I'd've had a hard time predicting.

Opening the blinds had let in a chill. I dropped my pillow to the futon, slipped my pistol under, and lay down. I covered myself with my overcoat. Thinking of John with his lightning bolts walking around the church made me chuckle. John had a good heart. I'm sure they would do something about the lightning bolts on his neck. Or, hell, they might even decide to leave them as an object lesson to others.

Toasty, I closed my eyes. The last time I saw Misty, they were still holding her in protective custody. They didn't let us talk. We'd pressed hands through the window.

I'm old . . . and a fool. No way could she have any interest in me. If we had children, I'd be sixty-seven by the time they were twenty.

On the upside, they'd have the energy of a twenty-year-old when it came time to change my diaper.

I slipped off to sleep.

I heard a noise from the hallway and checked my watch—same time as always. Today I was determined to get a watch that worked. In the meantime, I guessed it had to be six or seven.

More racket. Someone was banging on the outside door, and had been for a while.

I couldn't see the outer door from my office. I grabbed the pistol from under my pillow and stuck it in my belt. On the way to the door, I brushed my hair with my left hand. From the waiting room, through the clear pane of Jimmy Crates's replacement door, I saw a woman walking away. Her hair hung past her neck, but the black satin dress made it all simple.

I rushed over and opened the door. "Misty!"

Misty turned and looked into my eyes. She said, "I thought you were angry with me. For what Jeff did."

I scooped her up. She started crying. I started crying. And she was freezing. I carried her into my office, put her on the futon, and covered her up with my coat.

Misty squirmed under the coat, and then a silky black something appeared from underneath it and fell to the floor. I picked it up and realized I was holding her dress in my hand.

"Don't go crawling in here with that gun on," she said. "And shuck the rest of your clothes if you want to see where the tattoo ends."

-30-

Acknowledgments

BOB AND I WANT TO thank:

Deep and heartfelt thanks, first and foremost, to Andy Zack at Endpapers Press, without whose tireless efforts this book would not be in your hands.

Also, to all the people who provided so much care and assistance. Writing a book with a brain tumor is a tough and tiring task, especially when it's located in the speech and language area of the brain. Without the loving support of people like Bob's sister, Mary Sue Bailey; his sons Adam, Eric, and Sean Bailey; his parents, Margaret and Carl Hoops; those like Bob's brother and sister Gloria and Bill; and angels of mercy Debbie Jenkins and Heather McLees, it might well have proved impossible.

Thanks to Darby Grover for his friendship and critique over the years.

To David Poyer and Lenore Hart: Bob was always so grateful for your friendship, encouragement, and advice—and so am I! Thank you.

To Austin S. Camacho and his wife Denise: We appreciated your interest, your support, and your C3 conference so much! Thank you.

Bob always relied heavily on our writer's group and took every critique to heart. The Richwriters of Richmond, Virginia, have been going strong for over twenty years now thanks to chairman Joe Erhardt, who put in countless hours editing the third and fourth drafts of this book. Bob and I met here and got married at one of the meetings—in a bookstore. This incredible group of people held a special place in Bob's heart and will always hold a special place in mine. Thanks so very much to the members who critiqued pages, cheered Bob on to finish this book, and provided help when it was needed on short notice: Mark Pruett, Cathy Hill, Denise Golinowski, Archie Abaire, Julia Hebner, Kaye Carrithers, Ann Harmon, Richard Thomas, Sarah Harris, Robin Zeiger, and Annamaria Bazzi. Also a remembrance here for Rhoda Honigman, who passed away since the publication of *The Small Matter of Ten Large*.

Thank you to Bob's readers and fans. Nothing made him happier than hearing from someone who loved his books.

Deep thanks to the charter members of the GBM4Cure Glioblastoma Support Group on Facebook. They helped us through many a frightening episode, especially its founder, Debbie Moore; also Donna McCart, Judy Wright Dunbar, and Sandy Mayea Miller. I will always remember your advice and support as we battled glioblastoma alongside our husbands and fathers.

Thank you so very much, to those at Cullather Brain Tumor and Quality of Life Center, who provided crucial advice and care, and to all the dedicated doctors and nurses who helped Bob in his last battle. He desperately wanted to live long enough to finish this book. Your excellent care gave Bob two more years to keep writing, and with your support, he got it done.

Special thanks to:

Peter Alexander, M.D., neurosurgeon

Mitchell Anscher, M.D., radiation oncology

And very special love to Asadullah Khan, M.D., neurological oncology, "our wonderful Dr. Khan."

Bob always said that, when constructing the perfect paragraph, you save the best for last.

—Linda Lyons-Bailey